THE COST
OF HONOR

DIANA MUÑOZ
STEWART

sourcebooks
casablanca

For my children. The best parts of my life. The best parts of me.

Published by Sourcebooks Casablanca, an imprint of Sourcebooks
P.O. Box 4410, Naperville, Illinois 60567-4410
(630) 961-3900
sourcebooks.com

Printed and bound in Canada.
MBP 10 9 8 7 6 5 4 3 2 1

CHAPTER 1

DRUGS THAT MAKE YOU APPEAR DEAD HAVE SOME SHIT aftereffects. Temporary paralysis, monster headache, confusion, delirium, and dog breath, to name a few. Worth it for anyone wanting to remove themselves from their old life. Or so Tony had gambled.

Now, hours after he'd taken the drugs, he regained consciousness, cracked open bleary eyes, and slammed them shut against stabbing, red-hot-poker sunlight.

Not for nothing, a jackhammer had mated with a battering ram to create whatever worked the inside of his skull right now.

Licking dry lips with a sandpaper tongue, he tasted copper and salt. Blood.

He forced his eyelids open, blinked away tears. Above, a vaulted ceiling was crossed by ancient wood beams. His gaze rolled across the room. The mutilated backs of bullet-torn leather couches, blood-soaked yellow drapes, the smell of death's bowels, the lingering scent of gunpowder.

What the hell had happened here?

Like an old Ford on a below zero January morning, his drug-addled brain misfired, turned over, and restarted.

Oh fuck, right. That shit in Mexico. Take out sex slavers. Fake your own death.

That explained the sour stench, the empty pit in his stomach, and the stone silence. A roomful of dead sex traffickers weren't generally loud.

And just like that, the brutal event that had sent him to

this very room put on gloves, stepped into his mental boxing ring, and pounded him with heavy blows. His sister Justice. The shot. The kid. Brown eyes. Nervous as hell. So young.

Shit. He recoiled but was unable to stop the attack.

You'd think the jumpy, aggressive, snot-nosed guard was the one who was half-naked, unarmed, and being marched into the Mexican compound of a sex slaver to "perform."

So young he still had acne, the kid shoved Tony as he walked him and Victor to the golf cart that would take them inside.

Tony cringed. If Young and Pimply wanted to avoid the wrath of Justice, whose scope was on him and who took a threat seriously, he needed to stop acting like a macho idiot.

Because as agitated as this guy seemed, it was nothing compared to Justice, who wanted into the compound to save her boyfriend and destroy the sex slaver who'd killed her biological sister.

Reasons number one and two she should've been nowhere near this operation. From the very beginning, he'd said she was too close to this mission. He'd said it as she'd made mistakes. He'd said it as he'd come up with an alternate plan. He'd said it as she'd nearly gotten herself—and others—killed again and again. Hell, he'd even written it down in a letter to Momma.

But when no one in his family of female vigilantes had listened, he'd stop talking and had done something about it. He'd tried everything in his power to stop J's mission, keep her safe. Organized his plan. Sent word to Walid, let him know where to go to escape Justice. And…it hadn't worked.

He'd wound up in the role of betrayer. Now the only way to survive his family's wrath was to fake his own death. That was if he actually survived long enough to fake his death.

Tony's naked cheeks hit the striped vinyl golf cart seat and the compound alarm went off. That blaring pulse kicked the guards into action.

Wearing an FBI baseball cap and the attitude only a 6'3" jacked dude can manage, his inside man, Dusty, ordered him and Victor out and down onto their knees.

Come on, dude. Sure, Dusty had to make it look like he wasn't in cahoots with anyone, but that didn't mean he had to make Tony look guilty as hell.

Tony's knees hit the ground with a thud. Alarm. Jittery guards... Not a good combination. Young and Pimply bent over, got in his face, and lifted him to his feet.

"Knock it off," he told the kid in Spanish, gesturing with his hands. Maybe a little too dramatically. The kid startled, reached for his gun.

Tony's eyes widened. "Don't—"

Pop. Kid's head exploded. And then the next closest guard went down. All hell broke loose.

His stomach roiling, his mind reeling, Tony took off.

What the fuck. What the fuck. What the fuck.

He ran toward the closest building. He needed another plan. He needed another plan quick.

Victor caught up with him. "What are we doing now?"

We?

Actually, he could use Victor. Station him somewhere as backup while Tony made his way to Walid. If he could convince that psycho that he was on his side, tell him he was the one who sent the initial warning—he was—offer him his brother's real killer, get close enough to administer the poison, he could keep Justice and the rest of them from getting killed.

Lot of ifs, but it was a plan.

Tony groaned as the memories reasserted themselves in his mind, lodging their concrete presence in his brain—going to Walid, pretending to turn on Justice and Momma, an act even Justice had bought, and then the bloody battle in this very room.

The entire mission could've gone so much more smoothly. If only...

Didn't matter now.

The important part was Walid was dead. The guy deserved to die for his crimes, his abuse of women. Most importantly for hurting his sister Justice. She'd never forgotten. She'd grown up determined to take vengeance.

But as she'd gotten closer to that goal, she'd become obsessed. Everyone around her, including him, feared her quest would destroy her.

Though everyone in his family's secret society, the League of Warrior Women—because it was all adopted women 'cept him and Rome—had decided to let Justice give it a go, he hadn't.

Regret constructed a monument to his mistakes that stretched to the sky. How had wanting to save his sister's life turned him into a supervillain?

He shifted. A series of sharp pains reported back to him in stinging waves as his nerve endings fired brutal rebukes at him. *Yeah. Yeah. Just shake it off.*

Judging by the rising sun, it was near dawn. Made sense. The powerful drug he'd taken to make him appear dead had been designed to keep him out for hours, so his family, his sisters, would be long gone.

Thing about being a vigilante, you didn't stick around after a job.

A flood of relief swept his body as it really sunk in. They were gone. They'd left him. His two biggest fears had been his sisters would try to take what they thought was his dead body back home or bury him alive in the dry earth of Mexico.

As far as those two options went, the first had been more terrifying. The second meant he'd have gone to sleep permanently. The first meant they'd take him home, realize he wasn't dead, rob him of his memories, and replace them with who they thought he should be.

No fucking thanks.

His body came back online enough that he suddenly sensed the pain in his awkwardly bent leg. So numb he couldn't move it.

He reached down, grabbed a fistful of the green cargo pants he'd *borrowed* from one of Walid's guards, and moved his leg straight.

Leg must've folded under him when he'd fallen. Blood flowed back to the limb. Being stabbed hurt less. SOB. Dagger-sharp pins and needles lanced his thigh and calf. Biting off a curse, he rubbed at his leg. A figure crossed into the room.

No. Fucking. Way.

Why was this dude still here? The ex-FBI guy and Tony's inside man, Dusty, walked over to where Tony lay behind the couch. He was carrying a tarp.

"What the fu..." Dusty jumped back, dropped the tarp, and took out his gun. "You're not dead?"

So not what he wanted to deal with when his stomach gave him the middle finger and pins and needles jabbed his leg, teetering him between laughter and tears.

He wiped at his tearing eyes and sat up. Dizzy like that

time he'd stumbled onto a vomit comet after downing six-teen shots of tequila. Yeah, that had been a mistake. This might've been too.

He put a hand to his throbbing temple, drove his fingers up and around to his aching neck. "They teach you those kinds of expert evaluations in the bur...bureau?"

Throat was so dry.

Dusty kept his weapon out—not pointed at Tony, just out. Uptight. Maybe this was his first encounter with the living dead. "What's going on, Tony?"

I'm stalling, trying to figure out my next move. Probably shouldn't go with that. Dusty wasn't stupid. And their partnership had really been an exercise in both of them using each other. Dusty had pretended he'd wanted to become a vigilante in order to get an in with Tony's family so he could take out Momma's black ops organization, the League of Warrior Women. Tony had pretended he'd bought Dusty's ex-FBI cover so he could have some-one working here who wasn't a member of his family. Dusty had been a useful tool, but him knowing Tony had faked his death was not an option. "The poison I gave Walid must not have worked on me."

Dusty brought his gun down, frowned, and looked back toward the doorway. "Your sisters. We should call them, let them know you're alive."

This was a problem. Dude was big, like gladiator big. And Tony was in no shape to take him on. But he still had one advantage. Guy had no idea what was going on.

And it wasn't like Tony hadn't considered the problem that he might wake up in Mexico with someone nearby.

Oh hell. Rubbing his side, he worked his fingers under

the waist of his pants to his live entertainer G-string—most humiliating cover ever. He pulled out the syringe from inside a sex tool. "Just help me up."

Dusty put his gun away, shook his head, stunned. "Lucky son of a bitch."

Tony rolled his hand in a tell-me-something-I-don't-know manner. He didn't feel lucky. Felt like a total douche.

According to his chemist sister, Zuri, the first step in erasing a memory was getting someone to recall the memory. The drug he had would disrupt the stored memory, allowing Tony to replace it. "Must've been scary to walk in here and find me alive. You okay?"

Dusty came over and gave him a hand. "Guarantee you it's not a regular occurrence."

Tony took the offered hand, stood up, and brought his other hand toward Dusty's shoulder as if to steady himself. Actually helped. Leg was still kind of numb. He stabbed Dusty with the point of the instrument and at the same time pretended to fall.

"Sorry, didn't mean to scratch you."

Dusty supported him. "Dagger claw you got there."

Tony got his feet under him, slipped off Dusty's gun.

Dusty reared back, rubbed at his neck, stumbled. "You..."

Dusty fell on his ass, sat there blinking and blank. After a few more minutes, he was completely malleable.

Bending over him, Tony edited the story of what had happened, and whenever Dusty looked confused or uncertain of this version, Tony repeated, "Leave it be, man. Leave it be."

He did this until when asked what had happened, Dusty

would look confused, shake his head, and whisper, "Leave it be, man. Leave it be."

Once he was sure the guy's memory was disrupted, knowing that nothing happening now would be recorded, Tony put him into a choke hold and put him to sleep.

Poor guy. Well, he wouldn't remember any of this. Not for a while anyway. And by the time he did, Tony would be long gone, having set sail for warm beaches.

CHAPTER 2

RAIN ASSAULTED THE THIN, DESERTED STRIP OF BEACH along Roseau, Dominica. Though rarely cold on the island, the lack of sun combined with the wild weather created a deep, nagging chill.

Tightening the straps on her jacket, drawing the slick red hood into an outline around her rain-drenched face, Honor pushed through the last brutal gusts of the retreating tropical storm.

Seaweed littered the sand. Stacked lounge chairs clacked, and striped cabanas snapped in the tempest.

It seemed the sky and heaven cried with her, tears of sadness and fury. Honor ducked her head and made her determined way around a large puddle on the sand. The indents from her sneakers created smaller puddles as she walked.

Had it really been two years today? Two years since she'd lost Mom and had run here looking for a new start, a life without the ache of missing her.

Hadn't worked. Mom's death had been so sudden that the punch of that wound, straight through her heart, still gaped wide open. There wasn't a day when she didn't feel bereft.

But today especially, the anniversary of her death. The media, reminded of her famous mother's passing, had reached out through phone, email, and texts for quotes.

Unable to deal with them, she'd come to the beach looking for a distraction.

She'd found one.

A kiteboarder, rash and daring with a bright-yellow sail, glided across the rough ocean water. His dark hair flew back as his agile body, covered in a wetsuit, maneuvered with and against wind and waves. So beautiful he created an ache inside her. To be that free, that strong, that daring.

He kept hold of the kite's line as each gale whipped the large sail sideways, dragging him. Outcrops and rocks dotted the water, but he avoided them with ease.

Another gust and the kiteboarder flew up and up. She gasped. Her heart rose with him. Too high. He had too far to fall.

He slammed back down to the surf, angled his athletic body this way and that to skim the waves. He'd done it. She resisted the urge to clap. Mom would've loved watching him, another confident, courageous soul.

Unlike Honor.

Mom had stomped through puddles.

Honor hung back, worried about consequences.

Mom had gone boldly after love, spoken her desires aloud, and given her heart away again and again.

Honor secreted away her heart and her true desires.

With every risky new relationship, her mother seemed to forget the tears, the drink, and the therapy needed to get right after the last one had ended. Honor had never forgotten.

But when the winds of time had swept Mom's fierce soul back into the never-never, as Mom had always called it, it hadn't been her wild and crazy lifestyle that had caught up with her. No. She'd been hit by a car as she walked the streets of her quiet neighborhood.

One less brave and daring light in the world. Honor felt the dark coldness of that extinguished warmth in her skin, her bones, her heart. Now anything that was wild and free and exciting felt like a call, a siren song to her soul.

Like the kiteboarder. The way he worked with the energy of the waves, wove himself among them even as he wrestled his second opponent, the wind. As she watched, her breath fanned out in hot sheets of white against the cool wind.

He must be so cold, but he didn't show it.

Explosive and strong, he leapt with his kite into the wind. A thrill gripped her as he launched skyward. A moment later, he hit the waves, leaned his body almost flat against the roaring ocean as the sail jerked his arms straight.

He rode the waves steadily for a beat, and then the wind turned, snapped his kite, and yanked him backward.

Honor froze. The wind tossed him up, then beat him down against a black outcrop of rock. His strong body, suddenly flimsy and fragile, slipped from the rocks and under the waves.

Faster than thought, she broke from stillness and raced toward the ocean. She flung off her shoes, ripped her rain slicker over her head. Knee-deep in water, she stopped. Where was he? The sail bobbled against the waves, but where was he? Where?

There.

His body, facedown. A wave rose up and crashed over him. He disappeared. She took two leaping steps and dove. Using muscles conditioned by years of swimming, she plunged under the beating waves and fought her way to him.

Salt water stung her nose, esophagus. Again and again, she felt the push, the ocean's insistent, "Turn around."

She kept going. Surfacing, she bobbed in the water, got her bearings. This was where she'd seen him go under.

Diving with her eyes open, she scanned. Green and gray, a surreal muted picture. Something dark, darker than the rest of the ocean. Him? Lungs burning, desperate for air, she swam closer and deeper.

No more death today. Please. Her ears muffled with pressure, she reached out and grasped the collar of his wetsuit, capturing a fistful of his hair in the process.

She pulled, arms straining. He came even with her, and she grasped under his armpits and kicked up. Her head angled as high as she could get it. Air. She needed to breathe.

The weight of him slowed her.

Let him go or die?

She couldn't let go.

Wouldn't.

The edges of her vision began to dim. Too far. Not going to make it. She kicked harder. The glassy ceiling drew nearer. Please. So close.

She broke the surface. The kiteboarder was silent against her, his head bobbing in the surf. Legs as insubstantial as seaweed, she rolled onto her back and kicked toward the shore.

When her butt hit the beach, she gave an exhausted cry. Sweeping her feet under her, she crouch-pulled the kiteboarder onto the sand. Waves rolled into them, pushing. He was heavy.

"Let me help," someone said.

Gratefully, she looked up to find an older, bald man. Together, they dragged the kiteboarder out of the waves and dropped him onto the rain-soaked sand. She started CPR.

The bystander, hovering beside her, said he'd called emergency services and apologized for the inadequacy of his lungs. Asthma.

No air to respond, she pushed on the kiteboarder's chest. Drops of water slid across his handsome, too-pale face, but not one muscle twitched.

Please, please, please, she silently begged. Her knees ground in the wet sand as she pinched his nose, put her mouth over his, and forced air through her aching throat into his lifeless body. Crying now, begging God for intervention, she pushed again on his chest.

He convulsed once, hard enough to look like he'd been hit with electric paddles, coughed, and spat out water.

She helped him onto his side. He spat out more water. After another moment, he rolled onto his back, eyes closed, breathing heavily.

Breathing.

The bystander ran up the beach, waving to the EMT.

She'd done it. She'd saved a man's life. His eyes stayed closed, and she brushed the sand from his neatly trimmed goatee, cheekbones, and lips. Her fingers lingered against those full lips. The most perfect shape, perfect feel.

He was beyond handsome with a muscular build that filled out his wetsuit like a superhero. Her mother would've declared him "good enough to eat."

Lord. What was wrong with her?

His eyes popped open, blinked. Caught. She went still as a stone.

Deep hazel eyes ringed in the longest lashes she'd ever seen. For a moment, he seemed confused. His eyes turned to slits as if trying to puzzle something out. His lids rose, and his gaze cleared. "Silver eyes," he said, smiling. "Fucking beautiful."

Before she could respond or figure out how to respond, emergency services arrived. They carried him up the beach to the waiting ambulance with her dragging behind, gathering her jacket and shoes as she followed.

CHAPTER 3

HIDDEN BY THE DINGY BLUE TABLECLOTH, THE SIX-YEAR-old's heartbeat sounded loud enough to point fingers and wave arms.

Daddy continued to bellow, kick, punch her. The commonplace *thunk* and *thuck* and *umph* filled the small urban duplex, feeling different somehow. Worse.

This time, he wouldn't stop. Tony had to do something. Had to. Curling his fingers into fists, he charged out from under the table with a "Nooo!"

His bony shoulder barreled into his father's kneecap. Pain stabbed into his arm, but the unexpected action and his father's drinking worked in his favor. Daddy went sprawling.

Squirrel-running-from-a-dog quick, Tony spun away. Not fast enough. His father's hand latched onto him, dragged him back, hoisted him up, and carried him toward the laundry room. The dark door—a hole punched long ago in the plywood center—loomed before him.

Not there. He fought and twisted like a fish on a line. "Not in there. Not in there."

Mom had gotten up. She pulled against Daddy's arm. They were all three fighting. No use. Daddy was just bigger. Stronger. Tony was tossed into the laundry room. The door slammed shut behind him.

The dog came after him. All teeth and fury.

Tony yelled, jolted upright in bed, and remembered.

He was no longer a son to that bastard. He'd run away.

And after his father's death, he'd been adopted by Mukta Parish, aka Momma, one of the wealthiest women in the world. Thanks to her, he was no longer without the ability to fight back. Momma's organization, the League of Warrior Women, had trained him—along with his twenty-seven other adopted siblings—to be warriors in her social justice crusade. He'd been fighting alongside his family for over twenty years. Until he'd fucked up. Now, he wasn't really Tony anymore. Now, he was Lazarus. A dead man returned to life.

Ugh. He lay back, head pounding. Seemed like he'd been here before. Or someplace like it. This time, memory came quickly. Tropical storm. Kiteboarding. Idiot.

Hospital lights shouted down at him, hitting him like a fist full of "wake up, dumbass." Probably shouldn't have gone out. He groaned, rolled his head to the side, nearly lost the liquid in his stomach.

Hard to tell which sounded louder, his head or the heart monitor. His right arm ached like it had been slammed with a rock. It had. And there was no one to blame but himself.

This morning, he'd felt homesick, anxious, and frustrated at his inability to get off the island because of the storm. He'd gone out looking for something so deep, so wild and filled with adrenaline, he couldn't think anymore.

Basically, he just wanted to kill his thoughts. It had worked for a little while. He had a concussion to prove it.

"Knock, knock."

His gaze snapped to the door, skimmed her tanned legs, wrinkled white shorts, and moved up to his most favorite physical asset. What he told his sisters was a great smile. Only because a nice set of boobs always brought a smile to his lips. Heat shot through his body.

Not for nothing, she was gorgeous. Those eyes. Silver? He'd thought he'd dreamt them. The eyes of an angel. A fierce angel who'd saved his life and then brought him back from the dead.

Beginning to become a bad habit of his.

He waved her inside, tried to sit up. The room tilted. He pressed the button on the guardrail, inched upward with a whir of the motor. "I need to thank you."

Was that his voice? Sounded as rough as sand. As rough as his uncle Leland's. Uncle? Still didn't sound right. The man had hidden his relation to Tony for twenty years. For good reason.

Being the first male adopted into a secret society of female vigilantes was tough enough. Finding out he'd been adopted not because of who he was but who he was related to? Fuck, that'd hurt. And pissed him off.

His angel walked across the room. Fierce and hot with loose brown curls that caressed a delicate, almost regal neck. Or maybe it was the way she carried herself that was regal.

And, oh man, he felt something. Something big. Something wild and filled with adrenaline and a zing of lust that sent his heart monitor galloping.

Her silver eyes flicked to the monitor. No way to deny that. She turned her attention to him and held out a hand tattooed with a date that started at the base of her thumb and ran up toward her wrist. "Honora Silva. Honor for short."

"My hero has a name worthy of her." He lifted the arm with the IV drip and took her hand. The silk of her skin ignited flames in his palm that spread through his body. Could hold this hand all day. Wanted to. "Lazarus Graves."

He turned her wrist a little and read the black ink

tattooed there. Today's date. Two years ago. Slowly, she pulled her hand back, leaned against the bed, comfortable in a way that seemed unconscious. "Lazarus? Like the walking dead." She grinned. "Appropriate."

Huh. Kind of a smart-ass. He liked. "You got the States in your voice. On vacation? Determined to get every day you can from the beach, even during a tropical storm?"

"No." She pointed at her tattoo. "I moved here after my mother's death. That's why I was on the beach. A pilgrimage of sorts."

Something in Laz's chest moved forward, toward her. This had been a bad day for him. This had been an incredibly shit day for her. And despite her grief, she'd saved his fucking life. He put a hand to his chest. "I'm sorry."

Her shoulders slumped. Eyes downcast, she brushed aside tears. That was it. That body visible ache. That was what grief looked like. What he'd done to his family. Fuck. She shook her head. "You actually did me a favor. Made it so something good came out of today."

He took a minute, processed what she'd suggested—if not for her mother's death, she wouldn't have been on the beach, and he might be dead right now. "Guess I owe her my life too. Along with her fearless daughter."

A startled sound broke from her like a crack of thunder. "I am not fearless. Mom used to call me the Cowardly Lion."

His brows drew together. "You jumped into the ocean to save an idiot stranger during a tropical storm. I call that fearless. And the Cowardly Lion was tough too. Just needed to find the right situation to bring it out."

At this, she laughed, a laugh so surprised, and maybe delighted, that her head tilted back. Her chin lifted to the ceiling. When she brought her head down, her silver eyes were alight. Like twin moons. "I make chocolate for a living."

"Sweet and brave. Must be the luckiest survivor in the world. Who you makin' chocolate for?"

"I own my own cocoa farm, lodge, and agro-touring business. Along with Papito, my grandfather."

Okay. Not just making chocolate. He motioned in a tell-me-more gesture. "What kind of tours?"

"Tours of Morne Trois Pitons National Park, the Boiling Lake. Rappelling, hiking, climbing. That sort of thing. We have a lodge and individual chalets that we rent. We do tours of the farm too, not just the nearby rain forest."

She gave tours of Dominica and her farm. Smart way to keep a business afloat. "That sounds really cool. Kind of my dream job. Rappelling, spelunking, anything to do with the great outdoors and adventure, I'm your guy. A little jealous."

Self-consciously, she fingered the bit of blanket poking through the metal guardrail. "And you? Are you on vacation?"

He had his cover. Of course he did. And yet, she'd been so honest with him, saved his life. Plus, he just didn't feel like lying to her. "Ran away from home. Changed my name. Set sail. Forced to port with the storm."

Her eyes brightened. "But that sounds like an adventure story. I love adventures stories."

She opened her mouth to ask a follow-up. A question he was sure he didn't want to answer. Hell, why wasn't she running out of the room right now? Brave as hell. He beat her to the punch. "Your eye color—is that real?"

Her eyebrows rose. "Of course."

Sensitive. "That offends you? Me asking?"

"The idea that I am a person who puts in contacts to impress others offends me."

He liked the way she spoke, clipped and absolute. Kind of formal. Reminded him of the girls at the Mantua Academy, the private school his family ran. And used as cover for covert ops. Did she have a private education? "Never said it was to impress anyone. Maybe people who wear colored contacts just like the way they look. Like I like my tattoos."

She swished her chin around as if sampling his words like a sommelier tasting wine. Freakin' adorable. She must've found them to her liking because she nodded and moved on. "My eyes aren't that unusual."

Okay. She couldn't actually believe that. "They're silver."

"Some would call them a light gray."

"Some would be wrong. They're silver."

"I think my skin tone might lend to them seeming more silver than gray."

She had great skin. A touch darker than his own, it was a tawny island tan so pristine, her body seemed draped in silk. He longed to brush a knuckle across the swell of her high cheekbones, collarbone, cleavage. "Maybe if I saw you in a different light, they'd look less silver."

She laughed. "You could see me in a different light, but that might not change anything. As Robertson Davies said, 'The eye sees only what the mind is prepared to comprehend.'"

Yep. Well-educated. "I prefer Obi-Wan Kenobi. 'Many of the truths we cling to depend greatly on our point of view.'"

She raised a dark eyebrow over one silver eye. It gave her

a dangerous, seductive quality. Hard to resist. Not sure he wanted to.

A squawk from the hall announced visiting hours were over, but her gaze dipped to his bicep, to the tattoo revealed beneath the hospital gown. "And your tattoo, 'One for all.' Like the Three Musketeers. Does it have meaning beyond that?"

"It means my life for others. Used to be my motto."

"Not anymore?"

He wished she hadn't asked. She had. And the way he was feeling right now, grateful and turned on and fuzzy enough in the head that this whole conversation felt surreal, he told her. "I told you, I ran away from home. So I guess I'm looking after myself, making myself number one for a while."

To his surprise, she didn't frown or accuse him of being a totally selfish prick. She looked him in the eyes. "You say that like you're admitting a crime. You feel bad about it?"

Shit, yeah, he did. "That's not the way I was raised. I was raised to care. I do care."

"So why leave?"

Head pounding, he ran his fingers over his goatee. Every day, he woke up with this feeling of guilt. His stomach turning with the wrongness of it, of not doing what he was good at, what he could to help. "It wasn't really my choice. It was go or lose my mind."

She nodded, took a deep breath, like preparing to dive. "Do you know the Loco for Cocoa shop near where the cruise ships dock?"

"Docked at a makeshift pier. Haven't really been here long enough to learn the layout. Why?"

"Well, I'm there every other morning, Monday through Saturday. Or as my grandmother used to say, *Lendi to Sanmdi*. If you stop by, I'll take you on a personal tour, an adventure through the rain forest. Show you my business. Even share some of my chocolate."

Chocolate. Let's hope that was a euphemism for what he really wanted to taste. Hold on. "You asking me out?" Her cheeks pinked. He grinned. She was. Aw, man, worst time for it.

If they hadn't already, his family would soon figure out he was alive, be gunning for him, so staying in one place, especially this close to the States, was too dangerous. "Totally makes the concussion worth it, but..." This was going to kill him. "I'm not sure I'll survive another adventure."

She swallowed. Her eyes widened. "I won't let anything happen to you."

His heart tripped in his chest. "I think you saving my life once is enough."

In a move so sudden he nearly jerked back, she leaned over the bed and rested her lips against his cheek. Heat shot through his body, and something he hadn't allowed himself to feel for a long time uncoiled.

He wanted her. Wanted to feel those soft, full lips working against his body. Wanted to take her in all the best ways, slow and fast.

She smiled, a smile for the record books, a smile like an ellipsis—the start of something that had no end. Her eyes traveled down his body. "I saved your life. I think you owe me."

Wait. What did that mean? Was it his male ego or had she...? They locked eyes. And the blatant, unrestrained desire he saw there about knocked him out of the bed. Fuck yeah. He'd pay that debt. With interest.

He shifted his right leg at an angle, hid the reaction surging up between his legs. A boner tenting his sheets like a teen—not the first impression he hoped to make. Damn embarrassing.

She glanced down at his lips, licked her own. She leaned toward him, slow this time.

Like his heart, his monitor picked up its beat.

A nurse wheeled a blood-pressure machine into the room and with a no-nonsense shake of her head said, "Visiting hours are up."

Honor took a step away from him. Was that regret in her eyes? That made two of them.

She turned and headed for the door. Her high round ass, feline in its sway, caught his attention, purred at him. Or maybe that was his perverted mind at work again.

When she reached the door, Honor looked back, caught his eyes on her ass. She grinned like she'd just pinned him in her playful paws and threw back, "Try to stay out of the grave, Lazarus."

Fuck. That chilled him. He intended to. And that would be a lot easier if he left the island. Which meant, as hot as she was—hot enough to make him regret every life choice he'd ever made—this was the last he'd see of her.

CHAPTER 4

IN THE CRAMPED REAL ESTATE OFFICE OVERLOOKING A rundown neighborhood in Roseau, Dominica, Gray George answered the third line on her phone, the one that indicated someone was calling for a passport. "International Appropriations, Dominica."

She'd made sure to raise her voice when she pronounced her country, "Doe-mee-NEE-kah," as people often confused the island with the Dominican Republic. A bit of a tragedy when your mail went to an entirely different country.

The caller sounded Chinese, speaking in heavily-accented—and strained—English. "Hello, I'm calling about getting a Dominica passport."

She slowly explained the costs and the need to buy land on the island. She also assured him, as a real estate agent, she could handle the purchase of the land and the passport. *And if, by chance, he needed a tour of the island, she could provide that as well.*

Woman had to eat. No tour was necessary. He wanted the cheapest piece of land he could buy. Of course.

With the island recovering from a storm last year, so many swept in in the hopes of getting a deal. They didn't want to pay a fair price. They figured beggars can't be choosers. A difficult time to sell real estate, with both sides thinking the other was unreasonable.

If things didn't improve soon, she might need to take her sister up on the offer and move to Florida.

After gathering the man's details, she hung up and analyzed a computer screen filled with contact information.

Her phone rang again. Line two. Hallelujah. A good day. "George Travel and Real Estate."

"I need to speak with the owner, Gray George."

She rolled her eyes. This was how complaints always started. "This is her."

The voice on the other end paused. "Sorry, you sounded…" He didn't complete the sentence. He didn't need to. People often heard her deep voice and assumed her male. The man on the other end recovered and continued. "I'm an attorney, calling for a client who wishes to remain anonymous. He wants to make an offer on a property in Dominica."

"Can you give me the address or parcel number?"

"It's not for sale. But the owner will sell."

Gray slumped forward, her head almost touching her computer screen. Another person who thought they could waltz in and buy whatever they wanted. "I'm not sure—"

"My client wants the property owned by Honor Silva, the daughter of Natalie Silva. We're willing to offer four million for it."

Gray fumbled the phone as she sat ramrod straight at her desk. This was a joke. They had her on a radio program. She was being pranked. "What you're offering—"

"Ms. Gray, it's not just the property but the business that goes with it, Loco for Cocoa. There are many good reasons for this decision, and I can assure you all of them are sound."

"It will never appraise—"

"I have a feeling it will appraise well. Now, can you handle making the offer?"

For a moment, Gray couldn't speak. She quickly found her voice. "I require ten percent of such transactions."

"That's fine."

It was? She'd expected to bargain, to settle for much less. This would change her life. Her children's lives. "Send me the information, and I will make this happen for you."

"I expect you will for that fee."

An hour after she'd left the hospital, with the charming and handsome Lazarus Graves very much on her mind, Honor drove up the winding road that led to her mountain hotel and farm.

The raindrops had slowed, but her wipers *chu-whooshed*, *chu-whooshed* against the glass of her Honda Civic at the only speed they had, crazy fast.

A spin of her wheel directed her car up the long road that cut between the trees. Men with rain slickers tended the cocoa trees. She passed them and then the long, covered porch. Vats used for fermenting cocoa beans lined up under the steep, red porch roof. The architect in charge of this process—Uncle José's self-description—worked among the vats.

Expecting nothing, she waved to her Uncle José. He turned his back on her. Oh well, can't win everyone over.

A turn of her wheel, and she pulled up to the brightly painted green-and-yellow hotel with its charming wrap-around porch. Seated at one of the many wicker tables, Papito stood and moved toward her.

He wore his trademark white hat, white shirt, and white

pants. He called it his "costume." When he'd come up with the idea of doing tours to supplement their income—he'd done tours in Puerto Rico where he'd grown up—he'd also come up with this farmer persona. As silly as it had seemed, Papito had a great instinct when it came to people. His farmer persona was a favorite of the guests. Such a charmer.

Holding an umbrella over her, Papito greeted her with a kiss on her cheek. He smelled like cocoa butter and looked like a man twenty years younger, with a straight spine and thick, mostly gray hair swept into a ponytail.

"These roads are treacherous in the rain. You should be more careful, *mi hija.*"

Dios. What a worrier. Once they were safely on the veranda, he lowered the umbrella and shook it off. Honor greeted a few guests, then took a seat on a wicker chair beside Papito.

He pointed to a pile of papers on the table. "You need to read that."

Curious, she moved his ever-present cell phone off the stack and read. And then read it again. *Que es esto?* What was this? Someone had made an offer on the farm. A ridiculous offer. An offer that was twice what she'd put into this place after inheriting it.

Papito cleared his throat. "What do you think?"

She looked up. Her brain jumping around. "I don't know. This is a crazy amount of money. What do you think?"

Papito shrugged, put his phone down. "Don't ask me. You're in charge." He smiled. He always teased her, but now his smile faded. "José thinks we should take it."

Honor bristled. José just wanted her to accept the offer so she wouldn't be his boss anymore. Although, boss wasn't right. She shared responsibility with Papito. Only making the decisions she felt most strongly about on her own. She lowered the papers. "With the island's troubles, this could be something illegal."

His eyebrows rose. "Because the property is worth half what they want to pay?"

He was being generous. Two million was what she'd put into the property. There was little reason to believe she'd get that back right now. Not without building up the business.

"What other reason makes sense?"

"I thought…because of your mother. Today of all days, she is on my mind."

Her mother? "Why Mom?"

He reached over, flicked through the pages, and pointed. "You didn't read all of it. See here." He read it to her. "We reserve the right to use all branding opportunities associated with the product, including prior images and branding."

Crap. She'd forgotten. When she'd first started Loco for Cocoa as a teen—a business that had gone nowhere—she'd registered it under her mom's production company brand, Shameless Hussy. Maybe that was what this offer was about. She'd been approached over and over again by people wanting to use her mother's sultry movie star image to sell products.

One man had offered Honor ten million dollars to use her mother's Shameless Hussy branded silhouette shot where her "assets were highlighted" to sell car parts.

She'd been furious. He'd wanted to use an image her mother had cast aside, an image that in no way encapsulated all of who and what she was. "That makes sense, Papito. Two million for the business and two million to make Mom's memory synonymous with a trashy, stereotypical image." Honor pushed the papers away. "I'm not selling."

Papito sat forward, grabbed her hand. "You could negotiate, ask them to take out that part. This is a great payout. No one, including me, would blame you for taking such an offer. This life is not easy."

She flushed, hoped he didn't see it. The "not easy" part was financial. The tours were the only thing keeping this place afloat.

She looked around at the jungle that surrounded them. On sunny days, cocoa would be set out to be dried and conditioned by the nourishment of the sweetest sunshine on this planet. And yeah, she knew that the sun was the same everywhere, but it felt different here.

It smelled different, too, in the lush jungle, with the bouquet of flowers, the buzz of insects, and the laughter of people working the land.

Any other day, the money would seem the most important thing. She could take it and go back to her original vision, starting chocolate stores all over the world. But that took out the most important elements, the cocoa, the collaboration with Papito, the island.

Running the tours to supplement the business was barely enough to keep the lights on, but this was an anniversary. A day when a bold and adventurous spirit had been taken from the world. Mom would never have taken the safe route. "I'm going to say no."

His face still a little worried, Papito nodded. Pushing back her chair, Honor stood with a sense of relief and renewed purpose.

One problem though. Gray, the same woman who

hired local touring companies for the cruise ship tours, was the real estate agent. She had to tell the woman who was basically in charge of the one aspect of the hotel making money, the tours, that she wasn't going to accept an offer she was brokering. Basically, denying the woman a huge commission.

That should go over well.

CHAPTER 5

ONE OF THE THINGS LAZ LOVED MOST ABOUT HIS NEW life was that he didn't have a clock. He'd thrown the schedules out. So to be woken by his cell ringing at butt-crack a.m.—two hours after he'd snuck out of the hospital— annoyed and then terrified him.

Only one person had this number, the one person who knew he was still alive.

A pit bull of dread tore a hole the size of a lost lifetime through his heart. Guilt, regret, and fear roiled inside as he rolled over in his bunk.

He grabbed his Bluetooth from the side table, slipped it on over his right ear, and clicked it on, cutting off *Aladdin*'s "Friend Like Me."

Swinging his legs out of his bunk, he sat up. Beneath him, the sailboat swayed. "What's the bad news, Rome?"

There was a beat of silence, a steeling of resolve or a moment of dread or a lag in connection before Romeo's voice filtered in through his headset. "You're no longer dead."

"They know I'm alive?"

"Yep. Never seen Justice so pissed. And she spends ninety percent of her life pissed off."

Dread and relief slammed into him. Relief, because he'd rather his family pissed off at him than sad, mourning him. Dread because now they'd be looking for him.

And if they found him, they'd erase his memory. No

question. It wasn't that his family didn't love him. They did. But when you had twenty-eight lethal weapons all with emotional baggage—anger and revenge were two of them—you needed a threat great enough to keep them in line. A threat you were willing to carry out. "What gave me away?"

There was a long pause. "Short or long version?"

He should ask for the long one, but he didn't have the heart for it this morning. Pain pounded his skull like a tune being beaten on a Moroccan drum. "Short and sweet."

"Sweet? You haven't been gone that long."

With a grunt, he climbed out of his bunk and promptly hit his already throbbing head on the doorjamb as the boat pitched. *Fuck.* He stumbled to the bathroom.

Rome spoke into his ear. "Gracie fell in love with an FBI agent, the one that helped you in Mexico. Thanks to some crazy that is part of another longer story, they figured it out."

Gracie had fallen in love with Dusty? "She needs to be careful with him. She—"

"He's chipped. Been down to the dungeon. Restored his memory. He's not a fan of yours."

Better and better. Laz grabbed Motrin from the cabinet, glanced at the slight scar on his wrist where he'd been chipped. The League always knew where their operatives were. Not anymore. He poured three pills into his hand. "Dusty's in the League of Warrior Women?"

"Yep. Guess we found your replacement."

He popped the pills and dry swallowed. "Fuck you. How much time do I have?"

"Dude, you were adopted into a wealthy family of vigilantes. You got no time. Run."

Easier said than done. Running from the League—an entire system of highly trained assassins, cutting-edge technology, and well-funded global connections—required more than taking out his chip, more than false identities. It required going to a place completely removed from technology. The moon?

Crossing the small living area, he climbed onto the deck of his boat. Moored at a makeshift marina—constructed after the last hurricane—he blinked at the steam and sun.

He pressed his Bluetooth deeper into his ear as his connection went fuzzy. "Has Momma talked about erasing my memory?"

Rome took a minute. "They did Bridget."

Cold washed down his body. They'd taken his sister Bridget's memory? Obviously because she'd helped him carry out his plan to save Justice.

"Doesn't seem that bad. I mean, she's still herself. Just doesn't remember her part in the betrayal stuff. Probably do the same for you."

Kid said that like it was no big deal. Wasn't his head. "Fuck that."

"Then go deep, as deep under as you can. Like the Amazon. Or Greenland."

He'd go deep. Not stopping long at any country. Just him and his boat. Boats. His current one was the second he'd had. "Keep me in the loop but stay safe. Ditch this number. You got the other phone numbers I gave you memorized?"

"Yeah. I'll move onto the second number."

"Good. Don't risk yourself. You've done enough."

Another pause. Rome cleared his throat. "It's better now. Since you left. The aggression, the blame. Even the

Troublemakers Guild—the badass unit to end all badass units—have stopped looking at me like the enemy, like I'm someone who needs to be trained and kept in line. They're treating me like I'm a real person."

Laz's heart responded without his say. He'd shaken up his family enough to make a space for Rome? To get them to reevaluate the way the League worked? Or was the kid just trying to make him feel better?

Bending down, he opened his cooler and took out a bottle of water. "I'm glad it's better." He sipped the water. "But remember what I told you. They don't mean it, the suspicion. The anger. They're looking at you through damaged glass. To them, you will always reflect the pain they experienced through the hands of other men."

"That's dark, man."

"Just be careful. And thanks."

Rome snorted. "You're my brother. Dead or alive."

Laz tried to swallow over the lump that stuck in his throat. Unable to say a word—there were none to express how much he appreciated the kid's support, how much he regretted the necessity of leaving, how much he missed them all—he hung up.

CHAPTER 6

THE STORM THAT HAD FORCED HONOR TO PLAY HERO, had left damaged trees across roads, electrical lines torn down, and broken glass scattered. Now the blazing sun tossed orange light on the clean-up crews like a many armed goddess bestowing an apology.

With that warmth healing her through the open windows, Honor pulled into the asphalt parking lot of the stand-alone Loco for Cocoa chocolate store in Roseau.

Rounded like a cocoa bean, painted brown with a white roof, as if the raw cocoa inside the shell had been revealed, the store was undamaged. If only she could say the same about herself.

It was almost eight. Most days, she was here earlier, but she'd been unable to sleep last night after talking to the real estate agent brokering the bid on the farm, hotel, and touring business.

Gray had been annoyingly bleak, painting Honor as the dumbest person she'd ever met. She kept pushing her to accept. In the end, she'd even sounded threatening. Thus the sleepless night. Some people.

Pocketing her keys, Honor swung open the car door. Her cell rang. A quick look at the screen and she answered with a smile. "Hey, Junior. Shouldn't you be headed up into the mountains with the guests?"

"Yeah, that's the problem."

Uh-oh. Probably didn't want to hear this. "What?"

"There's just me. No one else showed up."

"None of the guests?"

"Oh. No. They're all here. But I'm the only tour guide. And I'm good. Cousin, you know I'm good, but I can't run the whole tour by myself."

None? "Are you telling me all three of our other tour guides haven't shown up? Even Tito?"

"Yep. And Tito was the only one who didn't text and tell me he was sick."

Spectacular. "I have gear in my car. I'll change and be there in a minute."

"The two of us? Is that safe?"

No. It wasn't. But she could not lose the tours. It was an iffy business, and the cruise ships did not mess around. It was hell to get on the list of approved tours, and if she was kicked off, she'd have to go through the grueling application process all over again.

Nightmare.

Especially since she'd be dealing with Gray. Not exactly a big fan right now. "I'll find us someone else. Get the guests to sign the forms, and load them into the truck. If you need to keep them happy, dip into the midpoint chocolate stash."

She hung up. Letting out a breath, she scrolled through her contacts. Not easy to find someone in Roseau who was free early morning on a weekday, who actually knew how to rappel and…

Wait. She did know someone. And he was close.

She shut her door, started her car, and tore out of the parking lot.

Returning from the store, one arm laden with provisions, Lazarus strolled toward the makeshift marina where his boat was docked. Despite wearing shorts and a sleeveless T-shirt, sweat dripped down his shoulders, neck, biceps. Sweltering hot. The kind of humid heat that often came after a big storm.

Mentally running through the list of things he needed to do, he veered around people cleaning up storm damage.

There was a lot of activity and noise, but he was on high alert, so he sensed someone coming up behind him. His heart began to pound. They'd found him already?

A bag in one hand, his weapon strapped in a concealed carry at his side, he prepared to turn, throw his goods at his pursuer, use the distraction to grab his gun and...what?

If it was one of his sisters, all he could do was threaten, because there was no fucking way he'd shoot. Rather die.

"Lazarus."

Every muscle in his body packed up its briefcase and quit for the day. He almost fell down. Not his sisters. He turned.

The heat that slammed into his body put the sun to shame. Damn. So hot wearing a brown Loco for Cocoa T-shirt, tan cargo shorts, and brown hiking boots. Her silver eyes beamed at him under her Loco for Cocoa baseball cap. His heart did flips in his chest, like a puppy when its master opens the front door.

Maybe he had time to pay off his debt before he left. "Hey. Whatcha doin' out here?"

She had car keys in her hand, seemed anxious. "I need a favor."

His heartbeat picked up to yes-please, right-now, boat's-over-there pace. *Down, boy. She probably wants to borrow a cup of sugar or something.* "Anything you want. I owe you my life, after all."

She shook her head. Her cheeks flushed. Freakin' adorable. He wished he could stay here a couple days, get to know her a bit better. He shoved that shit down and buried it in the pit that had grown in his gut.

Honor glanced at the supplies he carried. "But are you free today?"

Well, he did have to run from his furious, vindictive family. Sooner rather than later. "I've got time. What's up?"

"My tour guides haven't shown up. I can't run the tour with just me and my cousin. I need at least one more."

Oh shit. This wasn't an hour or two. This was an all-day thing. A job, basically. This would be a delay he couldn't afford. He hesitated.

"I understand if you can't. You're not recovered enough. I didn't mean to ask anything too extreme."

This from the woman who'd saved his life. And honestly, even if she hadn't…well, he might not be part of the League anymore, but that didn't mean he couldn't help someone when they needed him.

Anyways, probably the last place his family would expect him to be was in the Caribbean. "I want extreme, Honor. That's exactly what I want you to ask of me. You saved my life. I owe you."

She cocked her head to the side. "Don't tempt me. We could end up in serious trouble."

His mouth went dry. Probably hadn't meant that to sound dirty, but that was where he went. Swallowing, he hitched a thumb toward his boat. "Can you give me a sec to put my supplies away?"

"Of course. Thanks."

"No problem." Well, slight problem. This was a mistake. He should leave. Logic said leave. Hell, he was becoming as undisciplined as Justice.

CHAPTER 7

THE TOUR TRUCK, A SLAT-SIDED, OLD GREEN MILITARY vehicle, parked inside the pier gates, was crammed with guests and ready for takeoff when Honor arrived with the handsome Lazarus Graves in tow.

So handsome, it hurt her heart.

So handsome, he made her afraid.

So handsome, her desire shushed that fear.

Not even her anxiety could stand up to that need. Moving toward the truck, she waved to Junior.

Collecting forms from people on the truck, slim as a reed Junior had on his Loco for Cocoa uniform—brown baseball hat, tan cargo shorts, brown tee, and hiking boots.

Junior jumped from the truck and handed her the papers along with the keys to the vehicle.

Tipping up his hat, dark skin slicked with sweat, he cast a wary look at Laz. "Who's Robin Hood?"

Great. Junior watched way too much television. And had no boundaries.

Though now that she thought of it, Laz did kind of look like a muscular version of Robin Hood, with his wavy dark hair, neatly trimmed goatee, and hot, confident swagger. "He's a volunteer. Show some respect."

"Always thought of myself as a dark hero," Laz said and held out his hand. "Lazarus Graves. Newest tour guide. Quick study."

Junior shook his hand. "Let's see how quick. Can you

climb on the back and make sure everyone is strapped in? There's a mic back there, so you can talk, try and charm them."

Despite Junior being bossy, Laz gave him a big grin— seriously, the man had the best smile in the history of smiles. "Not for nothing. Charm I got."

Sure did. Honor's melting heart sped up. Laz could've made this hard. He could've gotten into it with her rude cousin, but he took it all in stride.

Laz lifted himself onto the truck, a tightening of arm muscles that caused her hormones to swoon like teen girls at a boy band concert.

Finding herself a bit discombobulated, Honor juggled keys and paper while walking to the front of the truck.

Junior followed, watching Laz uncertainly. "You sure about this?"

"We have no choice. You know how finicky the cruise ship business is. One mistake, and Loco for Cocoa Tours could be kicked off the approved tour list."

"But if someone gets hurt…"

She opened the door to the cab of the truck, put the papers on the front seat, and turned back to him. "It's okay. Really. I already grilled Laz. He knows how to rappel. And has experience with a ton of outdoor stuff. Heck, he might know more than me."

Junior's eyes traveled toward the big tread of the truck's tires. "If you're sure."

Honor stepped onto the dented metal truck step and climbed into the cab. "It'll be okay. If he can't hack it, we'll call the tour early and take everyone back to the chalet. Papito will fill them with chocolate and charm until they can't see straight."

Junior smiled, walked toward the back of the truck. "I've been there."

Hadn't they all? Honor slid the forms across the long, green-leather seat and put her cell into a small weighted tray beside her.

Junior banged twice on the roof of the cab, giving her the all-clear.

She turned the truck over with a roar that sent a rumble up through her body. With the big black plastic wheel comfortable in her grasp, she drove, bounced really, forward from the pier and through the chain-link gates. She waved to the guards.

After about five minutes in which her cousin had been using the microphone to welcome and inform the guests, she heard Laz's voice come through the speaker.

To her surprise, he began taking part as if he'd been dealing with big groups, giving tours to diverse personalities his whole life. He was a natural and won the cruisers over in record time.

She even found herself laughing as Laz engaged people, asked questions, and joked with Junior.

Before too long, they hit the winding road up the mountain, an older road that was more scenic for tourists.

Honor knew this road like the back of her hand. She knew before it happened that people would grow silent. They always did at this particular winding section, a view so lush with green, so startling in fertile beauty that speechless was mandatory.

In that moment of stillness, people from all over the world saw, were touched by what could not be denied. The hand of God himself had crafted every divine leaf, every sun-streaked bit of verdant green in Dominica.

The moment of awe passed, and Junior started the chant that would get them through the one-lane dirt roads that wound around huge stone outcrops. Every time they came to a sight-unseen turn, Junior would call out, "I'm loco for..."

And the group would call back, "Cocoa!"

Honor would hit the horn twice to start the chant. They'd explained to the group this was to let any trucks on the other side know they were coming, but no one ever went down this road. Only up. The chant was to keep people calm. A look down that steep side could be terrifying. Honor didn't flinch. She could probably drive this road with her eyes closed.

Some people had photographic memory when it came to words or ideas, but she had the same thing with trails and roads and scenery. Whenever she walked a place—paved or dirt or stone—its every dip, rise, curve, and swell became etched in her memory.

At the top of the ascent, she pulled the truck onto the roadway and a short while later slid to a stop at the head of the jungle trail.

Adjusting her hat, she climbed down from the cab. Laz rushed over to her with pure eagerness. He took her in his arms and twirled her around.

Setting her back on her feet, he stared at her with adoring eyes. "Honor, you catch my breath. The way you drive. The way you pause in the road right before a dip. It's like you're one with this earth. It's like..."

He stopped. Maybe realized what he'd done. Picked her up and twirled her around. He shook his head. "I'm sorry. I shouldn't..."

Her entire front longed to get close to him again. Unable to resist, she put a hand on his chest. "No one has ever noticed before. You're the first."

"I like being your first." He winked at her.

Detaching herself from the pull of him, she reached up and tugged down the Loco for Cocoa baseball cap Junior must have given him. He tipped it back up.

They exchanged a look that sent a deep longing to be closer to him, to hear his laughter as she rested her head on his chest, hear his heartbeat racing with desire. Hear his blood pushing want through every cell of his body.

The stare went on much too long. Laz gave her one last *want-you-alone* grin before he left her side and helped the guests down from the truck.

The guests milled about a moment longer before Junior hitched up his backpack and singsonged in a voice made for music, "I'm loco for…"

The twenty guests shouted, "Cocoa!"

And with her cousin waving them forward, they lined up and began to follow him down the trail.

CHAPTER 8

TONY HAD TO ADMIRE THE RAPPELLING STATION. THE cliff was high enough to give a thrill, a great view, but not so high as to put the fear of God in the clients.

Stationed at the bottom of a large brown and red cliff dotted with green moss that could give Ireland a run for its money, Laz worked as the belayer, securing the rappelling ropes for each guest and encouraging the more timid guests.

The thing about sailing to escape your vindictive vigilante family, was you didn't always get to stop and enjoy the view.

A day spent outside, hiking, ziplining, diving into warm pools of water, laughing, and hanging out with the enchanting and scorching-hot Honor Silva wasn't going to be easy to top. Or forget. Sucked that tomorrow he'd be all by his lonesome, sailing away from Dominica. And her.

Being here had made him feel like himself again. Probably because the activities reminded him of the underground training facility at the League of Warrior Women. Especially the climbing. As he'd explained to Honor, climbing was one of his skills. Another reason the kids he trained in the gym called him "Monkey Man."

Damn. Must not think of home. Brought down his mood. He flagged the blues for later, when he wasn't working. His calloused hands, worn rough by sailing, secured the belay device and rope giving slack when needed, but ready to hold steady if there was trouble.

Craning his head, he waited as Junior signaled that the last guest—a big guy named Roger but nicknamed Bud—was ready.

Laz fed the line and kept his feet wide enough to balance. Bud began to rappel.

Behind Laz, Honor had set up a folding table with chocolate and booze. The other guests, helmets and harnesses off, talked, ate, drank, and mingled loudly, barely paying attention.

Bud didn't need their encouragement. He knew what he was doing. He'd been in the military. And he'd been giving Laz a hard time all day. Still was. He called down, "Make sure you get right under me, catch me if I fall."

"No worries," Laz called back up, working the rope. "These rocks are super soft. Like cushions."

Bud laughed and continued to lower, walking himself back. He was slow at first but dropped quickly afterward. He was halfway down the thirty-foot drop when he tucked his feet into a rock, pulled fingers off the line, and gripped stone. Like he'd decided to free climb.

"You okay up there?" Laz called. Sweat rolled from under his helmet, and he blinked it from his eyes.

Junior encouraged from above, "Got some beer at the hotel."

His body weight supported, Bud's legs began to shake. Something in Laz's chest lurched to attention. The big man clung to the rocks, frozen solid. "Bud, you okay?"

"What's going on?" Honor said.

Laz startled, realizing Honor stood beside him. He shrugged. "Not sure."

Bud yelled down, "My beaner."

His carabiner? The piece of metal holding securing him and his harness to the rope? Shit. He exchanged a look with Honor. "Attach to the belay device. I can climb."

She looked nervously up the mountain. "I should."

Already grabbing her carabiner and locking her in, he handed off the safety line and unhooked himself. "Trust me. I got this."

Fingers accustomed to supporting his weight, he grasped hold of an edge of rock, pulled himself up, and began to make good on his nickname. He found handholds and footholds, almost without thought, scaling rapidly. It took only a few minutes to get up to Bud, but by the time he did, the guy's legs were trembling.

Not just adrenaline. If you weren't used to climbing, no matter how strong, and you weren't moving, shifting weight to balance, you'd find your weaknesses quickly.

When he was parallel with the man, he wedged his feet. "What's up?"

Bud didn't even turn his head. His fingers dug into stone, so hard Laz could see blood. "Need another beaner."

No shit. He could see that. No time to even tie a safety knot, palms slick with sweat, he kept his voice calm. "No worries. Got one right here."

Tugging up the rope from below—Honor automatically gave him the feed—Bud eased back from the rope, giving Laz the space to secure the new equipment.

His fingers expertly spun the clasp on the new beaner and looped it around the rope, and Bud relaxed. Laz reached for the old carabiner, and bam. It gave way, shot out. Laz managed to palm the bigger pieces. Bud slipped a fraction.

Damn. That was close.

Bud looked down below. "It's good?"

Dude wanted out of here. Couldn't blame him. Laz double-checked his equipment and, after signaling Honor, let him continue down.

Laz pocketed the broken beaner. Stressed and old. If Bud hadn't been paying attention, he would've fallen.

Laz free-climbed back down.

At the bottom, Honor was hugging Bud. "I'm so sorry. This equipment…"

She stopped her excuses. What could she say? The guy could've died.

Bud shook his head. "You need to replace these things. Keep an eye. I won't start any trouble, but that could've been bad."

She nodded, chastised and looking confused.

Bud gave Laz a bear hug and thanked him.

"No problem, man. Hope this doesn't spoil the adventure for you," Laz said.

Bud shook his head, scratched at his salt-and-red-pepper beard. "No. Just make sure you safety-check your equipment next time." He went over to the table and picked up a bottle of whiskey, poured himself a glass.

Taking the pieces of carabiner out from his pocket, Laz handed them to Honor.

Her silver eyes ran over the distressed pieces in confusion. "This isn't one of ours. Ours are new. We've only been doing tours about a year."

Junior called down, and Honor readied the lines as he rappelled. Once he was down, Honor held out the broken equipment to show him. "Didn't you check?"

Junior disengaged from the lines and looked down at her hand. "You said you checked them last night."

Honor held up one piece. Looked old. Anyone could see that. And Junior had had his hands all over it. "You didn't notice this wasn't one of ours?"

Sweat started to bead and roll down Junior's forehead. "The guy kept chatting with me. I was tired. I didn't notice. We are a few people short, you know."

Honor twisted the metal in the waning light of the day. It was nicked. Ancient. "What about when you opened the equipment locker under the seats in the truck. You didn't notice anything wrong?"

"No. The harnesses were there, stacked and ready. I just assumed..." He shook his head. "Sorry, Honor. You're right. I should've seen. That's not even the brand we use."

Honor pocketed the pieces of the carabiner. Her face was a cross between angry and confused. She looked at Junior. "Let's get everyone to the hotel."

After packing up, they took the group back through the jungle. Laz wasn't surprised to find some had no idea what had happened. They'd been talking and drinking, and danger had never seemed like it could be close at hand. That was the way it worked with most people.

And most people would probably dismiss what had happened as an accident. Not Laz. He dropped back to talk with Honor. "You leave your equipment in the truck?"

She let out a breath that sounded heavy with tension. Or regret. "Yeah. But I lock it up."

Still seemed a risk. Or maybe it just seemed that way to him. He'd grown up in a rather suspicious environment.

Kind of envied her a life where you didn't distrust as a matter of safety. But then again, it had cost her. He could see from her face and the shadow in her eyes that she didn't like this new reality.

And he hated to push it, but it was the paranoid in him that wouldn't let it rest. "You don't have anyone that would want to sabotage your business, right? I mean, first the guides and now the equipment. Seems kind of suspicious."

She laughed. "Where do you come from?"

That wasn't a no. "No place near as fun as being with you."

CHAPTER 9

IT WAS 3:30 IN THE AFTERNOON WHEN THE TOUR TRUCK rocked to a stop in front of Loco for Cocoa's lodge and surrounding chalets. Honor turned off the truck and put on the emergency brake. She dropped out of the truck and shut the door with a slam.

Laz and Junior were already helping the guests out.

Wearing his white button-down shirt, white pants, and white straw hat, Papito greeted the tour group. He looked timeless with his strong and athletic build.

Boys from the nearby village circulated among the guests, offering hand towels to clean themselves and handing out chocolate lemonade. Honor watched as people tasted, smiled, and sipped on their straws.

They liked it. Happiness warmed her heart. She'd invented this perfect chocolate lemonade recipe as a child. It had been her first experience creating things with chocolate. It had hooked her.

She still wasn't sure how *that* passion had led to her running tours. Today had been terrifying and exhausting. Thank God she could now hand the reins over to Papito.

His words rolled over Honor. "Welcome to the Loco for Cocoa Lodge. This hotel was begun by my wife, who inherited the land from her father, nearly sixty years ago. My granddaughter"—he motioned to Honor, and a few people made noises of surprise that he was a grandfather of someone her age—"expanded the business two years ago. One year ago, we opened our chalets and tours."

Honor found comfort in listening to him tell the routine story as if nothing had changed and all was as it should be. Everything had changed though. What Laz had suggested, about the issue with the climbing gear and guides being no accident, had hit her hard.

Could someone be trying to scare her into accepting that offer?

Papito led the group away, pointing out architectural details. Behind the hotel were six cottages, staggered down winding stone walkways, with pointed roofs and curled edges. Each front door was a different color, as were the small outdoor statues, seating, and flowers.

Laz looked around with interest, and Honor startled. That was right. He'd never been here before. How had he fit so perfectly into the tour, her day, her life that this place had always seemed to have him here?

He grinned at her. "It's beautiful. I love the combination of rustic and fairy-tale charm."

Her heart filled with joy. Bouncing happily on her toes, she pointed at the surrounding jungle. "It started out with the cocoa. My great-grandfather worked here. He eventually made enough to buy the property. Years later, my grandmother expanded her home into a hotel. She had high hopes of bringing tourists to Dominica for vacation."

As she spoke, they moved across the front porch through the handcrafted front doors.

"Wow," he said, staring at the handcrafted wooden front desk and matching banister and railing that wound up and along the open foyer. Made out of wood from the surrounding jungle, it wasn't hewed and cut, but rough. Branches of trees were bound together to make it look like the railing had sprung to life, curving and reaching out as if it grew there.

Honor beamed. "That's all original," she said. "Grandmother wanted it to seem like an extension of the woods."

"Who's the archer?"

Looking where his eyes had fallen—to the trophy case filled with trophies, a picture of her Olympic team, and her compound bow—she couldn't help the proud smile. "Me."

"Olympics?"

"I was an alternate."

Before he could say another word, she grabbed his hand. An involuntary *mmm* slipped from her lips. His eyebrows rose. Heat washed down her body, tugged at her center.

Clearing her throat, avoiding eye contact, she led him down the hall, showed him the dining room, the quaint library/conversation area, and pulled him out onto the back patio. Wedged between large-leafed trees and ferns, the chalets dotted the landscape.

"Kinda looks like a fairy-tale village."

That was how she thought of it. Her heart, like her step, grew lighter. She walked him down a stone pathway. Now that she thought of it, it wasn't as if he fit into the place all along. It was as if this place had always been waiting for him. Now, somehow, it seemed more complete.

And that was a crazy thought. A rash and dangerous thought. Because as he'd already explained to her many times, he could not stick around. He was sailing around the world. Maybe sailing forever.

Her heart trembled.

What was happening to her? She was not her mother. She did not rush into a relationship knowing it would end badly. She did not go boldly forward despite imminent pain. She could not afford to have her heart, still repairing from the loss of her mother, shattered again.

And yet, she wanted him.

CHAPTER 10

LOCO FOR COCOA WELCOMED AND INVITED LIKE A homey bed and breakfast but also had unexpected and unique areas that surprised Laz. Like this yoga room, built high and supported by the trees. Open on all sides, with wood floor, beams, and roof, it reminded him of a tree house.

Heck, it was a tree house. No walls, no *Boys Have Cooties* sign, but wood railings as sides, a pitched roof with numerous fans along it, and bug nets—currently rolled up—that could be dropped as makeshift walls. Yoga mats, blocks, and straps hung from the support beams.

His sister Bridget, a yogi herself, would freakin' love it.

Must not think of Bridget. Or the fact that her mind had been altered, that she'd been robbed of the most sacred part of herself, her memories. It made him angry enough to grind diamonds in his teeth.

"Do you like?" Honor asked, returning from flicking on the tropical fans.

He pointed around. "Never done yoga, but this is a great room."

"The yoga was Papito's idea."

"Dude does yoga?" *No freakin' way.*

"He hired the yoga teacher, Mia. She works here, teaching yoga, and also helps out at the shop. She's forty years younger than him. And I'm pretty sure she has a crush on him."

"That's it. I'm taking up yoga."

She laughed and, silent as a cat across plush carpet, walked to the edge of the room, looked out into the distance.

He watched her. Because he liked to watch her. He liked the way she moved, gliding along with her sleek curves and long limbs.

Her. This day. This place. All of it had gotten under his skin, in his blood, like nothing he'd ever experienced. Could just be the company.

Or the heat between them. Or something else, something...unexpected. Despite the tension of his lust, coiled and ready to explode, he'd never felt so comfortable with a woman in his life. Not even Justice. He walked over to her, looked out at the chalets below and the trees beyond.

Honor pointed out at the view. "You can almost see forever from here."

He could see the ocean. "That's incredible."

She turned unexpectedly toward him, closed the two inches between them, lifted her chin. Intrigued, he looked down at her. He knew what she wanted, what he desperately wanted, but he didn't move. He waited to see what she'd do. Wanted her to make that move. Wanted her to take what she wanted. He liked when she was bold.

Her breathing picked up. His too. When he stood his ground, color rose into her cheeks. He held steady. Not easy when all he wanted to do was crash into her, drag her body against his, claim her mouth, and run his hands all over her.

He silently sent her a do-it, please-fucking-do-it signal.

She stepped back.

Fuck.

"Would you like to see the chocolate store?"

CHAPTER 11

HONOR CURSED HER COWARDICE AS THEY LEFT THE YOGA tree house, walking down the ramp and onto the stone walkways between buildings.

Why hadn't she kissed Laz? She could see he'd wanted her to. Could feel the scorching heat between them. And yet as he'd looked down at her, too handsome to be real, she froze. Cowardly Lion indeed.

Keeping close enough to him that their arms rubbed together, she directed him toward her chocolate store, the Cocoa Chalet. She got their hands tangled and managed to hold his. He looked down at her, grinned. Okay, so she was trying to make up for the failed kiss. What of it?

"I've saved the best for last," she said.

His eyebrows rose. Nice to know her mind wasn't the only one so consumed with thoughts of sex that everything sounded dirty. Honestly, the jungle was steamy enough without the looks he kept sending her.

She stopped at the door to the chalet. "My store. My chocolate. Every recipe is mine."

"I can't wait to get my lips around your recipes."

Heat shot down her body, warmth tingled between her legs. Whoa. She squeezed his hand, moved so close the heat of his body warmed her whole side. "You're going to enjoy every minute of it."

He made a choked sound, and she felt a wave of triumph.

Yes, she definitely wasn't the only one consumed by sexy thoughts.

Inside, the cool air smelled of sugar and chocolate and spices. And well it should with cases of chocolate, shelves of wrapped chocolate, fudge and elaborate displays of green and gold boxed chocolates. Her assistant, and the hotel's yoga teacher, Mia greeted them with a wave as she continued to stack boxes.

As Laz looked around at the store, she closed her eyes, took a deep breath, and let it out with a satisfied sigh.

When she opened her eyes, she found him staring at her mouth. Heat rushed through her. She should've kissed him. Should've kissed him. Maybe now. She stepped closer.

The chimes over the door rang as a guest, an old family friend, Ford Fairchild, entered the store. Ford was a trim, bone-edged man, with a razor-straight nose, peeling from a bad sunburn.

Meeting Honor's eyes from across the store, Ford said, "Store's packed." He winked. Tried to wink. It was actually a blink. Ford had some quirky social awkwardness. She adored him.

When Honor had put the word out to her mother's wealthy friends in the States that she could use a few bodies to fill rooms, he was one of the first to respond. He'd been here for almost three weeks now, and Honor really appreciated his kindness.

Leaving Laz, she greeted Ford with a kiss to his cheek. "Is it true you're leaving next week?"

"Afraid so." He smiled, and a deep dimple appeared on the left side of his mouth. "My wife and daughter are due back from Japan, and I'm eager to see them."

"Your wife's shows are over?"

"Yes. A very successful trip."

His wife was an illustrator for graphic novels. Her work was extraordinary. She traveled a lot, going to conventions and even doing exhibits. Ford's coming here, to help Honor, was one of the few times he hadn't been with his wife and five-year-old daughter on tour.

"Plus, I need to get back into the office. We're starting our final season."

Grabbing his hand, she squeezed it. Ford was a screen-writer who worked on a popular television series. "I really appreciate you coming here. Giving up your time."

Mia, hair shorn to an auburn fuzz around her fair face, walked over. "Hi, Ford, did you need help with something?" Mia flicked her innocent honey eyes toward Laz, letting Honor know she had this covered. Honor smiled in gratitude.

She left them and caught up to Laz, who was examining the contents of the cases. "You like?"

He jumped at the sound of her voice. His eyebrows drew together. "You're like ninja quiet."

She'd often been told she was mouse quiet, but she liked ninja better.

"I do like," he said. "It's a great store."

It was. Long glass counters, green and gold touches in the ribbons and wrapping, the bright lights, and gentle invitation to shop were her chocolatier's dream. It was, in fact, a perfect candy store.

She was glad he enjoyed it, but one thing made her nervous. Well, many things about him made her nervous, but right now this. Getting him to taste something.

Time to bite the bullet. She pointed at the rows of dishes

in the glass case, white china, filled with different types of chocolate and truffles. "What's your favorite?"

He put down a chocolate bar whose wrapper he'd been reading. "My favorite? Would it disappoint you if I said I'm not a huge chocolate fan?"

Would it disappoint her? Was he kidding? "Are you trying to cause me physical pain?"

He laughed. "No. I love chocolate." He turned, moved closer to her, front to front. "Can't get enough. You have anything with some bite?"

Biting. Yes. What? She was losing her mind. Oh, he was so hot. But this was her chance. Her chance to make up for her missed opportunity. *Bold, Honor. Be bold.*

She leaned past him, into him. Her entire front caught fire. She gathered up a jar of chocolate sticks, took one out. Putting the jar back, she brushed his bicep. Hopefully he didn't notice her shaking hands.

She held up the chocolate stick. "I invented this."

"A small, chocolate straw?"

She pulled off the plastic wrapper. "It's a kissing stick. The middle is filled with a warm surprise, but as you can see, it's a little large for one mouth to suck on."

He grinned at her. "I think I might need a demonstration."

She grinned back. Oh good. That was what she'd wanted. "The things I do for my craft."

She put the chocolate straw in her mouth, up to the center, tilted up her chin. He dipped down and captured the other end of the stick.

Heat. Heat like she never felt before shot through her body. She clutched at him, had no choice, no way not to. Her body took over, closed down her mind. Closer. More. Closer. Now.

The chocolate reacted instantly, melting against their lips. Her hot and needy tongue licked the chocolate from his full lips.

The cayenne warmed her already tingling mouth, and she found her boldness in her desire. She probed the kiss, begged him to let her inside.

He did. Eagerly.

She moaned and moved into him. He put his arms around her. He'd given her the first move, but he was taking control now, demonstrating his own need.

His body was hard against her, mouth pulling at her, tasting her. The chocolate melted, leaving the cayenne slick between them.

The jingle of the bells over the door brought her to her senses. What was she doing? In the middle of her store?

She broke off the kiss, licked her lips, stepped back from him. They stared at each other. Their breathing heavy and much too loud. The heat in their mouths was nothing compared to the heat building between them. She couldn't have mumbled a single word.

What was this?

What was happening to her?

She'd never felt this way about a man. She'd thought it was a myth, this type of attraction—the kind that drove away doubt and common sense. She needed to take him to her room and rip off his clothes.

But was this unique for him too? Or did he act this way or feel this way with all women? A bolt of pain, real pain, pierced her chest. She had to be cautious. This was her first experience with these feelings, this desire, but that didn't mean it was his. Maybe he did this to all women.

He licked his lips. "Sweet." His voice was thick with need.

Though she wanted to grab another stick, take another chance with feeling his firm and eager body against hers, she found her voice and a better idea. "My grandfather usually finishes the tour around five, so we have some time. Would you like me to show you the rooms?"

His eyebrows jumped. His smile widened. "That sounds fantastic. Let's start with yours."

This man had just read her mind. Not that you needed to be a mind reader. She was sending up red signal flares that burst into the air between them spelling out, *I'm going to take you hard. You're mine.*

Honor called to Mia and let her know that she was taking off. Mia waved and continued with Ford and a couple who'd come inside.

Honor was ten steps out the door, nearing the hotel, with all Laz's hotness following behind, when José appeared out of nowhere. Okay, not out of nowhere. Out of a side door that led to the kitchen. But her uncle was kind of creepy. He blocked the path in front of her.

"Uncle José?"

"Honor, Junior just informed me you had a problem today. We should talk about it."

Nuts.

CHAPTER 12

ON THE WALKWAY BEHIND THE LOCO FOR COCOA HOTEL, Laz was pretty sure the timing of Honor's uncle José was comical enough to require a horse-walks-into-a-bar rim shot. *Ba-dum-tish*.

Thanks for the cock-block, dude. Honor handled José with calm grace. She nodded to him and turned to Laz. "Don't go anywhere."

He couldn't help the snort of laughter or the full stop gesture of his upraised hands. "Even if my car was here and headed straight for me."

She smiled, then her face darkened as she turned to José. For his part, José looked equally annoyed. Even hostile. They walked off together.

And though Laz had no intention of leaving the hotel, that didn't mean he'd actually stand stock-still. Especially when he had an interest in this particular conversation.

And there it was. That raised to spy and cross every line flag that he couldn't help but carry. He knew, some part of him knew, that the average person didn't spy on a conversation between a woman and her uncle, but that wasn't going to stop him.

He ran on the balls of his feet and caught the door they'd entered before it clicked shut. He came into the hall, hugged the wall, and kept his eye on them as they turned a corner.

He followed.

Spying on regular people was easy. Not like spying on his

sisters or bad guys or law enforcement or anyone with any kind of situational awareness. Laz parked himself outside the office door they'd entered, and using the setting on his burner phone, along with a small ear device, he listened to the conversation.

His phone showed him some game he'd never played in his life. It actually ran through the game while he pretended to play. He hit the button mindlessly as his concentration was elsewhere.

Uncle José, it turned out, was really pissed off. No sooner had the door shut than he was raising his voice. "I told you, Honora. A thousand times. We don't need tours. We would do just fine with filling the rooms, selling the chocolate like before."

Guy seemed almost happy that they'd had the accident. Or supposed accident.

He heard Honor sigh. "Uncle José, the chocolate is good, but few people are interested in coming to the rain forest and sitting in a hammock. That is what Grandmother tried."

"Yes. But the chocolate is better. You are just listening to Papito. This is his doing. Why else wouldn't you take the offer?"

What offer? There was a long pause. Laz didn't know Honor, not really, but he pictured her right now with her hands balled into fists. Hard to blame her.

"The offer made to buy the property and business is large. But not if you take into account the two million I've invested—"

"You've invested money." He spat the word. "My blood is here. The arthritis in my fingers. My sweat. The kink in my back. Things you can't equal. That has paid off as much as your dollars. I ferment the beans."

"Uncle José…"

Laz took out his earpiece and walked away. It was that or bust in and punch the guy. What a total ass. This guy was acting like *she* was ruining *his* business.

Fuck. Could Honor be in real trouble here? He rubbed at his face. Something wasn't right. He could feel it in his bones. Or had his upbringing, the one that taught him to pay attention, made him paranoid?

Making his way out to where Honor had left him, he sat on a stone bench and waited for her to come back.

That conversation between José and Honor just ate at him. He couldn't stand to see a man bully a woman like that.

Great, Tone. You were raised with a bunch of kickass women, and you revert to character the moment you leave?

Shit. Justice's voice in his head. And yeah, he fucking got that. Honor was capable of defending herself, not like the women they rescued—trapped by circumstance, poverty, brutality, conditioning.

But it still reminded him of his mom. Of the night she'd died. Of the night he'd watched her die and had been unable to do anything to stop it. Of the years after that he'd pretended not to know his father had killed her.

To this day, it was his greatest shame. Not just being unable to defend her from that abuse. Keeping quiet. It was why, when he'd seen Justice about to go off and get herself killed, he'd risked everything to keep her safe.

And it had cost him. His integrity. His relationships. His life.

Fifteen minutes passed before Honor came out. Her face pinched and angry. Okay, and this was not his only concern here, but he so wasn't getting laid now. Fuck.

Honor walked over, and he stood. He reached out to

her. She reached too, grabbed him by the hand, tugged. And said, "We don't have a lot of time."

Dumbstruck and more turned on than he'd been in his entire life, he let her lead him into the hotel.

She walked him through the hotel, dining area, then kitchen, where she let his hand go, acted like she was still giving a tour while trying not to make eye contact with her staff. Guess it wasn't easy to be the boss and have a sex life. Especially with someone who had just served as one of your employees, even if it was just for the day. With a brisk and boss-like "Follow me," she led him up a back staircase.

At the top, she unlocked her room with a key, an actual key. Fuck. A two-year-old could pick that damn lock. He'd bring it up later. Much later.

Inside was the exact place he would've pictured her in— soft and comfortable, a big bed with a plush comforter, a series of dark, wood-framed windows, and a sitting area with a desk.

And a cabinet filled with archery trophies, along with a series of small to larger bows. Cool. She really was an archer.

She shut the door and dropped all pretext, grabbing his waist and pulling him to her. Her face was still a little cross, but now there was something else too. Fear.

He got it. This was all moving so fast. Necessitated by the fact that time wasn't on their side.

That, he could make better. He lifted her chin and slowly, slow enough to set a different mood, bent to her lips.

He kissed her gentle and sure, taking his time, learning her lips, the feel of them, how she responded, how she tasted, the sweetness of her mouth.

Their breathing picked up. She made small sounds of

need. He grew so hard against her, his pants became uncomfortably tight. Best feeling ever.

Slowly, he worked against her. And she opened wide for him. Moaned hot into his mouth. Grasped at his sides, making soft, demanding tugs for him to get closer.

Her need came alive, robbed her of her fear, and he welcomed it.

He'd known it. Known that she was wild underneath—brash and needy. That truth was what he wanted from her.

CHAPTER 13

THIS WAS THE MIDDLE OF HONOR'S WORKDAY. SHE HAD guests from the cruise ships walking around, one of whom had nearly been killed or at the least seriously injured. She'd just gotten into another fight with José about her business management. And here she was in her bedroom, rubbing herself against the thick, hard, throbbing part of a man she'd met only days before.

Didn't matter. She could not stop. He was so hot and hard and sexy. So sweet. And attentive. He gave her room— that was the best way to say it. He gave her space to be herself and explore him. While he enjoyed tasting her, he let her set the pace. She felt him giving her that space, as if saying, *Go on now. Just how you want it.*

And she knew exactly how she wanted it. Furious after her exchange with José, she wanted to be with someone who would let her take the lead and respect her enough to give her that control.

She had no idea how Laz knew that she needed that. But he did. And his response and encouraging patience were setting her on fire. Rubbing against his hardness, she kissed him until they were both breathing heavy and tearing each other's clothes off.

The clothes came off in record time. Naked, they crashed back together. He put his hands on the sides of her face, kissed her, long and deep. She whimpered, arched into him.

Laz pulled away, stepped back. *What?*

He reached down and put his hand against her center, cupping her. The palm of his hand hard against her clit. Moisture pooled between her legs. She gyrated against his hand.

A knowing, challenging look settled on his face. "Ask me," he said.

She hesitated. He kept his hand there, tight, cupping her, his finger teasing her folds in a way that was patient and demanding.

When she hesitated, he kissed her. A kiss for the ages. A kiss like fire. A deep and probing kiss, an expert and sucking kiss that drew need from her in a swell that broke through all her inhibitions.

Breathing heavily, he pulled back, looked at her pointedly. "Ask me for what you want."

She didn't hesitate this time. "Get on your knees. Taste me," she said.

He grinned and dropped to his knees.

His arms came around her, gripped her cheeks. He brushed his tongue against her clit.

She jerked with pleasure, and he moaned vibrations against her clit as he licked and sucked her. Incredible. The way his hands clasped her butt cheeks, as his tongue ringed her clit and his mouth covered her with vibrating, sucking heat.

She moved against him. Encompassed on all sides by him, appreciated, worked, worshipped by him—that was the way it felt. She grasped his hair for strength. Had to. She could no longer feel her legs.

The building pressure, the tingling need, the hot warmth made her whimper. He was everywhere, his hands, his tongue, but she was in control.

"Harder," she said. And he drove his tongue harder

against her, squeezed her ass. "Yes. Suck me," she said, and he sucked her so expertly, so sweetly, so perfectly, she threw her head back and had to bite her tongue to keep from screaming his name.

The pressure built and built until the eager insistence of his tongue teasing her, the working of his mouth igniting her was too much, so tight and ready and...

The orgasm broke over her in a wave of pleasure that loosed her tongue. She cried out, came against his mouth as his hands—cupped around her ass—held her shaking body tightly to him. His mouth sucked and wrung every last tremor of delight from her.

When she came back from the bliss, tingles still dancing through her, she found herself strangling his hair and stopped.

He rose to her. Breathing heavy, he kissed her ear. "Never been this hard in my life. Honor, I need—"

Her two-way squawked to life. "Guests are coming back. Ready in ten."

Junior. Telling her the guests were coming back and would be ready in ten minutes to head back to the ship. How had the time gotten away from her?

Laz moaned, almost a curse. "That's my ride."

She smiled against his lips, grasped his hard-on tight. "You're not leaving here like this."

"Honor."

She put her lips close to his, whispered, "Shh," and began to stroke him. Judging by the hiss that escaped him, he hadn't been expecting that.

She worked the long, thick length of him, tightening and releasing, fast and hard. He dropped his head, moaned a pained sound. She stopped. His eyes popped open. She smiled at him. She was still in charge. "With me."

His eyes swam with want, with need. He placed his hand over the top of hers. When he did as she asked, she said, "Just like that."

With his hand over hers, his eyes hot and fierce upon her, she stroked him. He followed her lead.

Together, their hands moved along his flesh, faster and harder. His beautiful, muscled body so strong and capable, naked and willing, and his hard-on between them as they stroked and quickly found a rhythm was the hottest thing she'd ever seen.

Honor alternated between watching their hands sliding along his cock to watching the pained pleasure sliding across his face to letting her eyes dip over every beautiful muscle in his ripped body. She grew moist again.

Her eyes rose back to his face. His ripe lips were parted. His eyes wild and needy, as he watched the way her full breasts bounced with their movements.

She picked up the pace, and he cried out, tightened his hand around hers. And together, they pumped, a hard, fast, breathtaking beat that filled the room with sound and heat.

And he came. Came with a cry as loud and lost as the one she'd issued.

She released him. And they crashed together again, spontaneously. They kissed. A kiss that felt like more than just now. More than just tomorrow. It felt like forever.

She clung to him fiercely, wanting that feeling to be true and knowing it was a lie. This was goodbye.

After dressing, Laz grabbed Honor's hand and began to lead her out. She pulled back. "We can't go down there together now."

"Why not?"

Her eyes opened wider, round and innocent. "My grandfather will suspect."

She seemed to take that very seriously. "Okay. I'll go out first." He stopped. He knew he shouldn't push it, but he couldn't help it. All her guides not showing up, the near accident, her uncle's anger had struck a chord of warning. Not just a chord, a gong.

"Honor, are you sure that there is no one who would want to bring down your business, competition on the islands, maybe family who wants you to run the business a certain way?"

Her eyes slitted at him. Yeah, he'd admit it, that wasn't subtle. For a moment, it looked like she'd say something, but something behind her eyes thought better of it. "Don't worry about it."

Nah. He didn't work that way. "If you're tryin' not to drag me into something, worried cause I have to leave, don't be. I'm asking here. What crossed your mind?"

"You do have to leave."

"Honor."

"It really isn't anything you need to worry about."

He opened his mouth to tell her to think again, but whatever she saw on his face had her shoulders dropping, her leaning closer, whispering, "Okay. Okay. We had an offer on the business, farm, chalet—the whole thing. It was a crazy offer. Way more than it's worth right now. I declined it."

That put what José had said in context. "But how could that accident force you to sell?"

"If we'd lost the cruise ship business, I'd probably be forced to sell. I've put every dime I had into the business. My own and my inheritance. I need that business to keep the hotel up and running."

Shit. The choices, stay or go, bounced around in his mind like a pro wrestler flinging against the ropes during a match, each option pushing off, hurtling back, until one option got knocked flat down. "I think we should investigate before I set sail. Interview the guides, talk to whoever made the offer—"

"I don't know who made the offer. Only the agent."

"Then we talk to the agent brokering the offer. Okay?"

"You said you have to set sail tomorrow."

He had. He would. After. "I've got the morning free. Let's just check it out. I'd feel better if I knew before I set sail what's going on here. Trust me, this is what I do, what I did."

"You protected people? And now you're trying to make sure I'm safe?"

He nodded. Yeah. For all the good it had done. "Yeah. And I still owe you a life debt, so don't mess with me."

CHAPTER 14

Sitting before a wall of computer screens in the operations center for the cyber unit of the League of Warrior Women, Gracie wasn't sure this was the best use of her time. The best use of her time, especially at one a.m., would be to be with Dusty—who was downstairs manning the bar of Club When?

But not the best use of her time didn't mean it wasn't absolutely necessary. They had to find Tony. They had to stop him. They had to be ruthless.

At the Mantua Home, the mansion she and her siblings had grown up in, the home that had always seemed a safe haven, things had gotten bad. Not things. People.

Their secret society of vigilantes ran on a strict set of rules. Adherence to those rules was essential in order to keep the group in line. Turned out, when you adopted twenty-eight kids, all of whom lived complicated lives and had damaged pasts, you needed structure.

Tony faking his death, disregarding the rules, and leaving for parts unknown had blown that structure out of the water. Especially for two of the younger units, who had gotten behind the whole my-way vigilante lifestyle big time. Rome's unit, Vampire Academy, had actually tried to organize their own black ops. And the Troublemaker's Guild... their name said it all. Those three. Sheesh.

Of the two, Gracie was most worried about Rome's unit. Tony getting away with seemingly no penalty, had that group trying things that could best be characterized as indulgent and accurately characterized as reckless.

So that meant finding Tony, which she wanted to do for her own peace of mind and to slap him upside the head, now had a radically different need. It was needed to save her family. Her siblings. The League.

And as much as she loved Tony—they all did—they had to take his memory. There was no other way to reinforce the culture that had kept the League secret and operational for over forty years.

Her computer beeped and flashed warning. The screen in front of her read, "Accept secure video chat? Yes. No."

Time to get down to business. She hit Yes.

Three livestream boxes materialized on her screen from places all over the world.

In parts unknown, Justice with her Native American features, straight nose, straight black hair, and straight no-nonsense attitude. From Pennsylvania, Dada, whose joyous pregnancy brought a glow to skin so lustrous and dark that Gracie was pretty sure even the night sky was jealous. And from Laos, Bridget, yogi extraordinaire, with her disheveled hair, patient smile, olive skin, and recently altered memory. But shh, don't tell her.

For a moment, Gracie's heart leapt. She really loved them. Justice's box highlighted. "You're not going to believe this." Dada's box flashed color. "Why can't you even say hello? We haven't spoken in weeks."

Gracie could feel her too-pink skin heat her face. Redheads definitely didn't have all the fun. Here we go. "It's late, ladies. Let's get down to business."

Bridget's box lit up. "I'm with Dada. I want to know

how everyone is doing. There is a lot of stress around this, around Tony's actions. We need to take a minute to connect, remember why we are doing this. Remember who we are."

Justice snorted. There was a weight of silence. *Remember who we are.* Bridget's memory had been altered, so she no longer remembered she'd been a partner in Tony's betrayal.

Kind of sucked. Gracie had argued against using M-erasure on her. But Bridget, seeing how the actions she and Tony had taken were undermining the group, had insisted. Her sacrifice had helped a little bit, but even Gracie, no fan of memory erasure, had to admit only getting Tony would fix the problem, restore order to the family and the League.

"Bridget," Justice said. "This isn't a family get-together. It's a mission. No need to get into hurt feelings."

"Feelings are the problem," Dada said. "We are a family of misfits, broken girls and boys from all over the world. Our impenetrable, unbreakable loyalty connects us. Tony destroyed that when he dropped bombs on our school campus."

Bridget sat forward. "Betrayal is a strong word, a loaded word. He didn't intend to hurt anyone. Just scare Momma into stopping Justice's mission."

Bridget wanting to clear the air made Gracie's stomach hurt. She was basically a walking reminder of how you could neutralize a threat without killing a person.

"Bridge," Justice said, "Maybe you're confused because you meditate two hours a day and eat sunlight to survive, but no one ever dropped a nice bomb."

"Don't belittle Bridget," Dada said, her momma-gene kicking in.

Dada's mouth opened, and her box blinked with light then dimmed as Justice's outpaced her.

"Forget kindness. This is about Tony. And I get it. It fucking sucks. But we've seen what his betrayal has done to our family, the League. And we've all agreed that nothing, no one is worth the chaos and fear that's taken over the Mantua Home. We stand up for our ideals and fight when others can't or won't. No compromise here."

Gracie let out a breath. Justice, who'd been arguably hurt the most by Tony's betrayal, was now the most militant. She and her husband, Sandesh—whose sleeping outline Gracie could see on the bed in the background of Justice's video feed—were stalking the globe looking for him. "What do you have, Justice?" Gracie asked.

Justice moved closer to her computer camera, so close her fierce, dark eyes filled the screen. "Turns out, our brother likes to sail."

CHAPTER 15

THE RHYTHMIC WHOOSH OF ROSEAU'S OCEAN WAVES slapping the shoreline spilled in through Honor's open windows. The drive was slow, like island life. It was hot out. She liked it hot. Just like she liked her men.

Speaking of hot men… Standing with his back against a brown storage shed, Laz waited for her. He seemed to be surveying the area, keeping his back covered. Who was he really?

Not Lazarus Graves.

He'd told her that. In the hospital, that information had seemed light and fun. He'd made it feel that way. Now…she was worried. For him or about him, she wasn't sure. Had her hormones dismissed something she should've been wary of?

I don't care. I'll pay whatever price there is to pay to be near him. A shudder ran through her. A premonition that the price would be too high or the growing thrill at her own boldness? What was the difference between boldness and recklessness?

She pulled to the side of the road, her car leaning slightly as two wheels met the sandy shoulder.

Laz strolled toward her, not strolled, stalked with limber, packed muscle ready for action. Not nearly as casually dressed today as yesterday, he had on tan pants, boots, and a matching T-shirt with a short-sleeved button-down. Too hot for a top shirt. Was he wearing it to conceal a weapon? Probably. Yikes.

Although she'd been on the archery team in college, she had little experience with guns. Truth was, they scared her.

If she hadn't known Laz—the unruly dark curls, the stern set to his jaw, the intensity of his walk—her first impression would've been that he was dangerous.

And that he was sexy. With the ocean behind him, those shades, that body—it was like watching a cologne ad. And the voice-over would say, "Temptation. No woman can resist."

The man was the perfect blend of muscles and leanness. His body last night. The "All for one" tattoo below his ribs. The cut of his muscles. The tightening of his abs as she'd, they'd, stroked him.

She would never forget it. The memory was so vivid, it had her slick with desire.

A desire heightened because he was kind and sincere and smart and funny. All that should've been a good thing, but he was leaving.

He opened the door, got inside, shut the door, and leaned toward her. She leaned the rest of the way. They met in the middle and kissed. It started light, but the heat between them made it longer, deeper, wetter.

She pulled from the kiss. "Are you sure you want to spend our last day researching when this whole thing is probably a coincidence? I can park. We can go to your boat."

He groaned, moved away, leaned his head back. From the side of his sunglasses, she could see him close his eyes as if in pain.

She watched him. "Laz?"

"Just give me a minute to get the image of us on the boat out of my head." He adjusted himself in his seat, and she thrilled to see the reaction pressed hard against his pants. He let out a breath, turned to her. "Can you put the air on?"

She did. Some people only like it hot in the bedroom.

He brushed a strand of his wavy hair behind an ear. "I can't leave here knowing I did nothing when you might be in danger."

She swallowed a big, hard ball of complicated and disappointed emotion. And she shouldn't give voice to it. It was silly, but this connection between them had annihilated her normal, calm control. "Do you have to leave?"

He put his hand over the top of her hand, which rested on the emergency brake in the space between the seats. "I want to stay, Honor. I mean if last night was the opening act, I really want to stay for the next scene. But staying isn't an option. One way or the other, it's best that I go."

Heat that felt a lot like rejection stung her cheeks. She pulled her hand out from under his.

Laz didn't say anything else, offer any more explanations or apologies as she pulled onto the road and put up the windows. Humid air, smelling of the sea and oil, drifted in through before the artificial cold of the car's A/C took over.

Although Honor was tempted to let what had felt like rejection cloud her judgment, there was another part of her, the stronger part that went over what Laz had said again.

It wasn't his choice to leave. He wanted to stay. He was here this morning accompanying her to Gray George's office. He was here helping her. Letting go of her own issues, she let that truth sink in, and since she'd given her brain room to work over things, realization dawned. "What are you running from?"

Laz bent forward in the seat, reached under, moved the

seat back with a rumble from the components, stretched out. "You know why clichés are so popular?"

"No."

"Because they're true. So here's a cliché for you." He gestured with one of those strong, capable hands as if he were actually handing her something. "The less you know, the better."

Normally, that kind of dramatic statement would make her laugh, but his face was complicated with real emotion. And it felt anything but funny. "Is it…the police?"

"No. Kind of the opposite of the police."

The opposite of the police? People outside the law? "Are you going to be okay? Should you leave now?"

His lips tucked up at the edges, a forced smile, filled with longing. "Trying to get rid of me?"

No. God, no. But she didn't want to be the cause of him being in danger. "I want you to be safe." And though she shouldn't say it, she couldn't help a small, bitter, "Besides, I didn't think I had a choice either way. Keeping you or letting you go."

"You don't," he said, not cruelly. "I don't either. What little choice I do have, I'm exercising this morning. In the hopes that we'll either find nothing and I can leave knowing you'll be okay or that we'll find something, anything suspicious, and you can go to the police. Maybe hire someone for security."

She couldn't afford to hire anyone. She'd poured every last dime into Loco for Cocoa. She couldn't afford to get her hair cut. But she wasn't going to tell him that. If they turned up something, she'd figure out her next step.

CHAPTER 16

THE WEATHER-WORN HOME/BUSINESS HAD WELL-TENDED small shrubs and flowers around a square cement porch. Honor knocked on the white door, propped open by a box fan.

Gray, a fiftyish woman with silver hair, square jaw, and brown skin, sat behind her desk.

She wore a stylish, sexy leopard-print dress, perfectly feathered makeup, and long, painted nails. But she seemed tired. Or maybe stressed.

Talking on her cell, Gray looked up from her computer screen and waved them inside. The office had plaid drapes, faux potted plants, and a chandelier that might've once hung over a dining room set.

Gray hung up, clapped her hands together, a sound so loud, Honor startled. "You have changed your mind. You are here to accept!"

For a moment, Honor found herself ungrounded. And it wasn't just Gray's deep voice that always seemed so at odds with her appearance. It was that Gray seemed so genuine. As if she'd truly expected Honor to come here today and accept the offer.

Shifting her feet, Honor explained. "No. I appreciate the offer, but I'm not interested. I'm—"

"Let me come out to your home. Let me explain to your grandfather. This is a foreign investor. Stupid. You will never see this again."

A foreign investor? "I don't need you to explain anything. It was my decision."

The cell began to ring. Gray ignored it and stood. She towered over Honor and was even taller than Laz's nearly six feet.

Gray's big hands waved away Honor's words. She sat on the edge of her desk, leaned back, and pursed her lips. She looked at Laz. "Why don't you tell her to take the money? You two would be much happier. With that much money, you can start a farm elsewhere."

Laz put his hands in his pockets, hunched a little. It made him somehow seem less muscular, less intimidating. "Maybe we could talk to the investor directly."

"So you can cut me out of the deal? No."

"Wasn't thinkin' that. Just want to meet the guy. Can't be sure he's the decent sort."

Her cell rang again. Gray picked it up, looked at it, hit a button, and put it back down. "I don't understand. This will make you wealthy. This will change your fortunes. You want hard work and uncertainty? Who knows when the next storm will arrive and knock out everything? Who knows if the tourists will keep coming? Who knows if the ships will keep using your business?"

This last part, she delivered with a bit of warning in her voice. It wasn't lost on Honor that Gray was in charge of those deals.

Honor knew she should tread carefully, but she was annoyed beyond measure. "I know this deal going through would have brought you money, and I'm sorry for that, but I'm not selling."

Gray *tsk*ed and sat back behind her desk. "I'll let him know you require more money."

Honor fisted her hands at her sides. Gray hadn't heard a word. "The decision is made. Don't come back with any more offers."

With as much calm as she could manage, not much, Honor turned and stalked out. She walked down the street, aware that Laz hadn't followed. No way was she going back in there.

He came out five minutes later. She gave him a what-took-you-so-long frown. He smiled, put his arm around her waist, and guided her toward the car. "That could've gone better."

"Why didn't you follow me out? I was making a dramatic exit."

His arm tightened around her waist. "I noticed. But dramatic exits don't help when your goal is information."

True. "What did you discuss?"

"I asked about the offer. When it had come. Where the foreigner was from."

"Where?"

"America."

Oh. That was good to know.

"I asked about her commission. A bunch of stuff she wouldn't answer."

The hand on her waist dipped lower, rested at the top of her butt. She liked it there.

"I figured she wouldn't answer those though. I was just stalling."

"Stalling, why?"

"I had a device in my pocket that collected data from her phone."

Oh. That was why he'd put his hands in his pockets. "Is that legal?"

He looked down at her, his deep hazel eyes a bit startled. "No."

Well then. Not sure what to say to that, she took her keys from her pocket and unlocked the car. They climbed inside, and this time, she didn't wait to turn on the air. She cranked it up.

She sped away feeling like a thief, an illegal data thief. Laz waited until they were on the road before asking her, "What's your take?"

Annoyed probably wasn't what he was looking for. The woman had made a lot of assumptions about Honor, her family, her and Laz. She shrugged, tried to be clinical and not emotional. "She seemed genuinely happy about the idea that I was there to accept the offer."

"Genuine can be faked. What else?"

"She's busy. Her cell rang a lot."

"Super busy. Got three businesses here, right? The travel agency, the real estate, and passports."

"Passports?"

"She had paperwork on her desk."

She frowned. "I hadn't noticed."

He shrugged. "To be expected. Lot of emotion for you there. She practically threatened your business, the tours."

No kidding.

"But what did you notice? Anything about her physically?"

She turned the corner, headed toward the home where one of her guides rented a room. "Why does her physical appearance matter at all? I'm not here to make judgments."

"No. You're not. Judgment is unnecessary. Observation is not judgment. Don't confuse the two. In observing, we notice things, even things that might make us uncomfort-able. We don't judge. Don't add *this is good* or *this is bad*. That screws up objectivity."

"I'm not sure what you're suggesting."

"She was tall. Had a deep voice. A bit more masculine than average. On a hot day at home in her office, she was dressed to the max. Hair. Nails. Makeup. Clothes. Jewelry."

"So?"

"Could be transgender. Happy to be in her skin, to be a woman. It's not a chore for her to dress up. She likes it."

"Or maybe she's just tall with a deep voice."

"Maybe. So we observe that. We observe she doesn't fit neatly into a gender box. And if the people of Dominica are anything like the rest of the world, some people might put a value judgment on that. Judge her unkindly."

"Some would be *pendejos*."

"Some would. But we're not worried about them. We're thinking of her. On a fairly poor island. No air-conditioning. Run-down. With three jobs. A lot going against her. And did you notice the picture? A kid, seemed to be in a hospital gown. Maybe got a sick kid she helps."

Honor started to feel ill. She hadn't picked up on any of that. She was too busy listening to what Gray was saying. She flicked on her turn signal, waited for a break in the oncoming traffic, and turned. "This deal would bring her money."

"She has motivation. Sure. But if she knew how much the tours meant, why didn't she cancel the tours?"

Honor touched the brake slowly and coasted to a stop at a red light. "It would look suspicious. The customers didn't complain."

"But if she knew the accident was likely to happen, couldn't she have gone to one of the guests and asked directly?"

Good point. "So it probably wasn't her?"

"She's desperate but still playing by the rules. That makes her less likely to have done anything to harm you and your tours. But"—he held up a slim black device—"this will give us her recent contacts and email. So maybe we can find out who made the offer."

"You mean before you leave?"

A long pause, a pause in which he looked out at the small colorful homes they passed. "I'll make sure you get the information. Even if I'm not here. Let's go see what your missing guides have to say."

CHAPTER 17

LAZ WATCHED AS HONOR PARKED IN FRONT OF THE LAST guide's apartment complex. They'd spent most of the morning tracking two of the three guides down, and his suspicions had been raised. High.

They'd gotten the same response—sick, not feeling well—from both guides. The same exact response and descriptions. From the time they'd woken up in the morning—six a.m.—the medicine they'd taken, herbal concoction, the symptoms. Headache. Fever. Chills.

It was as if someone had written the script for them. And both were just fine now. Not only that, both guides had quit. And he'd noticed one of them now had a nice new-looking moped.

A bad feeling gnawed Laz's gut. Not only about time ticking away but about what he'd be leaving her behind to deal with when he went.

"You okay?" Honor asked, switching the car off.

He wasn't okay. Someone had messed with that equipment. Someone had paid the guides off. Someone wanted her business and her gone. He took all that as seriously as a man raised to imagine the worst. "I'm worried about you. Mostly worried that I won't be able to stick around, help you out."

She did that thing with her jaw, like she was tasting his words. "I guess we're even then, because I'm worried about you too."

She had him there. They got out of the car and walked

toward the apartment building. Three stories, with an open-air walkway with a white railing, partly rusted in places. The building was painted seashell peach and had green trim. Looked like the kind of apartment building you might see in Jersey.

Gaudy. Brought a smile to his lips. Reminded him of Momma. And though he'd spent the last two years astronomically pissed at her for ignoring his opinion and for the casual way she'd let Justice bungle her operation, he loved and missed her.

Of course, he was also scared shitless of her, considering she wanted to alter his brain, his memories, and neutralize any damage he might cause to the League of Warrior Women.

Honor walked in front of him with her shoulders tight. There was a necessary tension between them right now. He didn't like it. But he wouldn't have it any other way, because he was leaving.

Soon.

He'd gone out of his way to remind her again and again. And he felt like an ass every time, but he couldn't stand the idea of leading her on.

As Honor approached the building, he scanned the street. No one around. Since the only security on the building was a broken wrought-iron gate, they skirted it and went up the open-air cement stairs. Two floors up, down a narrow cement hall, they saw no one. No cameras either.

Honor knocked on Tito's door. That was what she'd called him, but he'd noticed his name on the mailbox outside had read Thomas Balder. There was no answer.

Honor knocked again, called his name. Still nothing. She shrugged. "I guess we can come back later."

He raised an eyebrow.

A soft pink feathered her cheeks. "I meant I can come back."

No fucking way would he have her come back here on her own. He leaned toward her, whispered in her ear. "I'm going in."

She pulled away from him, forehead wrinkled. "That seems extreme."

Sure. But this was the only guide who hadn't called. "Can you go down, move the car, take it a few blocks south, and wait for me?"

Her eyes darted around, then back to his face. "Okay."

When she was far enough away, he approached the job. Now if this had been his old life, he'd have done more recon. And he'd have had something other than the baseball cap and sunglasses to obscure his face. He hoped the guy was out and not just taking a shit.

Pulling out his tools, it took one-point-seven seconds to B and E. He cracked open the door and stepped inside. The smell hit him before he'd even closed the door.

He retched, covered his nose with his T-shirt, and walked through the apartment. Ransacked to hell and back. Broken TV, scattered glass, he avoided the worst. This hadn't been quiet. No one had called the cops?

He found Tito, a large man with chalky brown skin, shaved head, and black painted nails, in the bathroom. His head was in the toilet. His body beaten to hell.

Sad as shit. Honor had talked about this guy like he'd been a friend.

He checked the rest of the apartment. Kitchen was a mess, just like the rest of the apartment. Back in the bathroom, he searched through the medicine cabinet—if this guy had a habit, it might explain what had happened here. And right now, he wanted any reason other than his connection to Honor.

Guy had enough hand lotion to start a massage business. Some suppositories and a couple of butt plugs. Nothing that indicated drugs.

A knock on the front door ricocheted down the hall, followed by a deep voice announcing the police. Laz's nerves tensed. His heart decided to flush fuel through his body. Crap. He'd been careless.

Who'd called the police? The other guides? A neighbor?

Couldn't get caught in here. Having a murder charge put on him wouldn't exactly be keeping below the radar. One thing his family would pick up on right away was his prints being pulled by authorities in Dominica.

A quick sweep of the laundry-littered bathroom. No place to hide. Or run. The bathroom window, a portal really, was the size of a toddler's head.

The police knocked louder, threatened to break in. Grabbing a pair of navy silk boxers from the floor—don't think about it—he slipped them on over his baseball hat.

Last time he was this sloppy. Plan. Make a fucking plan. Bolting out of the bathroom, he raced across to the bedroom.

There was a *slam, slam* from out front, followed by a splintering and crash as the door was kicked open.

The window had a fucking crank on it. It squeaked as he opened it, but he managed to wedge his body halfway through.

"Hold there," a police officer said, coming into the room. Gun still in his holster.

Guy was kidding, right?

Laz forced himself through, scraping his side, caught the edge of the window, lowered himself down, and dropped into the alley below. He hit and rolled and was up and running with the officer squeezed sideways in the window screaming, "You there, stop now!"

Not likely.

Having gotten rid of his hat and the—shudder—dead guy's boxers, Laz jumped into Honor's idling car and instructed her to drive.

He ducked down as she took off. She drove silently for a while. The only sound the air-conditioning and the tires *thwump, thwump*ing against the blacktop. After a few minutes, her eyes darted over to him. "What happened? I saw the police."

Since they were far enough away, he sat up, adjusted the vent to his face. "Yeah. Someone called the police on me."

"Oh my God. I shouldn't have let you break in there. Did you even learn anything useful?"

Damn. Shit. "I did. Can you pull over up here?"

She pulled into a local eatery, a chicken joint, with—no lie—a live chicken running around the parking lot. She parked next to a pickup truck and turned to him.

He grabbed her hand, laced his fingers with her long slender ones, held tight. "I'm so sorry, Honor. He's dead. Your guide, Tito."

The skin around her eyes wrinkled. "I don't understand."

A lump formed in his throat. Christ, this sucked.

"Someone killed Tito. Your guide. He's dead. I'm sorry. I know he was a friend of yours."

When it hit home and she started to shake, he took her into his arms, whispered to her, ran his nose along her soft, wet cheek.

"He was the first guide we hired," she said in a voice strained with tears and disbelief. "He encouraged me when I first started, helped me figure out how to organize the tours. He was a good man."

She lifted her head, rubbed the tears from her face. "You don't think his death is related to the offer on Loco for Cocoa? My refusal to take the offer?"

He gave her a soft, compassionate look. "Anything's possible. His death might be coincidence—"

Honor turned from him, put her grieving head on her steering wheel for a moment. "You don't believe that."

"No. I don't. I think he was, as you just said, the most loyal of your guides. The others were paid off not to show up. He wouldn't be paid off. Got himself killed. But that's a theory. Could be more there. He could've known something. Could be a coincidence. We can't rule anything out. We have to be methodical about this."

"We?" Her head jerked up. She turned. "I can't allow you to stay. It's not right. I'm taking you to your boat."

She put the car into drive and exited the parking lot with a determined press of the gas pedal. "If this is true, if this happened because of my business, I'll figure it out. I'll work with the police. You can't stay here. I saved your life. And that means something to me."

Laz waited for her to finish her speech, waited for her to get curious, waited for her to glance over and look questioningly at him. When she did, he said, "What kind of person would I be, Honor, if my comfort, my safety, my problems came before yours?"

"But I could ask you the same question."

His eyebrows rose. True. "You're..." He shook his head. It was hard to walk this line, the one that said her safety was more important than his. Especially since now if his family found him, they wouldn't just be taking the memories of Mexico. They'd be taking the memories of Honor. No fucking way. "When I was a kid, I learned about order of importance. It's a way of determining what to do first or who to protect first."

"How does it work?"

"Well, one of the ways is we ask ourselves, between the two of us, right now, who is in the most immediate danger?"

Her silver moon eyes traveled over his face. "I can't answer that, because I don't know what danger you're in."

Woman was a ballbuster. Just his type. "Can you trust me enough to allow me to determine that?"

"Can you trust me enough to tell me?"

"Isn't a matter of trust. Remember the cliché. The less you know, the better. If there comes a time when that's reversed, I'll tell you whatever you need to know to keep you safe. Promise."

"So you think I'm in the most danger between the two of us?"

He put his hands together like he was gripping a bat and swung like hitting a ball, made a click sound and the roar of the crowd. "Yep. You. For now. If there comes a time when that switches to me, we'll act accordingly. Okay?"

She steered the car around a man riding a ten-speed

bike, towing a two-wheeled trailer filled with unpainted pottery. "Are you sure, Laz? You barely know me. I mean, we haven't even slept together yet."

Yet.

Heat caroused through his blood, like a giddy drunk veering all over the place. "I like the 'yet' part of that statement. And honestly, that's a reason for staying, not going."

She laughed. Quieted. Seemed to think on it. After a moment, she nodded. "I'm going to accept your offer. Because, well, bluntly, I'm afraid. And because other things." She didn't specify the other things, but her tone was such that his blood lunged toward his groin. "But you have to promise, if you are in danger, you will go. No question. No looking back. Just take off. Promise?"

He stared out the window. Damn, he really liked this woman. He turned to face her. "Can you drive me back to my boat to get my stuff? I'd like to be your newest tour guide."

Honor gritted her teeth. "One problem with that."

"Which is?"

"Papito does all the hiring."

CHAPTER 18

HONOR'S MIND SPUN, BUT SOMEHOW SHE MANAGED TO safely drive Laz back up the mountain.

Tito had been murdered. Probably because of her business. And—this was awful—she allowed Laz to stay, to put himself in danger not just to help her but to help herself to him.

Well, at least he knew that. Because though they had many secrets, not the least of which was his real name, they were honest about the sexual desire between them.

Once they crested the hill, she parked in the gravel employee parking lot. When the bags were out of the trunk, scattered around their feet, Laz cast a glance her way. Her throat went dry. There were no words. No words for how he made her feel, safe and warm and needy. So needy. She fisted his T-shirt, pulled him close, and kissed him.

The warmth of the sun, the chirping of insects, and the sound of Laz moaning against her mouth filled her with a heady, frantic want. She wiggled against his hard body then broke the kiss. "This is wrong. I feel like a bad person."

He didn't ask her what she meant. He just addressed what she meant. "I wanted to stay. I made the choice. And part of experiencing a brutal and sudden loss like with Tito is realizing one day, we all die. It makes us long to connect, to celebrate life, to indulge in the things that make us feel most alive. I'm all in, by the way."

He smirked. The Big Bad Wolf had that kind of smile.

The kind that should be registered as a lethal weapon. And she was all for throwing caution to the wind with him. Had no choice in this. Except…

"I haven't been with a man in two years. Since I lost my mom. But I'm still on the pill. Take it religiously." She blushed, hoped he understood what she was asking. She was clean. Protected. Was he?

Laz closed his eyes. Groaned. "Give a guy a warning." He adjusted himself, and she had to bite her own smile. For a long moment, they stared into each other's eyes. His hazel focus promised her things, deep things, loving things, forever things. "In my old line of work, I had routine tests. Haven't been with anyone since the last time I was tested."

He didn't say how long that had been, and she was curious, but with a wink, he asked, "How long do you think it's going to take me to charm Papito into giving me a job?"

"Not long." She kissed him again. This time, their make-out session got some attention from the farm workers, who whistled.

And then there was a crude, "Like your mother."

Honor froze. *José.*

She blushed, stepped away from Laz. She looked at the retreating José.

"What's his issue?" Laz said.

"He resents me. A resentment that passed from my mother to me. He saw her as the spoiled movie star who never really cared about anyone but herself."

"Your mom made movies?"

Swatting away a fly, Honor cringed. This was the part she hated, the part where she had to become less of herself and more the celebrity kid, defined by her mother, what people thought of her mother. "Mom was an actress. Natalie Silva is her birth name. Her stage name was Kiki Hart."

"Your mom was Kiki Hart, the actress?"

"Yep."

He shifted, and she could see him reevaluating the situation. The situation. Not her.

"She made two movies here in Dominica, right? *Stranded* and the sequel. I saw a commemorative plaque in town."

She nodded. "About ten years apart. I wasn't around for the first. I was here for the second. She brought the crew, movie people here, was able to fill the hotel with them. But when she left, she didn't look back.

"José remembers. Now, I bring in guests, most of whom knew my mom, were old friends of hers, and he sees the whole thing playing out again." She looked toward the retreating José. "I should probably go talk with him."

He shifted. "Want me to go with you?"

She did, but that wouldn't help anything. "No. Go get that job."

And plan to spend the night in my room. She wasn't bold enough to say that last, but she was bold enough to think it. Time was running out. They had days, not a lifetime. Though the heat and attraction she had to him could fill a lifetime.

This man had her mind focused on one thing. Sex with him. He felt that good against her. She couldn't wait to find out what he felt like inside her.

He kissed her again, a small kiss on her nose. Even such a small touch of his lips had her body flushing with heat.

He gathered up the four bags and walked down the road toward the hotel. She watched him go, because he had a butt any human with a pulse would stop and ogle. He should do a calendar. Really. It was that perfect.

Releasing a sigh filled with as much longing as self-reproach—she was at her work, her home, surrounded by her employees and her family—she walked the opposite way, toward the covered porch where José fermented beans.

Clad in rubber boots, mud-green pants, and a brown shirt soaked in sweat at the armpits and around the neck, José looked up when she got closer. And then he looked down.

So rude.

The sound of the insects in the trees dimmed to her ears as her face heated with the rejection.

With a grab for patience, easier to catch the horsefly buzzing around her head, she moved toward him as he bent over an enormous white barrel. He slid the barrel into place, tapped on the lid with a rubber mallet, and moved to the next vat.

Sidestepping, she purposefully blocked his access. He took a step closer, a bit menacingly.

For someone who spent much of their life stooped, he was still tall. Over six feet, with muscular arms, white-streaked black hair, and chestnut-brown eyes—the color of bark soaked in rain.

She swallowed her agitation. "Uncle José, I wanted to speak with you about the offer made on the property. I know you're upset about my decision—"

"Do you smell the fermentation?"

Kind of hard not to. "Of course."

"I don't. I no longer can tell the difference between the smell of fermenting beans and the soil and the trees. I have to judge by color, by time. For me, this job, this farm takes. For you, with your marketing and talent and cooking, it gives."

This again. "You work hard. I see that. I truly appreciate what you've done, but I'm asking you to trust me. This family and farm are five years away from having a thriving business, and—"

"And if a storm comes? Or if the U.S. raises tariffs? Or if any one of a thousand things happens?"

"There are risks in taking the money too. You saw the offer—"

"What risk? That I will be rich? That you will have to split four million dollars with me and Papito?"

What? How did he think all that money would be split among them? "We wouldn't split all four million. It would be four million minus my two-million-dollar investment and any taxes or fees."

José squared his waist, leaned forward. "You act as if this place had no value before you came. A value given by my years of hard work. You're trying to cheat me. Like your grandmother."

"Grandmother never cheated you. She was the kindest person I know—"

"You only see what you want to see." His tanned and lined face grew red-brown with anger. "Like with this young man. He is nothing, not family, and he will run too, like the tour guides, at the drop of a hat."

"Tito didn't run." Her chest tightened with rage and pain. "He's dead. He was murdered."

José's eyebrows rose, and for a moment, she thought she saw fear or regret in his eyes, but it quickly passed. He rubbed a hand across the rigid white and black hair lining his chin. "If you hadn't come here after your mother's death, I would be living a different life."

What? She wiped the tears from her eyes. Who did he think would've paid the taxes, made the necessary repairs, paid the employees? Of course, José would hear none of it. Ever.

With a shake of her head, and a bone-deep sadness, Honor walked away. It was useless. He was incredibly angry at her, and his sense of helplessness—like everything was everyone else's fault—only made him angrier.

CHAPTER 19

WORKERS WITH LONG POLES TOPPED WITH CURVED blades moved through the surrounding cocoa trees, slicing the fruit from the branches and depositing them into baskets. Laz watched their expert work as he approached the hotel.

He deposited his bags, filled with the security equipment, at the foot of the front steps. On the porch, Papito interviewed a twentysomething for a guide job.

When the other guy walked off, Papito came down the steps, introduced himself as "Papito Ramone Silva." He then clapped Laz on both arms and said, "And why is the young man with a thing for my granddaughter visiting me?"

A thing? Guy was observant. Still, that 'thing for my granddaughter' bothered him. Maybe because it made him seem small. Like a passing thing. Though he was just passing through. But the emotions he felt weren't small. In fact, they seemed larger than the limited time he'd spent with Honor, and the limited time he had left with her. "I'm here about a job."

Papito's eyebrows rose. "As a tour guide?"

Laz nodded. "I've got experience."

His thick brows settled again over clever midnight eyes, he leaned back and listened as Laz made his pitch. The old guy was still smart as a tack, and Laz would've explained his fear for Honor, but right now, without any reason to know who was after Honor and why, he had to keep everyone on the suspect list.

THE COST OF HONOR

When he was done, Papito held out his hand and said, "You have the job."

What? He'd accepted Laz's offer without even looking at his faked resume. These people. He'd have to double-check every single person they hired. Not that he hadn't been going to do that anyway.

They shook hands, and Papito raked knowing eyes over Laz's bags. "I think you need a room."

"Pardon?"

"Don't worry. The room is free."

Call him a suspicious guy, but this seemed on the border of too-good-to-be-true territory. He had all his stuff with him and had intended to bargain for a room. Still, he wasn't sure he wanted to jump that fence without knowing where he'd be landing. "So you're giving me a job and a free room. What's the catch?"

Papito spread his hands wide. With his long silver-white hair, white pants, and white shirt, he looked like the most honest man in the jungle. Or at least the most comfortable. "After losing my other guides, I learned I need to offer more in order to keep workers. Does this bother you?"

No. Honestly. He liked the idea. More than liked it. Besides wanting to be here to help with security, he'd missed being with people. Still, he hadn't seen Papito offer the last guy a room. "I'd feel better paying."

Papito's thick eyebrows drew together. "And if I were to tell you that your employment was conditioned on you taking the room for free?"

What was his game? Did he understand why Laz had come here? Was he worried about Honor too? "Well, if a free room is a condition of my employment, I guess I'd say show me to my room."

Papito rubbed his hands together like a villain who'd just put the first step of his master plan in motion. Kind of funny.

"A good man. Good man." He picked up two of Laz's four bags. "I'll show you. You'll like it. I promise."

Grabbing the other two bags, Laz followed. He hoped the guy wasn't depending too much on him. Wished he could tell him that he couldn't stay. But if the guy knew he could only spend a week here, he wasn't likely to give him the job.

More than that and his sisters would find him. The thought made him want to run down this mountain and hop into his sailboat.

No one was fucking with his mind.

Crossing into the foyer, Laz followed Papito up the beautiful hand-carved stairs and around a corner. He had to put a spring in his step to keep up. "I don't know what you're taking, but you've got some stamina."

Papito laughed. "I will give you some. A tea with fermented cocoa beans." He turned and beamed at Laz. "It puts vigor in your equipment too. I never need Viagra."

Yikes. Not necessary. "Uh. Thanks."

They went down a hall painted a muted green and decorated with photos of people eating chocolate. Made him want a cookie.

At the end of the hall was a room with double doors. Laz stopped as Papito took out a key and began to open them. Wait. "No. Man. I'm not taking a suite. You can—"

Papito spun around. "This is your room. Don't argue with me. I've already proven I'm the better negotiator."

He met Laz's eyes. He meant business. Give this guy an inch and he'd take a mile. "Okay. Okay. I'm no match for your determination."

Papito nodded. "Exactly."

Inside, the room was colorful, lined with detailed white molding. The round bed had a large light-green comforter, and there was a jungle theme on the walls.

Papito put down the bags and moved across to a set of French doors that led to a deck. A deck? Nice.

Papito unlatched and slid the doors all the way open. "The couple who was here left this morning. You are lucky."

Seemed lucky. A two-person hot tub seemed very lucky. Honor in that hot tub was a must. Laz shifted, reminded himself not to picture the guy's granddaughter naked. Felt guilty enough. This room had to earn them some serious money. "It's beautiful. Really wish you'd let me pay you something."

Papito waved aside the comment. "We have no guests scheduled for this room. And look. Here. This is the best view."

Laz stepped out onto the deck. It was a great view. He could see over the trees and out to the horizon. Laughter from below drove Laz to the edge of the deck. He leaned against the white railing and looked down. Honor played soccer with a group of boys. She was good, had great ball control.

And those legs. She had lean and muscular legs. The kind of legs he dreamed of having wrapped around him as he pushed into the soft, saturated warmth.

As if sensing his deeply inappropriate thoughts, Papito cleared his throat and called to Honor. She looked up.

One of the boys she'd been playing soccer with took the opportunity to steal the ball and zigzag past her. He made a goal and began to jump up and down in triumph. Honor cupped her hands to her mouth. "What are you doing up there?"

He held up the key. "This room comes with the job."

Honor shook her head. "Papito, you gave him the honeymoon suite?"

Honeymoon? Damn. Laz looked at the key in his hand. It was silver, attached to a red heart charm. He looked at Papito. Guy was more devious than he looked.

Papito's eyes twinkled. He walked out with a "Dinner is at eight. Don't be late."

Laz looked down at the key again. Odd that the key was a way to let him in and out, because it felt like he'd just been tossed in prison.

After unpacking his bags in the honeymoon suite—room seriously needed a television—Laz cleaned up, changed into cargo shorts and a loose button-down—all the better to conceal-carry—and went downstairs.

He found Honor beside a series of long, rectangular wooden platforms, almost like a raised garden, but instead of mulch and plants, they were topped with cocoa beans, being spread out by women using soft wooden rakes.

He greeted the women, made sure to remember their names, find out more about them as he remarked on their work, walked around, and asked questions.

Honor slid a longing look at him, a look that sent a wave

of heat smashing through his body, like Godzilla through Tokyo. She said, "You got the job."

It was a moment before he could answer, swallowing the images of Honor from last night, the taste of her on his lips, the hold she had on his hair, the arch and thrust of her body that was seared into his memory. "Yep. First you saved my life, then you got me a job."

Because they asked, he quickly explained why Honor was his hero. He exaggerated his ineptitude, only right, but accurately portrayed her heroic deeds in a way he hoped flashed as brilliantly to them as she did in his mind. And when he told them the part where he'd looked up and was sure he'd seen an angel, they began to clap.

One of the women, gestured at Honor and said, "And on that day. See, your mother still looks out for you."

Honor's eyes turned into two full moons, shocked. Raising her hand, she waved goodbye, then charged away as if beating back flames nipping at her feet.

Laz hurried after her, caught up, and grabbed her hand. "You okay?"

"Did you understand what she suggested?"

He did. "Yeah. Like your mother had hooked us up from the grave."

Nearly at the hotel front steps, she stopped. Her hand was loose in his, almost not responsive. The sun shone off her soft, dark curls. "I'm not superstitious. I'm not." She angled her head. Her eyes flashed with the sun. "It was more than just coincidence, right? It feels like more. *We* feel like more."

Fuck. It felt like more to him. She'd saved his life. It wasn't just that though. He got what she was saying. This thing between them… It was like a shooting star, a tsunami of feeling. So deep that he'd stopped thinking his sisters would take his memory of what happened in Mexico and had started to think, if his sisters found him, they'd take his memories of Honor.

Would they hurt Honor? A knife of alarm sliced through him. "I can't stay here, Honor. I can't."

She took a whole step back, like he'd pushed her.

He rushed to fix it, to be honest. Because that pain in her eyes gutted him, and he knew it would be there when he left. So right now, he owed her whatever honesty he could give her. "Yeah, it's different. I feel it. If I had a choice, I'd stay." He added the word, the stupid word that felt true but logic told him couldn't be true. "Forever."

They shared a long look, a deep and connected warmth. His throat grew tight.

"Honora," Papito called, coming from the stone walkway that skirted the side of the hotel and led to the chalets and the chocolate shop behind it. "Mia is still in the store."

"Crud. I forgot." Honor waved to acknowledge Papito, who stopped, turned, and retraced his steps. She turned to follow but softly whispered, "Do you want to try my favorite chocolate drink?"

He did. He wanted to try her favorite everything. He wanted to get as much of her likes, wants, and desires as he could before he set sail.

They walked along the brick path that extended around the property. Out back, at the curved bamboo and wood bar, with a dozen rattan bar stools under a thatched, pinnacled roof, Honor stepped up onto a bamboo footrest and whispered to the bartender. She handed something to Honor, who tried to hide it from Laz's view. "Don't peek."

Too late. She wasn't that quick, and he was observant. Vodka.

Speaking of being observant, he saw two men at the bar who looked new. Both around Laz's age, early thirties. Lighter skin, muscular builds, dark hair.

Laz leaned down to Honor as they continued on the brick path toward the chocolate shop. "Who are the big guys at the bar?"

She looked back, frowned. "New tour guides? I don't know." She kept walking.

He kept pace with her. "Honor, that doesn't work when someone is trying to fuck with you and your business."

And judging by what had happened to Tito, might try to hurt her.

Her brow furrowed. She looked back at the men. "Okay. I'll find out."

She opened the door to the small store, stepped inside, and inhaled deeply. "This is what heaven smells like."

He was pretty sure heaven smelled like Honor, who, he had to admit, did smell a little like chocolate. And cocoa butter.

As soon as Mia had left, Honor put the vodka behind the counter, low enough that no one entering could see, and began making the drink.

Laz wandered the store, looking at displays.

A jingle of the bells over the door and one of the kids who'd been playing soccer with Honor and a guy who, judging by his brown skin, might be his father came inside. Around twelve, with dark hair, the kid rushed over to her. Laz recognized the look in his eyes—infatuation.

"Hi, Honor," he said.

"It's Ms. Silva," his father corrected, crossing his arms as he stopped by a large tower filled with shelves of boxed chocolate. Dude was strung tight. The boy's eyes dropped. He stuttered an apology.

Honor smiled at the man. "It's okay, Don. Chocolate stores were made for informality."

Who was Don? A fortysomething with black hair and a bit of a paunch. The kind of guy who didn't look physically dangerous and yet set every hair on Laz's arm to standing.

Honor began to bring out candies from the glass case for the kid. That saying about kids in a candy store was definitely true. Laz set himself up in a corner and used his encrypted phone to access the secure site he'd set up with Romeo.

He'd need Romeo's help with the information he'd taken from Gray. And he'd asked the kid to keep him informed if the family found out any new information on him. No news was good news.

Except when he got into the site, there was an email. He opened it. Thick dread squeezed his throat. A dread that tightened with every word he read.

You sail? Kind of surprising. They think you're in the Caribbean. Keep moving. They've set up a special ops team, like a regular mission.

Shit. He kept reading. Justice had tracked him and discovered not only his first boat name but his first pseudonym.

She didn't know he'd changed boats since then. And names. He finished reading the message.

If you still want your memory, run. Run fast.

If he still wanted? He couldn't let them take his memories of the Brothers Grim operation. What he knew. What they called betrayal was him rescuing Justice, him keeping the family code—*no League member will ever allow another member to irresponsibly risk themselves, the security of a mission, or the secrecy of the League.*

He rubbed at his ribs, at the "All for one" tattoo. If they took that information from him…they took him. Who he was.

And Honor? Dominica? His throat dried. He wanted. No time to waste waiting on Don and his son to leave. No time to cozy up to Honor and taste her favorite drink. Shame. With an apology, he waved goodbye to Honor and left the store.

Outside, the croaks of the noisiest frogs Laz had ever heard filled early evening air along with the smell of moss and trees and flowers. It would be the kind of night to sit outside, park it by a fire, and share a drink with… Not tonight.

He walked the winding trail from the Cocoa Chalet to the main hotel.

His sisters would already be checking the Caribbean islands. Of course they'd check. But that wasn't an easy check. Lots of places to hide. Who was on the ops team? Romeo hadn't said, but Laz had asked in his reply.

Had a few things going for him. Including the fact that the "marina" Laz had parked his boat at didn't take credit cards or names. It was cash only. There were plenty of islands for them to check, but they wouldn't start at tourist traps. They'd go for more secluded areas. They'd search mountains. They'd come here.

He'd thought maybe he could stick around for a week.

Hoped. Wanted. But now… He needed to find and elimi-
nate this threat to Honor fast.

And if that didn't work?

It had to work.

He walked across the redbrick patio, past the outdoor
firepit orbited by tables, and over to the bar. He'd intended
to find out who the guys at the bar were, but when he got
there, they were gone. Another guy was sitting there. Ford.
Fortysomething, in shape, with the kind of good looks that
suggested an easy life. Or at least one of wealth. Sitting next
to him, Laz held out his hand. "Lazarus Graves."

The man stared at Laz's outstretched hand, then startled as if realizing his part of the social contract required
response. He grasped Laz's hand, pumped once, quickly
let go. "Ford Fairchild." Another moment of processing
and the man laughed. "That's a great name. Are you a new
guest?"

"Nah. Newest tour guide."

"Really? Honor didn't mention they were hiring new
guides."

Why would Honor mention that to a guest? "So are you
a guest or…"

Ford motioned the bartender toward his drink—looked
to be whiskey—then without asking what he wanted,
ordered a beer for Laz. "No. I'm a guest. But an old friend
of Honor's mother's. Old enough, I butt in where I don't
belong."

Butts in where he doesn't belong and picks drinks
for absolute strangers. "Were you one of Natalie's movie
buddies?"

Guy looked like an actor. A flash of shock, maybe

surprise, and then Ford's smile widened. "I'm a screen-writer. Not an actor."

Laz nodded. The bartender put his beer in front of him. Whisked Ford's drink away and replaced it with a fresh one. Laz took a sip of his beer. He lifted it and read the label. "This is actually good."

Ford smiled. "That's why I ordered it for you. I talked Honor into adding it to the bar, but no one ever orders it. I was starting to feel bad. And as good as it is, after three weeks here, I can only drink so many."

"Well, I'll do as much as I can to help you out." Laz took a longer pull. "Three weeks, huh? That's a long vacation."

"I'm able to work remotely." He took a sip of his drink. "To be honest, I've loved the island since I first came here as a teenager."

"You've visited Dominica before?"

"Years ago. My uncle financed two movies here. I was an unpaid assistant during the first." He smiled at the memory. "It was summer. I was fifteen and had a huge crush on Kiki Hart. So when she spoke with me, befriended a kid with more con-nections than friends, I thought I'd died and gone to heaven."

He laughed, a little sadly. Too sadly.

"Sounds like you never got over that crush."

Ford sipped his drink, stared at the ice bobbing in the amber liquid. "There are few people who you meet who genuinely change the course of your life. She was one of them. The world is a sadder, darker place without her."

Guy was really carrying a torch. Or was he? Natalie Silva had to have been twenty years older than this guy, and he did have a wedding ring on. Laz was about to ask about that when Papito showed up.

Holding a cardboard box filled with flowers in glass vases, Papito gave him a wide and genuine smile. "We have two new guides. Inside. Would you like to meet them?"

"Sure would." He got up from his seat, put a tip on the bar large enough to cover both him and Ford, thanked him for the drink, and followed Papito back into the hotel.

After meeting the newest guides and a few other guests, Laz went back to his room, gathered a pocketful of small, nearly invisible cameras, and prowled the hotel, placing them in discreet and strategic locations.

Back in his room, he sat on the couch in the honeymoon suite, his gun on the seat next to him, laptop on the coffee table, checking the feeds.

Wasn't sure what Honor would say about the cameras, but he didn't have time to be respectful of her patrons' privacy. He had to streamline his mission. Streamlining meant breaking rules, breaking into Honor's computer to get her guest list, making assumptions, prioritizing files based on stereotypes. Guy traveling alone ranked higher than Don Toltz, that guy traveling with his kid Cole.

Definitely not PC, but he needed to send Rome shorthand. There was no way Laz could protect Honor, interview people here, pretend to be a tour guide, and do all the cyber work too.

Have to rely on Rome, a teen. Damn, really missed the League's resources right now. He wrote a quick note to Rome explaining he should start with the most obvious security threats and work his way down. After organizing the files, he sent them off and rechecked the cameras.

His laptop ran camera shots in a corner of his screen. People here and there. That kid, Cole, running down the hall. Not a kid running for fun though. The father chased him, caught him by the arm, and shook him hard.

Laz tensed, shoulders, jaw, fists. This didn't seem a normal kid-running, dad-pissed parental reaction. It reminded him of his rough childhood with his father. The controlling nature of it. And maybe that was wrong, but he put the guy higher on the list. And sent a follow-up message to Rome.

A few minutes later, there was a knock on his door. Checking the camera, he got up and opened the door. Honor smiled at him. "Room service."

Sounded good. He let her in, but she didn't have any food.

"Question. The names on your hotel registration for the next few weeks, there's been no changes? These have all been set up in advance?"

"Yes."

"And there's no one who'd made a reservation recently?"

"Nope. No one. Can we have sex now, or do you want to grill me more?"

Did she just…? He shut the door and kissed her.

CHAPTER 20

BEING BOLD TURNED OUT TO BE A LOT EASIER WHEN there was no time and you were doing so to fulfill a desperate need.

And Honor needed. She needed the heat and hardness that was this gorgeous man. She needed his eager touch and deep kisses. She needed him like he was sunshine, laughter, chocolate.

His hungry, possessive kisses made her head spin and her hands shake. Pulling frantically at his shirt, she couldn't get even one of his buttons undone. A whining, frustrated sound escaped her.

He smiled against her mouth, unbuttoned his own shirt, shrugged out of it, and slipped his T-shirt off over his head.

Her fingers rushed to the swell of his muscles, his abs. Soft skin. Hard muscles. She kissed him, undid the silver button on his cargo shorts.

When she pulled back from the kiss, his eyes dipped to where her hands were. Those eyes didn't leave as she unzipped, pulled his shorts down his body, and then went back for his boxer briefs.

With her kneeling, he stepped out of them. She stood and held his clothes to her chest and stared. So beautiful.

The kind of man she'd seen in magazines. Not one she'd ever thought to have her hot hands on.

"You okay?"

Okay? "This might be the best moment of my life."

Tossing his clothes, she rushed back up to him, kissed him, stroked him until a bit of moisture seeped from the slit of his cock.

He stopped her caressing with a whispered, "Slow down." And lifting her hands high, pulled off her shirt.

Slow was not in her vocabulary right now. Her hands dropped back down, hungry for him. And somewhere in her groping need, as he kissed her neck, licked, he managed to unclasp her bra. She shrugged free.

He looked down at her. "I can't…I don't have the words for how perfect you are."

"Really? I've always thought they were a little large."

His eyebrows rose in complete and honest shock. He caressed her breast and made a deep and appreciative sound. "God, Honor. Perfect."

His other hand undid the button on her shorts. He unzipped them, helped her slip them off, and then pulled her panties down. She stepped out of them. As he slowly stood back up, his hands traced up her body, over her calves, her thighs.

Oh. That felt so good. He moved his fingers between her naked legs, to where she was wet and aching.

"Fuck yes," she said, as much moan as word. He thrust a finger deep inside her, rubbed her clit with the heel of his hand.

She was losing her mind. No slow. She couldn't wait. "No more teasing. Take me. Please."

With a hooded gaze, he slipped his finger out, brought it to his lips, tasted, savored. "Not sure what I did right in my life… Not sure…"

Without warning, he scooped her up and carried her

to the big, round bed. As he lay her down, she saw herself naked in the ceiling mirror.

"Yes. Look at you." His voice was husky, filled with demand and wonder. Hard and needy, he devoured her with his eyes. "Look."

She squirmed. Uncomfortable. He waited. Slowly, her eyes drifted back to the ceiling. He whispered. "See what I see. Soft, sleek legs. Round, full breasts. Smooth, curvy hips. The V between your legs, warm and wet. Do you see how unworthy I am?"

The sincerity in his eyes... Tears filled her throat. She felt perfect. Felt this moment between them as strongly as she'd ever felt anything in her entire life. Anything.

He crawled up the bed, brought his hot body over hers.

She welcomed him with hands that shook. Her heart trembled as well. They kissed. And the world, every trouble and threat in it, became insignificant.

She moved under him, arched into all that sweat and muscle. Sure and graceful, his fingers ran over her nipples, teased, stroked her body to a taut, impatient need.

Writhing, mindless, she grasped at him while his deep voice danced in her ear, praising her, filling her with warmth.

"No more teasing," she demanded. "Hurry. Now."

With a choked, "Honor," he pushed into her with a look of pure pleasure pinching his features.

She cried out with relief, exhilaration. "Oh. That feels so good. Fast now."

Taking her at her word, he moved with a hypnotic, pulsing thrust of eager male hips. And the music of his dance, the rhythm of his swaying hips played her.

She didn't call his name as the pleasure built and built.

Laz wasn't his name. She grabbed at his strong biceps, kissed them, whispered. "*Querido*, that feels so good."

His thrusts went faster. Her body adjusted to the hard and deep length of him. The pressure unbearably good, unbearably... Her core tightened. Her writhing hips rose to meet him.

She moaned. Lost her mind. Lost herself to the pounding beat of their connection, the joy of sharing and...

She came, shaking with the orgasm, as he pumped and rode into her, pushed so deeply, she broke apart with moans and liquid warmth spilling from her.

In the mirror, she watched his thrusts, watched the quick, deep movements, the muscles in his back, his ass. And then he kissed her with a longing as deep and demanding as his thrusts.

He came a moment later. Kissed her as he came, kissed her as his thrusts slowed, kissed her as moisture from his eyes rolled down and onto her face. How was this happening?

After the last deep push, the last shaking tremor, he lowered across her. She wrapped her legs behind his knees and held him when he tried to lift off. "Stay. Stay in me."

He did. He curled his head next to her, breathed in her ear, caught his breath, wiped his tear from her cheek, whispered, "How is this happening?"

She almost laughed. This, this thing between them was too big to fit in the rest of their lives. This joy of each other, this unbelievable connection and bliss. Everything else was an intrusion.

She clung to him, wanted to tell him that they should just enjoy it, enjoy what time they had, but she couldn't. This weird and strange intensity, the electric zing between them required more than silly words. It deserved songs, hymns, poetry.

Was it because they both knew it was temporary? Was that why she felt so swept up in him, his scent, his body? Was he thinking the same thing as his body stilled against her, weighed her down? As he kissed her head, her cheeks, swept her hair back, was he thinking the same thing?

Laz scooped his arms under her, rolled with her so that he stayed inside her, but she was on top of him. He looked up, winked. "Really wanted to see your ass in that mirror."

She burst into laughter.

Before her mind caught up, Honor's eyes popped open. Moonlight streamed through the window, revealing her in the mirror above. Her cell was ringing. She rolled from Laz's embrace, grabbed her phone from the nightstand, answered with a whisper so as not to wake him. "Hello."

For a moment, no one replied, and then a mechanically altered voice said, "Do you think he'll protect you? He won't. You're fucking dead. Your body is already rotting. Just like Tito. Just like your mother. Did he like it? Did he like fucking a corpse?"

Tossing the phone away with a scream, Honor raced across the room and made it to the bathroom just in time to spill the contents of her stomach into the toilet.

She was shaking and retching when Laz rushed to her side. He dropped to his knees, rubbed her back with one hand. When she was done being sick, he said, "Who was it?"

He had her phone in his other hand. She took the phone, punched up the call log, and read, "Unknown number."

"Recognize the voice?"

"It was disguised. Mechanical. The person threatened me. Said I was already dead."

He drew her close, pulled her into his lap, as if to reassure himself as much as her. "Tell me exactly what the person said."

She shook her head. She couldn't repeat those things. Wouldn't. Repeating them might make them real. Wiping at her mouth, she tucked her head into his shoulder and said, "Can you teach me self-defense?"

CHAPTER 21

THREE HOURS AFTER THE PHONE CALL THAT HAD WOKEN him and Honor from a deep, satisfied sleep, Laz had to force himself from their bed. He kissed her once. So tempted to kiss her again, he ached. *No. Don't.* More than that and he wasn't getting up.

It was still dark out. The room was humid but not oppressive with a refreshing breeze blowing through the open doors to the deck. God, Honor smelled fantastic.

Don't think. Just get the fuck up. Protecting her means getting your ass up.

With as much care as pulling the precarious piece in Jenga, he removed himself from her sleeping form. She shifted a little, made a small sound of protest, and drifted back to sleep.

Climbing out of bed, he set the bedside alarm clock for thirty minutes from now and dressed in the fading moonlight, watching her breathe as he did so.

He couldn't put words to what he was feeling. Putting words to it, well, it sounded fuckin' ridiculous. Not for nothing, it was still there. He more than cared for her. More than liked her. He... No. That was impossible. Fairy-tale stuff.

Shit. He left the room, securing the door behind him with sensors that he'd set up. If anyone but Honor—who he'd taught to disarm it late last night—opened this door, they would set off an alarm loud enough to give them permanent hearing loss. And alert the entire hotel.

He made a note to put an alarm on her room as well. Cursed himself for not already doing it.

Walking through the hallway, hearing the creaks and cracks that the day seemed to hide, he made his way down the back stairway and through the kitchen. A man was already there, bent at the wide steel oven, inserting tins of bread to be baked. Laz slipped out before the guy could see him.

He made his way to the yoga center, walking up the planks to the tree house room. He flicked on the lights, dimmed them, took off his shoes, and began taking out mats to set up a training area. When he was done, he checked the secure site through his phone. No messages from Rome.

He began to warm up with a few squats and basic Muay Thai kicks and hits. Moving his body in the forms felt amazing. Like coming home. Forty-five minutes later, he stopped and checked his watch.

She might not be coming. They'd been up late, and he knew she had to be at work by eight. Wouldn't blame her if she'd stayed in bed.

He went toward the side of the tree house that faced the hotel. Some staffers were out there—

"Hey."

Laz startled, spun, grabbed her, nearly putting Honor into a choke hold. *Shit.* He let her go. "Sorry. How do you keep doing that?"

She slipped off her shoes and laughed. "I perfected my skill when I was home schooled."

"You were home schooled?"

"Yep. Which meant hanging out a lot with my mom on sets. I'd get bored, so being naturally quiet, I used to follow adults around, mimic their movements. If they turned, I turned. Honestly, I got so good at it, it wasn't fun anymore."

He gaped at her. She was dressed in loose sweats, black fitness top, with enough cleavage to distract him—though he doubted she could help that. "That's incredible."

She pulled her hair back and tied it in a ponytail. "I was always good at hiding." Her face grew tense. Her jaw tightened.

God, he wanted to protect her. But whatever he felt, whatever this big, scary feeling was, that was one thing he couldn't do—protect her. He could, though, teach her to protect herself.

If someone had asked Laz three weeks ago when he was guiding his sailboat through a storm and responding to every crisis with detached and focused calm, he would've said he had a lot of patience.

But that was before Honor. Before she shredded his control with her eager demands. "No more teasing."

Before his concern for her sent him racing to set up security, racing to imagine every danger, racing to research threats. Before someone had called and threatened her life, threatened her while he held her, sure in his embrace that she was safe. And before he knew her, knew his time with her was precious. She was precious.

And this morning? His fear for her was testing every thread of patience he'd thought he had. He needed her to get this stuff down yesterday.

They'd been at it for an hour and a half. Time was almost

up. She had to get ready for work. So did he—they were leading a tour for hotel guests this morning. Not to mention the yoga class would be here at eight.

Still, he didn't feel like they should call it quits until she got something right. He'd need a magic wand to make that happen. He had no idea how it had all gone so wrong.

The lesson had started out well enough. He'd begun with verbal self-defense instruction. Telling her that fear could be a gift and not to ignore her gut-level warning systems. Explaining about situational awareness, explaining that every human—no matter how much bigger, stronger, and meaner they were—had similar weak spots. Telling her that these weak spots weren't the same in every situation. Because a weak spot is the one you can get at most easily.

Then he'd come at her a few times, not attacking, just asking her to determine in each distinct instance—when he adopted different styles and came at her different ways— where his most accessible weak spots were.

She'd done well, taken it all in, asked the right questions, given the right answers. So he'd moved forward. After warming up together, he'd demonstrated a few easy self-defense moves.

It had been like trying to teach the Tin Man in *The Wizard of Oz* how to do a spin kick. Even now, with her sweating and cursing and trying her very hardest, she couldn't get it. He had no idea what to do with her. She was so bad at self-defense, he'd had to break it down into the simplest of moves. Like shove me.

Who couldn't fucking shove someone?

And holy shit, he was getting frustrated, as frustrated as her face said she was. It was hard for Laz to believe someone so fundamentally in touch with her body and sure-footed could be so stiff and unsure, so wooden and unresponsive when it came to fighting.

He watched her as she turned from him, crossed the room, took a paper cup, and filled it at the watercooler. She sweated through her top. Her body shook. Couldn't say she wasn't trying. She took this seriously, was putting in the effort.

She just had a mental block on the physical actions of fighting, the idea of causing harm to someone.

He needed to try something else, try getting past her hesitation and self-consciousness. Maybe make her angry enough to stop overthinking everything. That was so not in his own best interest when he was sleeping with her. And, just as importantly, wanted to keep sleeping with her. Every chance he got.

She tossed the cup in a wicker wastebasket and came back to the mat. He kept his tone blank, emotionless. "Let's try again."

"What's the point? I suck."

"Not gonna make anything better if you put yourself down."

She wiped sweat from her brow, bounced on her bare feet. "Are you trying to tell me I don't suck? I thought we were being honest with each other. I'm hopeless. I can't be taught."

Her words caught him off guard, dragged him back to the gym underground at his family's mansion, dragged him back to a training mat with Leland. Uncle Leland. He'd said nearly the same thing to Leland during his first week of instruction. And he had responded with nearly the exact words Laz now told Honor.

"Fuck that. It's not true. Unless you want it to be true."

He moved into her, lifted up her chin, and kissed her. Gave way to the fairy-tale feeling, the stupid, impossible, racing, hot, full, and desperate feeling. All of it went into the way his lips worked against hers. Then he stopped, kissed her on the forehead, and said, "Do you want it to be true?"

She shook her head.

"Tell me what you want to be true."

She leaned into him, breathed against him. "I am Honor, fierce and capable and strong."

He kissed her atop her head . "That's just the start of the list, Honor. Just the fuckin' start."

CHAPTER 22

AFTER HE DRIED OFF FROM HIS SHOWER, RUBBING THE towel around the back of his neck, Laz visited the secure site. Romeo had gotten back to him.

Teeth clenched so firmly together, air would've had a hard time slipping past, he opened the email. Nothing about his family's pursuit. His lips eased apart. But Romeo had gotten back to him about the information Laz had taken from Gray.

As he read, he leaned closer to his screen. Nothing on the offer maker. But Gray was busy. Lots of calls. One name stuck out at him, stuck out and jabbed him in the eye. José Silva. Now what was he doing calling Gray?

Only one way to get that answer. Talk to José.

On each side of the road, the agro farm grew out in rows of cultivated trees. Among the trees, slim male workers, shirtless and sweating, hacked with long bladed poles at the ripe fruit. The whisk of a blade was followed by the slice and crash as the fruit dropped into a basket. Above the noise, what must've been a thousand birds sang in the trees.

Stones embedded in dirt crunched under Laz's boots as he walked. The sun warmed his face. And that warmth, any warmth these days, made him think of Honor. He didn't want to leave her. Wanted even less to lose his memory of her. Just the thought caused a fierceness in his chest, like an animal that bared its teeth and growled at the approach of a sensed-but-unseen threat.

Who was arguing? Laz stopped, turned his head, and gazed down the short path through the rows of trees. It was for the tours, but after a hundred or so feet, it gave way to a cleared path of dirt.

Down that dirt path José argued with Papito. Papito placed his hand on José's shoulder, looking just like a father trying to reason with a wayward son. José knocked Papito's hand off, turned, and stormed away.

Papito tipped back his hat, took a handkerchief from his pocket, and wiped his brow. It was then that he saw Laz and shrugged as if to say, "I just can't with this guy."

That seemed to be the consensus.

José didn't even make eye contact as he passed Laz and stalked toward the fermenting station. He transmitted to Laz exactly what he wanted him to know. Basically, *you mean nothing to me and my life. All will be the same after you are gone.*

Well, that might be true. But if the wear and worry of José's body testified to anything, that back to normal wouldn't make that guy any happier.

He looked much older than Papito, who had to be twenty years his senior. José's countenance said he worked a lifetime in each and every day. And that each of those moments was an insult and a burden. One he never forgot. Or forgave.

A few clean strides and Laz had caught up with him. He walked beside him, held out his hand. "Lazarus Graves."

José stopped, eyeballed the extended hand for a moment. "*No entiendo.*"

Really? Last he checked, names translated. He dropped his hand, switched to Spanish. "*Soy el nuevo empleado*."

"I meant I don't understand that name. Awful. Did your parents not realize you would have to go every day into the world with it?"

This guy was the opposite of Papito. No charm. "Yeah. Well, guess we all carry the burdens of someone else's decisions."

José's eyebrows rose. "Until we decide not to."

Guy didn't look like he'd decided anything but getting up, getting dressed, and doing the same exact thing for the last forty years. Or maybe he had. "Why'd you call Gray George, the agent brokering the offer on the farm?"

José put his hands into the frayed pockets of faded olive pants, the color of limp celery. "Who said I did?"

"Gray."

José hitched his shoulders back and stopped cold. "That is a lie."

So he thought Gray would protect him or the fact that he'd called? Was that because they had a personal or business relationship? Interesting.

José eyed Laz suspiciously. "Why are you here?"

"Wanted to say hi. Get to know Honor's *familia*."

José gave him an annoyed, "*Pfft*. Then don't bother with me. She and I are not family."

What?

"Laz? Are you ready for the tour?" Honor called.

José spun, walked away. His head and shoulders down.

Laz joined Honor, dressed in her tour gear with tan cargo shorts and a backpack on. Looking like this man's dream hiking guide. They headed back toward the hotel and the waiting tour group. Their hands brushed. A sweep of fire lit his insides. "So José isn't related to you?"

She turned and looked at the retreating José. "He said that?"

He nodded.

Her brow creased. "We are related. But he's not my uncle."

"What's that?"

Before answering, Honor stopped to direct a group of preteens and teens from a nearby village, standing off the side of the road, milling about, looking confused. "Classes for making soap and skin cream from cocoa fats and oils are down there."

She pointed down the road to where Papito now stood. The old man waved his hand, which also contained his cell phone. The kids moved off. She watched them and shook her head. "Another thing José can't stand. Teaching others how to make a profit from our lands."

She let out a breath, partly defeated, partly annoyed.

Laz couldn't blame her. It seemed José had a problem with everything she did. "Why would he say you weren't related to him?"

Bringing her eyes from the group walking down the road and back to him, she said, "He's being dramatic. A slight from the past. My grandmother loved him but never considered him blood."

"Why not?"

"Ugh. This is going to sound harsh to your American ears."

He raised a *you're-an-American?* eyebrow at her.

Smiling, she hitched her thumbs under the straps of her backpack. "Honestly, it sounded harsh when I first heard it. You see, José is Papito's nephew. Brought here as a troubled boy from Puerto Rico as a favor to his sister."

"He's your second cousin, but he grew up as a son, of sorts, to your grandparents?"

She nodded. "Yes. But my grandmother, who inherited the farm from her father, was adamant about this land going only to a blood relative of hers."

"Ah. I see. José took offense. Has a chip on his shoulder because of it."

"Partly from that. And partly because when my mother inherited, she ignored the property for years."

"Why?"

"Mom was a huge romantic with a romance problem. She always picked the wrong guy. She was thirty-eight when she finally decided enough was enough and went in vitro. And grandfather—he's old-fashioned about some things— held it against her."

No family, apparently, no matter how idyllic the setting, was without issues. He chewed on it for a couple of minutes. All this brought to mind how little he knew about her relationships and the business here. "Mind if I ask your grandfather about it?"

Hands tense on the straps of her backpack, she gazed out at the trail ahead, the tourists and guides waiting there, before answering. "No."

That no sounded anything but confident. He felt for her, he did, but he needed to press buttons, ask questions. They lapsed into a silence loud with their footfalls on the earth and quiet with impending threats. Her family. His family. And whoever wanted the property.

Ahead, the tour group, which included Ford Fairchild, Don and his son, and another couple, milled about talking.

"So what about Junior? Is he family?"

"Sort of."

"Sort of?" Laz couldn't help the jump in his voice.

She laughed. "Junior, who is also named José—thus the nickname—came here for lessons, like those kids we saw. This was years ago, before Grandmother passed. At the time, my grandparents realized Junior was basically living on his own, so they took him in. That probably seems weird to you. Family from all over, not all of us related."

Sipping from his water flask, he nearly choked. He'd been adopted into a family of kids from all over the globe. He coughed, wiped his mouth. "Uh. No. Not at all. *That* I get."

She eyed him, picking up on the suggestion in a way that made him curse his casualness. He looked away. He'd given too much away already. But that was what she did to him. She undid him, broke him open. He wanted to let her in, share stuff with her.

Exchanging hellos with the group, Honor made a point, before they started out, to remind them of the length of the tour. Eight hours. She specifically warned the only person there with a kid, Don. He assured her, with all the testiness of a father who didn't like to be questioned, his kid could handle it.

Honor smiled graciously as she began the hike. Don didn't return the smile. Laz's radar went up. Not that he needed a radar. This guy.

That scene in the hall might've been a snapshot of Don and his family, but it was one that proved accurate as they walked. Guy never stopped advising, warning, instructing his son, Cole. Cole, do this. Don't do this. Do that. Don't do that.

Kind of exhausting, but the hike eventually took the spit

out of the guy. He wasn't a champion hiker, and when he quieted down things got better.

In fact, Laz hadn't been this happy in a long time. Maybe ever.

It was nice here. Peaceful. The jungle forest was so green, even the rain couldn't dim it. But that wasn't all of it. It was being with Honor. It was the kid. The group dynamics. The spontaneous jokes and the connection. It was the outdoors.

As they continued on, the vegetation got less and less. And a smell straight out of hell hit him like a wall. "Might want to warn a guy. Specially when he's walking behind you."

Honor turned around, walked backward a few steps, laughing. "It's the sulfur pools." She waved around. "Welcome to"—she lowered her voice—"the Valley of Desolation."

Steam rose along barren, brown ground, creating a misty area that, along with the rain, gave the feel of entering an entirely other world.

"Sort of like the Fire Swamp," Cole said.

"Yes. But you won't find any rodents of unusual size. Papito calls it a land of a thousand lands. He says that you can be happy on this island but never comfortable. It will turn on you as surely as a storm."

She bent down and dipped her finger into the hot mud, then walked to Cole. "Do you mind?" she asked. He shook his head, and she put two dark streaks under his eyes. Like a soldier on a long march.

He smiled up at her. Kid had it bad. And he had great taste.

CHAPTER 23

THEY'D ARRIVED AT BOILING LAKE FIVE HOURS AFTER they'd set out. An hour behind what it normally took, and they still needed to head back. Now everyone had split off into groups. They all seemed fine, but Honor worried about Don and his son.

Well, mostly Don. He looked exhausted. She'd have to make sure they did less chatting and stopping on the way back.

Dropping her backpack on the drying, brown earth, Honor took in the misted blue water of Boiling Lake. It stretched out below, a beautiful threat.

Taking a seat next to Laz, she extended her legs. And secretly tried to move as close as possible to him. It was that kind of pull, the kind where closeness was an absolute need. She could feel the heat of him even through his cargo pants.

This entire trip had been one long test of her self-control. She leaned her head against his shoulder. "This is one of my most favorite places on the island. It reminds me of better days with my mother."

"No need to answer, but I was wondering...how did she die?"

She had no problem answering but knew people were often surprised by how her mom had died. Her mom had lived a big life, so people assumed her death would be the result of the risks she took—skydiving, ice climbing, or hiking the Amazon. "Hit and run. Never caught the guy either. I know it sounds vindictive, but it seems wrong that the person who killed her is out there living life, not in jail, not suffering, while my mom is not here."

Laz's face was no longer playful or curious. He looked worried. "No leads?"

His face had gone so still, so serious. Her heart began to pound. "No. I even hired two different investigators to find the guy."

"What'd they discover?"

"Not much. Mom lived in an affluent neighborhood, so all the homes had security footage, but neither investigator had been able to come up with any substantial leads."

"That's weird. With all that security footage, your average hit-and-run driver is gonna get caught. Have you seen the footage? What about the car?"

A chill ran the entire length of her body. She had learned so much from him, learned to see the world differently. "Are you suggesting…it wasn't an accident? That it could be related to what's happening here?"

"Not sayin' that. Just putting pieces of the puzzle together. Some might not fit, but we need to look at all angles."

Her throat grew dry and thick with dread and regret. Fists of anxiety pounded against her chest. Had she let her mother down? "But how could her death be related to the offer on the business?"

"No idea." His hand moved down her arm, his fingers intertwined with hers. "Tell me about your mom. She seemed pretty dynamic."

Honor cringed. "Her career wasn't her. Not really."

"Whaddya mean?"

"My mother's image wasn't real. You know, in her

younger days, she played party roles, sex symbol. That was her persona. Early on, she was fine making a living that way. She told me, 'Honor, I had three choices: bitch, bimbo, or saint. Bitch doesn't pay. And I couldn't pull off saint.'"

His brow furrowed. "I remember her as some kind of activist."

A host of complicated feelings welled up within her. Best to get it out there. "As she grew older, she became disenchanted with the industry, and she took on fewer roles. Invested her money in causes. Began to make documentaries. Most of her money went into these exposé documentaries. Of course, those she spoke out against branded her as old and bitter. Her documentaries got little attention after that. She put them online for free."

"What did these exposés take on?"

"Feminist issues, chauvinism, sexism, abuses in Hollywood. It earned her a lot of hate." Her shoulders tensed, and she ordered them to release and relax. "They were constantly throwing her former image into her face, the dopey sex goddess, as if as a warning to the rest of womankind. Look, see what happens when you lose your sex appeal, you get crabby and angry. She didn't care. She fought back by standing up, despite the critics."

"I think your mother and my mother would've been good friends."

A flare of frustration ignited through her. Here was one more thing she didn't know. Was anything in her life knowable right now? "I wouldn't know. You won't tell me about your mother."

He looked past her. And her eyes strayed to follow where his gaze had gone.

Cole and his dad were playing a game of catch with an apple they'd brought. That was a little dangerous near the lake. Did Don understand that 92 degrees Celsius was 197 degrees Fahrenheit?

Laz looked over at her. "Sometimes people are protected so much, they've got no idea when to be cautious."

Honor felt the sting of that. The accusation that she had lived a sheltered life. She hadn't once questioned her mother's death. She had been naïve. Even so, the suggestion pissed her off. "And sometimes people are protected so little, they can't figure out how to relax and trust."

He startled. His brow creased. With a move as quick as it was graceful, he got up and walked away. He stood at the edge of the cliff, looking through the rising steam out at the mist-soaked mountains and winding trails.

She went after him, equal parts sorry and frustrated.

As she approached, he looked down at her. "I'm sorry, Honor."

He was sorry? "About?"

"Suggesting your life has been easy, protected. I'm just frustrated, wanting…I guess something that can't be."

The swell of emotion caught her off guard. She'd expected him to tell her she'd misunderstood, that she had no reason to bite his head off. But he was telling her the opposite.

"It's okay," she said and put her arm around his waist. He put an arm over her shoulders. "So if my mom's death is linked to this, it could be bigger than we thought."

He squeezed her closer. And then quietly, "Yeah."

"I have files."

"Files?"

"I have all my mom's files and notes at the hotel. Maybe there's a clue."

He leaned down and kissed her on the cheek. "Fierce and beautiful and smart. Wish I could share more of my history with you."

Again, her throat grew tight with emotion. "You share enough. The truth of who you are now. No matter what our future holds. This, right now, is enough."

CHAPTER 24

THE GROUP THAT RETURNED FROM THE HIKE DIDN'T have nearly the same cheerful mood they'd had when they'd set out. They were quiet, plain old bushed as they made the final push down the trail. Even Don was quiet. Only took a nine-hour hike.

Truth, Laz was more tired from Don's near constant anxiety over what Cole did or didn't do. Talk about helicopter parenting. According to Honor, her mother wasn't anything like Don.

He'd need to do research on Natalie. Wouldn't be the first time not knowing who's who in popular culture bit him in the ass. Kind of strange that she'd been hit by a car, and they'd never found the driver.

Probably not related to what was happening here, but this could be messier than it appeared. Still, how could someone making a generous offer on Honor's property be related to the hit and run?

Unless, could the person who hit Honor's mother be trying to make up for his or her actions by offering her an outrageous sum of money for her property? Crap. That didn't make much sense. He'd never felt more adrift, never missed the resources the League provided more. He needed a team.

The sky turned to dark. Nearly out of the woods, off the trail, and a crack of thunder erupted nearly on top of them. The sky opened up and gushed rain.

They hit the trail's end and set off at a run for their chalets or the hotel.

Honor turned to him as they ran, grabbed his slick-with-rain hand. Her silver eyes pinned him like steel, like a spike to his heart. "Do you want to see some of my mom's films? Or her files? They're in my room."

He did.

Laz really liked Honor's room. Lots of earth tones and dark furniture, with a big bed. California king. Lady knew the way to his heart.

Once the door closed behind them, she pulled him to her. Hands on his shoulders, she brushed eager lips across his. He moved his tongue into her mouth, savored the feel of her soft, wet tongue against his.

After a moment of hot kisses, she pulled at his damp cargo pants. "Take these off. I want to give you head."

His eyebrows must've shot to the roof, along with his body temperature. "That might be the nicest order anyone has ever given me."

Never been a guy, in the history of damp, stuck-on pants, who'd gotten out of them gracefully. He tried. He really tried to be cool in the face of his raging cock and his shaking hands. Nearly made it. But as he worked his cargo pants over the tops of his feet, they caught him up, and he crashed to the floor.

Finished taking off her own clothes, with no problems, Honor's hands flew to her mouth. She looked at him for a moment, sitting on the ground, pants around his ankles, hard-on at full attention. She burst into laughter.

Most men, men who hadn't grown up in a house full of women who'd regularly laughed at them, might've been bothered, embarrassed. Not him. He saw this for what it was. An opportunity.

He winked at her. "Looks like I'm going to need your help."

She smiled, dropped to her knees, and pulled his pants off. She tossed them across the room as if they wouldn't be needed for a long time.

Worked for him.

On her knees, she cat arched that beautiful body by his feet, licked his toes. What was…? Oh, that felt good. Ah. That felt great.

Using nothing but the tip of her fine, sweet tongue, she positioned herself between his legs, worked her way up his right calf, the muscles in his thigh.

The delicate flutter, the slick, soft moistness moved up and over his body, along the inside of his thigh. He arched in expectation and clenched his fists.

With her crouched between his thighs, he had no choice but to spread his legs. She ran her tongue over the swell of his balls, sucked one into her mouth, and gently worked it over with her soft tongue. "Honor…that…"

A moan chased his words back down his throat as she swept her tongue to his other ball.

Woman had the instinct of a goddess. If she'd been in his own body, she couldn't have known how to make him feel better.

With an audible plop, she dropped him from her mouth and slid her tongue up and then down his cock while cupping his throbbing balls.

Pushing toward her mouth, he begged with the thrust of his hips for her to take him fully into her mouth. She didn't disappoint.

The moment her lips came down and wrapped velvety warmth around him, he nearly came.

He moaned loud and long, watched the sway of her body as her tits bounced with the rise and dip of her head. She began to move faster.

Seriously…going to come. Reaching down, he slowed her by winding his hands through her hair. It was that or lose it.

Her eyes looked up. Those silver eyes locked directly on him. He swallowed. "Too good. Going to come."

She smiled around his cock. A wicked smile that said he was in deep trouble. Pulling against the hold he had on her hair, her mouth dropped down, taking in nearly the whole of him.

Fuck. Never seen a woman do that before. She began to work the length of him with an enthusiasm, a genuine pleasure that killed his restraint.

He grew so hard and thick in her mouth, it began to hurt. She dipped and sucked. The friction built, the tension that edged him toward orgasm.

He needed to slow her down, take control.

She ran her tongue along the seam of his cock, then began to move it with a speedy, fluttering vibration. What the hell was… He bucked into her mouth and came, came like a flood, came like it'd never end, like the orgasm would carry on for days.

When he was done, she swallowed and smiled like the cat who'd eaten the canary.

And man, he was dead tired, so satisfied. But she obviously didn't know she'd thrown down a challenge. Or that he'd grown up in a family where a challenge was *never* not accepted. Game on.

CHAPTER 25

ON THE WARM, DARK FLOOR OF HER BEDROOM, HER SKIN slick from the heat between them, Honor curled against Laz's chest. Kissing her, he rolled, scooped her up in his arms, and carried her to the bed.

Thunder broke in the sky, and rain pelted the window as the storm continued.

With a gentleness that made her feel precious, he placed her on the bed, leaned over her, and kissed her. *Mmm.* He smelled like sex.

His warm hands traced down her body, sought between her legs, stroked. In no time, she was saturated and reaching for him. Then he stopped.

Grabbing his hand, she protested, pouted, but he pressed his forehead against hers. "What can I do for you, Honor? What can I do to show you...to make this moment last forever in your mind? Last for all the days that I won't be here?"

The thought of him leaving filled her with intense grief. She pushed it away. If all she had was this moment, she wanted every second of it. Grief could wait.

He stood there in his perfection, every blessed inch. And he waited for her to tell him. She wanted... She swallowed. "Will you dance for me?"

A smile played on his lips. He kissed her fully, nodded. Wrestling his phone from inside a deep pocket on his cargo pants , he turned it to a soft song. Oh, she recognized the artist, Shawn Mendes. And the song, "Mercy."

As the soft acoustics filled the room, he lifted one arm and... She thought he'd do a disco, a teasing, joking Magic Mike dance, but his other arm floated up. He lifted his foot in perfect pirouette—like the most graceful male ballet dancer—and spun.

And he danced. Like a heartbeat. Like a prayer. Like he meant it.

Tears sprung to her eyes as she watched him. His body was an instrument, and he serenaded her.

Honor had heard women say there was nothing beautiful in the male form. None of those women had ever been in this room, watching this flawless man spin and move and slide. The curtains blew in a rainy breeze, scented with green and jasmine and cocoa.

The cut of him, the strength of his hard lines, the bunch and pull of muscles, set her aflame. He wrote with the spins, fades of his legs and arms a poem to her. And she felt it, him, everywhere.

When he was done, sweat slicked his body. The room filled with his soft breaths. And her heavy ones. He returned to her, crawled on top of her. So beautiful, her breath caught.

And as his body had danced for her, his lips and fingers danced over her. She writhed under him.

Kissing her, a fierce and flowing kiss, he slipped a finger inside her already throbbing core. She pushed hard into him, encouraged him deeper. His lips traveled down her body to her nipple, biting lightly.

He teased her nipple as one skilled finger, curled inward, found the bundle of nerves inside her body. He stroked. Oh. "Yes. There."

His mouth praised her, loved her as his finger danced

inside. The tension built, tightened. She tossed her head, moaned his name, and as his mouth came down and captured her clit, cried out.

He was everywhere. Inside and out. Sucking and strumming. And she was mindless with need. The tension so high, she was seconds from having it crash against her.

With an expert pressure, he bit her clit. She screamed, came, came hard with her body throbbing and shaking and her mouth murmuring nonsensically.

For long moments after, she shook with aftershocks. He didn't stop his exploration, though his fingers gentled, a tenderness that showed he was in exact rhythm with her.

If he'd continued too hard or too fast, the pleasure of those aftershocks might've been lost, but his softness let every last shock of pleasure flash and whisper through her.

When his finger slid from inside her, he licked her clit and ringed it with his finger. Her hips shot up. He rolled his thumb, slick and hot, against her. Holy…What was he… The orgasm slammed into her, bowed her, startled her, shattered her. "Yes. Oh. Yes!"

She moved hard against his strength, and he caught her, wringing every last ounce of pleasure from her body.

The orgasm slowed. Stopped. Satiated, stunned, she could barely keep her eyes. Every muscle in her body released and sighed. He gathered her to him, kissed her on the head, and said, "I liked the way you danced for me."

She smiled, wanted to say something poetic and right, but only managed, "Wow."

———————————

Sitting up in her bed, her mother's old laptop open between them, Honor watched as Laz viewed her mother's last completed documentary. A silhouetted figure was on the screen, describing in an altered voice abuse suffered at the hands of a well-known director.

Laz paused it. He stared at the screen. "I'm often amazed by things like this, big truths about abuse, and on the fucking internet. Just out there. In the public fucking domain. And no one does shit."

"This is ugly. People don't want to see it. Much easier to believe the lie."

"The lie?" He waited. Could see a bunch of things working in his eyes.

Honor ran a finger along the silver computer's edge. This laptop contained so much of her mother, of her work, of her determination, but it didn't contain the whole story. "Years before my mother got pregnant with me, she had a drug problem. She went into rehab. When she started making documentaries, someone put out this video of her, totally stoned... She became Kiki the drug addict. Weirdo. Making all that crazy noise about the movie industry."

Honor hated that video. The tears she'd shed knowing that was how some people would always see her mother. As if her mother was only that moment in time, even though she'd been clean for decades.

"There was so much hatred directed at my mom after that. People accused her of making stuff up, trying to revitalize her career by drawing attention to herself. And worse stuff. Angry things. I was afraid. I stopped telling people my mother was Kiki Hart. I couldn't take the shame, anger, hatred."

She brushed aside a tear. "Told you I was a coward."

Laz pushed the old laptop away, shoved the files from the two detectives Honor had hired to the end of the bed, drew her into his embrace. He whispered, "Don't matter how many times you tell me that, Honor, I'm never gonna believe it. And I can see why you wouldn't want to claim that false image. To you, your mom was the woman posting the videos, trying to make a difference, Natalie Silva."

A chill of relief worked down her skin. And a tightening of shame filled her throat. "There was that. But I don't want to lie and pretend that some of it wasn't pure fear and selfishness. Mom did a good job of protecting me. Homeschooled until high school—an elite private school. I even attended a small elite college, pursuing my passion for food and gastrological chemistry."

She tucked her head into his shoulder. Inhaling the spice of his body, she curled into the warm reassurance of his steady presence.

Even though the tears flowed, she couldn't stop talking. She hadn't known all this was inside her, all this pain. "After Mom became so hated, I was shell-shocked. I just wanted her to shut up. It wasn't doing any good, speaking out. It's like people who hate are so loud. And people who don't hate, naturally, just aren't."

"I'm sorry, Honor. She deserved better."

She did. And she didn't deserve to die the way she had. To be murdered. Because more and more, she was becoming convinced that that was what had happened. "Do you think one of the people who threatened her murdered her?"

He wiped a tear from her eye. "The hatred from online kooks isn't usually deadly. More likely, if she was murdered, it was someone with a more personal reason. Are all her documentaries online?"

"Not all. She died before she could finish the last one."

He stilled. Something she was beginning to understand he did when he found an item that drew his attention. The way a hunting dog freezes and points when it sniffs out game. He sat up, pulled the laptop back. Fingers working the keyboard, he opened some files. "I noticed before, the amount of money she spent here was crazy. Tens of millions on research. What was she working on?"

Honor sat up next to him. "Not sure. I know she had a big-name star willing to go on camera to expose someone using movies to get close to kids. But I don't have names. By necessity, she did all the filming in secret, kept everything under wraps. And I didn't press. Honestly, I didn't want to know. Until she died, I had no idea she'd basically spent her life's savings on her last film."

"Where can I find that film?"

She shrugged. "It's gone. After she died, I toyed with the idea of releasing it, but…" She waved at the paper files, the thumb drive, external hard drive. "If there was ever any kind of completed film, I was never able to locate it."

He continued to search through computer files. "Her files are extensive. Lots of passwords to online locations. Some hidden on the Dark Web."

Rolling onto her side, she readjusted her pillow, propping her head up. "So it's going to take a while." Part of her dreaded going through the files, seeing what her mother had been up to. And part of her wanted to know every little thing about it and how it related to the threats to her now, the offer on the property.

Ugh. She felt restless with the need to do something, discover something. Everything seemed a mystery right now. Especially the man hard at work on the bed beside her. Blankets partly covered one leg, blue boxer briefs on, muscled stomach creased as he bent over the laptop.

Lifting her head, she looked down at Laz's exposed leg. "How did you get the scar?"

His eyebrows went up. His body tensed.

No. Nope. She grabbed his thigh, squeezed. "I really *need* you to answer this."

Putting the laptop on the nightstand beside him, he rolled onto his side, smoothed her hair. The night was cool and smelled of the rain and all the deep, earthy scents churned up into the air. "A dog."

His eyes drifted closed. She tensed, wanting to grasp onto him, shake him, shake something about him, some truth from his mouth, but she felt him still, focus.

She stilled too—all but her heart, which picked up its pace. She could feel the tension inside him, feel it growing, feel when he decided to let it go. "I don't think he intended to kill her. Just got carried away one time."

Honor had to force her clenched hand open, force her nails not to dig into his thigh. "Kill who?"

"My mom. My dad was an abusive guy."

His father had killed his mother? She closed her eyes. Opened them with a horrible thought. "Did you see it?"

He looked toward the open window and the almost full moon. "No. Would've. But at one point..." He scrubbed at his face with his hand. "I went after him. He dragged me out of the room, shoved me into the laundry room. We had this vicious mutt."

That was the scar.

"Tore the shit out of my leg. Kicked it off, crawled into the dog kennel, and locked the door. So no, I didn't see him do it. But I heard. Even over the dog growling and attacking. I heard. The cries, the crash, the thud. And later when he came into the laundry room and got some cleaning supplies. I saw her on the floor." His head lowered, as did his voice. "Pretended to be asleep in the cage."

"How old were you?"

"Six."

Six! Honor had to swallow twice, then clear her throat before she could speak. "Did you have to testify? Did he go to jail?"

She couldn't have caused a greater reaction in him if she'd held a hot poker to his side. He jumped out of the bed, stood in the moonlight, all taut muscles and wild beauty.

He ran an agitated hand through his hair and began to collect his things. "I need... We'll talk tomorrow."

Her entire body in a state of panic, she got out of bed. The pain, the conflict was obvious on his face. Had she caused that? She couldn't let him leave. She walked over, tore his pants from his hands. "No."

The smallest hint of anger darkened his face. "Give me my pants."

Pulling them behind her, she shook her head. "No."

"Fine. Your guests will get an eyeful." He tried to step around her.

Honor wasn't sure what came over her. She looped her leg around his and brought him down, like he'd taught her. Except she got caught up with him, and as he began to fall on her, she cried out.

He twisted, grabbed her as he fell, so she somehow ended up on top of him. How, she had no idea.

His back on the floor. His warm front to her front. His hot breaths pushing against her lips. Anger lined his face. And she suddenly felt wrong, for forcing him to stay, for not respecting his need for space.

She swallowed. "I'm sorry. I just… It's painful to watch you go. It hurts me. How can I sleep knowing you're out there, in pain, and that something I said caused it?"

His face softened. He let out a breath, brought his forehead to hers. "This isn't your fault. Nothing you caused. You changed everything, Honor. You don't even know. You changed everything."

He rolled, gathered her to his side, tucked her against his body, held her tight, and whispered in her ear. "He didn't go to jail. I never told anyone what I saw. Not until now."

Oh.

She heard him swallow. And when he spoke again, his voice was low, clouded with pain. "He pretended he didn't do it. And I pretended I didn't know he did it. It was a matter of survival."

"And you've lived with this the whole time? Never told anyone?"

"Until you, I didn't…" He swallowed. "No one ever asked."

"No one has ever asked about your childhood?"

"Nah. My adopted family…they all got stories. Mine," he said with a shrug, "just wasn't… I don't know."

"You were adopted? By who?"

Silence. A closing down. "Don't matter. None of it matters. What's important is that now, I live my life in a way that makes up for not saying anything—or trying."

It did matter. She wanted his story. She wanted his truth. "Does this have anything to do with the meaning behind your tattoos?"

He kissed the back of her head. "Just lie with me a minute. Okay?"

Ugh, so frustrating. She wanted to know. She cared. But she'd pushed him enough. So with her shoulder against the floor, his heat to her back, and her head pillowed on his bicep, she breathed deeply, swallowed her questions, and slept.

CHAPTER 26

LAZ HADN'T PLANNED ON SLEEPING ON THE FLOOR OF Honor's room. It just kind of happened. But when her alarm sounded, he came fully awake. A streak of sunlight through the windows caressed the outline of her hips. She had the kind of toned body that looked so good naked, clothes seemed like they should be banned.

She rolled, threw a shoe at her clock, silencing it. A former archer, she had a good aim. She made a sound of deep regret. In a voice that reminded him of an old commercial, said, "I need to get up and make the chocolates."

He wanted her so badly. "How long do you have?"

She sighed, nuzzled his neck. "I have orders to fill, and my self-defense instructor is a pain in the ass. I need to get up."

She did? Then why was she doing that. She went from nuzzling his neck to nibbling his ear to tracing her lips across his jaw and taking his lips.

For a moment, he wasn't sure what was happening, and then his body silenced his brain and he forgot to care. He rolled onto her, rolled his tongue into her mouth, began to tease and stroke her body—a manipulation meant to get her too hot to leave him.

She moaned under him, pushed against his chest. "I can't. I have to make chocolate."

Damn. He rolled back. She sat up, kissed his lips, once, twice, and then swept her tongue into his mouth. And then she climbed on top of him, her wet core throbbing against his hard-on.

What was going on? Was she going to stop now? Fuck. Who cared? This was the best feeling in the world. This hot woman on top of him, soaked, sliding against his cock.

She moaned again. Again said, "I can't." And then she lifted, grabbed his cock, and pressed herself onto him. His eyes sprung wide at the exact moment hers did.

"Honor, are you—"

His eyes rolled back in his head as she slid slowly down. "You're so thick and hard and ready," she said.

All he could do was hold absolutely still, afraid she'd startle and bolt if he moved, but she continued to slide down until he was fully sheathed.

She kissed him again, open-mouthed and desperate, and with no more warning than that began to ride him. Fast.

Body bouncing, hips pumping, ass thrusting up and down, she made frantic, mounting sounds of need and want. All he could do was grab her waist and hold on for dear life. That and focus on something other than the heave of her tits, so full and ripe.

Focus on something other than her sighs, her moans, that building heat. Focus. He was two seconds from losing himself inside her.

She threw her head back and came, even as she continued to pound him. Wonderful, blessed moments later, she slowed, bent down, kissed him on his lips.

He started to roll, to get her under him, but she stopped him with a push of her hand against his shoulder. He lay back down. She began to move off of him, and a small sound, definitely not a whimper, broke from his mouth.

But she bent and kissed him, kissed him with her tongue probing him, and then she turned around, got both feet under her knees, grasped him and plunged down.

"Fuck. Honor."

She began to lift and lower at a pace that was excruciatingly good, an impossibly fast pace that she kept with her hands on her thighs and her ass thrust in his face.

So beautiful. So hot.

He arched to meet her when she descended, and the sound of her labored sighs tightened his skin, coiled his body. Until there was only her, that slick, surrounding heat, and nothing left but to release himself hard and hot into her soft, waiting body. With crazy, stupid gratitude on his lips, he whispered, "Thank you...thank you...thank you."

She rode him until the very last ounce slicked the skin connecting them, and then she lifted off, turned, fell onto him, and breathed hot and heavy in his ear.

He waited a minute before asking, but he had to ask. "Momma always told me that when a woman says no, she means no. But you said you can't, but you did. Not that I'm complaining. I'm the happiest man on the planet right now, but just so we get this straight. No means no, right?"

She laughed, punched him in the shoulder. "Of course no means no. I wasn't saying I can't have sex with you. I was saying I can't leave you. I knew I should, but I just couldn't. You are irresistible."

He laughed. "If I had known that was what you meant, I would've been a lot more participatory. I was afraid to move. Wasn't sure what you were doing."

She winked at him. "Worked for me."

CHAPTER 27

LAZ WAS A DESPERATE MAN. HE HAD TO KEEP HONOR here, trying. But she was losing all her patience, and it was all he could do to get her to stay in the yoga tree house.

Couldn't blame her. Though she'd done a good job of taking him down last night in her room, she'd reverted to her usual stiffness in the self-defense class. And these were slow, careful lessons. Lessons designed to imprint the movements, not mimic the speed of an actual fight.

This was beginning to feel like a waste of time. But he'd never found a student he couldn't teach, and he damn sure wasn't giving up on this one.

Honor rolled her neck, wiped sweat from her eyes, caught her breath before taking his hand. He pulled her to her feet. She smelled of her sweat and chocolate. All he could do not to nuzzle into that scent.

He backed up. Maybe he could slip past her mental block by startling her, shaking something loose. It had worked last night. She probably didn't even realize how much she'd startled him. She was that damn quick. That damn quiet. But it had taken her not being in her own head to do it. So could he do that to her again?

Maybe if he tried the way he'd been taught. The way he'd taught the kids at the Mantua Home. He liked to think of it as the *now-whatcha-gonna-do* method.

Shortly after being adopted, he'd arrived at the Mantua

Home, a mansion on a hill in the center of the Parish boarding school, the Mantua Academy.

He'd been walking around, getting a feel for the huge
home, when Justice had jumped out from around a corner
and nailed him in the chest with a kick. He'd stumbled back
and fallen on his ass. She'd laughed, cocked a grin. "Now
whatcha gonna do?"

Pissed, embarrassed, he'd gotten up and charged at her.
She'd taken him down in one-point-five seconds. Being
taken down by an eight-year-old when you were twelve was
hard to swallow. Tough as charred steak.

Especially when he'd come from the streets and a violent home, so he'd had some experience with reacting to
violence. But scrappy and angry failed against trained and
calm every time.

Laz let out a breath. All right. "Try to get past me."

Her brow drew down, then she sighed and relented. Dancing
around a little, she waved fists around like a cartoon boxer, hit
him weakly in the arm, no follow-through. She dodged.

He tripped her, brought her down to the mat, and put a
knee into her back. "Now what do you do?"

She shook her head. "Okay. I get it. Get off."

This was killing him. "Whatcha gonna do?"

"I don't know. You haven't taught me that yet."

Wrong. He had. He'd taught her how to get out of this
exact situation. He didn't have her right arm, was leaning
close enough to let her put an elbow into his face. Was
barely holding her. She just wasn't willing to do it, to hurt
him, to hurt anyone.

But last night when he'd been leaving, she'd acted. She'd
acted when she thought it meant saving him from pain.

Maybe that?

He got down closer. "When I was eleven years old, I ran away from my abusive father. This situation, the one you find yourself in right now, I found myself in with a stranger. And guess what? Saying 'get off' didn't fucking work." He swallowed. Saying it out loud, the brutality of it, suddenly made his throat tight, made all those old feelings bubble up. "Fight for that kid, Honor. Defend him. Show me."

She moved like he'd lit a match under her, genuinely taking him by surprise. She slammed her elbow into his face. Hard. For real. *Fuck.* She twisted, knocked him off, sat on his body, made as if she would punch him.

He held up hands. For a moment, the red rage in her eyes took his breath away. The side of his face throbbed with heat. That was gonna leave a mark. "Honor."

She blinked.

"You did it."

Her eyes opened wide. She rolled off. He sat on the mat next to her as she sat up, rubbed at her arms and tears. Great. He'd made her cry.

She sniffled. "What did you do?"

"The first time? Wasn't much I could do. The second time? Well, that time, I had a knife, made sure when that same guy came after me, he saw it. Made sure he could see how hard I'd fight. He left. After that, spent the nights sleeping behind a dumpster."

Her eyes were wide, shocked. "I can't get my head around this stuff. Your life."

She wiped another tear. He'd genuinely startled her, hurt her. "I'm sorry, Honor. I shouldn't—"

"No. It's okay. I want this. I want to know. It's just different from how I was raised. I was kind of sheltered."

Maybe there was a clue there. "When was your last fight?"

Her eyebrows rose. "My last fight?"

Okay. Maybe *fight* wasn't the right word. "When was the last time someone physically threatened you, got in your face?"

"The other day. My Uncle José."

Laz balled his fists. "He threatened you?"

"Not exactly. He kind of blocked my way. He didn't touch me or make it seem like he'd hit me or anything."

Laz let out a breath. "How many fights have you been in? What's the most violence you've ever experienced?"

"Violence? Like me hitting someone or someone hitting me?" She looked down. "Never."

"Tripped. Shoved. It doesn't have to be hit."

She looked up at him. Her silver eyes wide and curious. "Where *are* you from?"

The real world. "Are you telling me you have never been hit? Not as a kid, not in school, not playing soccer, not shoved, not tripped, never?"

"I was pushed into a pool once. But as a joke, not with malice. As for sports, I danced. Did swim team. And, of course, archery. Not hunting. I would never. I didn't play any sports that required aggression."

An archer that had never killed anything. Weapons training, teaching her to shoot to kill, would be a problem. "So never violent. Not once?"

"Never. And up until this very moment, I thought that was normal." She eyed him. "What about you? When was your first time?"

He looked over her head, could hear the clink of breakfast silverware and glasses in the courtyard below. People were up and having breakfast. "I guess I'm your polar opposite. Can't remember a day without violence."

Her silence drew his eyes back to her. He watched her fumble with her distress, grasp for something to say. They locked eyes for a moment. He watched her accept what he'd told her, realize it wasn't something that needed sympathy, because here he stood, unbroken. She smiled, a bit sadly. "Well, give me a chance to catch up. You have lived a *lot* longer than me."

He laughed. How much longer? "How old are you, Honor?"

"Twenty-six. You?"

Shit. She was young. "Thirty-four."

"Nice. Tone."

He flinched, scooted back. His heart jumped into his throat and kneed his Adam's apple. "What'd you call me?"

CHAPTER 28

ON THE FLOOR IN THE YOGA TREE HOUSE, THE SUN working its way inside, sweat dripping down her back. Insects buzzing outside and the sound of utensils, of people talking and eating breakfast drifted up, but Honor's focus was completely on Laz. What had she called him?

She shook her head. "I didn't...I said nice tone. Your tone. You said your age like it made you smarter."

His face became completely blank, impassive. Her heart started to pound. This meant something. But that made no sense. What had she said? Nice tone? Nice. Tone. Tone?

She considered those words, chewed on them with a swish of her jaw as she flexed her toes up and down against the squishy blue mat.

Laz began to collect his things as if nothing had happened. Something had happened. What in those two words could... "Tony?"

He spun.

Her hands flew to her mouth.

Of course. Of course. Goose bumps washed over her in such a fierce rush, she had to repress a full body shudder. Him. It was him. Water rushed to her eyes. "Tony? Is that your name?"

He stared at her with eyes that went wide and moist with some unnamed pain. It was. His name. For a moment, he was unmasked to her. She made a small, pained sound.

As much as they shared, and they shared something far

deeper than anything she had known in her life, there was a giant emptiness between them. The emptiness that was him. Who he really was.

Saying his name, Tony, counted. She hadn't expected it to be so important. But it felt huge to her. A lump of emotion rose in her throat.

She opened her mouth to say it again, to feel his name on her tongue, like she had felt him against her body.

He closed his eyes, put up a hand, a stop gesture as if it caused him physical pain. "Don't call me that again, Honor. As much as…as good as it feels, it's not safe."

He opened his eyes, giving her as much of his truth as he dared. It wasn't enough. Suddenly, it wasn't enough.

Now that she had a piece, a taste of his truth, she wanted it all. What had happened to him after he ran away? Where had he ended up? What or who was he running from? The moment she'd said his name, it was like a small bell in her heart had been rung. *Tony.*

She stood, walked over to him, wrapped her arms around his neck, and kissed his cheek. She put her lips against his ear. "Tony. Tone."

She felt him shudder, felt moisture roll from his eyes. He groaned, wrapped his arms around her. "Fuck. Don't. Please."

His words were a plea for her to stop, but his body, his warmth begged her otherwise. So one more time, she whispered, "Kiss me, Tony."

He did, full on the mouth, wrapping her tight in his arms. Hot and wild and as needy a physical response as the looming threat against him, the barrier from his past that kept, would keep them apart. Her heart swelled, battered against her chest.

What was happening to her? What was this?

Barely eight a.m., the sun was already high in the blue sky spreading out over the trees, birds chirped their hopeful songs, and Honor felt as if her entire world had changed from the one she'd known just a few days ago.

She pulled back. He stared at her. She at him. "What is this?"

He shook his head. "I…I don't know." He smiled, awed and sad. "Like something from a fairy tale."

The sound of someone whistling drifted into the room, and a moment later, the yoga teacher appeared. Mia waved at them as she entered. She had on cream-colored yoga pants and matching top, with her hair tucked into a swami-like hat. She began turning on the diffusers around the room. Tea tree. It kept out the bugs.

Honor stepped away. Laz rubbed at the back of his neck. "Want to get something to eat?"

She wanted to go back to their room, his room, the honeymoon suite, and whisper his name, whisper it in his ear while he poured himself, his truth, into her. She nodded. "Yeah. I'm starved."

On their way out, Laz smiled at Mia in a way that was all charm. "Sorry if we delayed your class prep."

She shook her head. "They won't be here for a few minutes. You could stay if you want."

Honor laughed. "I can barely use my arms right now."

Mia shifted slightly, tilting her head to the side. "What are you guys practicing?"

Whoops.

Laz took over. "Is that a hint of a British accent I hear?"

Mia smiled. "Yep. I'm an offshore financial expat. One of many on the island."

"What's that mean?" Laz said.

"The Caribbean has a lot of havens for business. It attracts people who use the lax laws to do things other countries deem illegal. There are a few places, like Dominica, where you can get a passport. Can even register ships under Dominica's flag. Years ago, before I embarked on my journey of rediscovery, I was not the most honest of people."

Laz's mouth dropped open. Honor didn't blame him. She'd had the same reaction to Mia's openness the first time she'd met her. The woman had no secrets. Including things she should probably keep secret.

Laz's mouth snapped shut as a few guests arrived. He smiled. "Have a great day."

They walked out. Their hands entwined. Laz leaned toward her. "Awkward, but it sure makes searching for bad guys easy."

She laughed and realized, though she only had a bit of his truth, it was enough. It was him. She had the truth that he was here, fighting for her, helping her despite whatever danger he faced. She let out a breath. "Sorry about today's lesson. I'll be better tomorrow."

He brought his mouth to her ear and with a voice dripping in warmth said, "If you get any better, I might not survive it."

And that, right there, his reaching out to remind her that he found her perfect, despite her imperfections, her fear of violence, her bumbling was just one more reason her heart had followed her libido in throwing caution to the wind. Now, if her head would only get with the program and stop worrying.

CHAPTER 29

As they crossed the courtyard to the hotel, Laz couldn't help the wave of guilt. He'd given Honor his name. Could that put her in danger? Fuck. Should've played it cooler. Should've…but it felt so good having her say it, having her accept him, the real him. Hadn't expected that.

And it was one name. A first name. How could Honor knowing his first name change anything?

It couldn't. When he figured out the threat to her, he could leave knowing that even when his family caught up to him, they'd leave her alone. The only way they'd ever mess with her was if they suspected she knew about the League. And he wasn't going to put her in danger that way.

"What's going on?" Honor said.

He looked. The breakfast seemed to be hectic. A group of people stood together by the edge of the patio. Papito was there, talking with the group. Seemed to be some kind of meeting.

Honor hurried over. He followed as she went up to Papito. "What's going on?"

"A boy is missing."

"What boy?" Laz said. "A guest or one of the kids from the village?"

Papito's eyes switched to him. "Guest. Preteen. Black hair and brown eyes. His name is Cole."

Shit. The kid who seemed to have a crush on Honor. "I saw him on my way to the yoga center this morning."

"Where? Where did you see him?" The father, Don, came up to them. He looked daggers at Laz.

"He was outside here, hanging out." Laz called up the mental image. "He had on mesh shorts. Red. A T-shirt. White with red stitching, a Nike swoosh on it. Tan hiking boots. And a backpack. Heavy enough to suggest he carried a good amount."

The group of people gaped at him. Don's face soured. "You noticed all that and you didn't stop him? You didn't ask yourself what a boy of twelve was doing preparing for a hike?"

"I did. Asked him. He said he was going on a hike with you."

"And you just left him?"

It wasn't like Laz was in the looking-after-your-kid business, but he didn't say that. The guy was obviously distraught. And truth, Laz was pretty upset too.

This probably didn't have anything to do with the threat to Honor, and most likely it could be as the dad said—a kid going on a hike by himself. Then again, the kid could be in serious danger. More danger than just a kid alone in the rain forest, which wasn't exactly safe.

Laz pointed to where he'd seen the kid last. "When I got up to the tree house, I looked out, saw him starting at the sign that leads to Boiling Lake."

Honor looked in that direction. "It's a long walk from here," she said. "But if I set out now, I'll find him and have him back in no time."

The father protested, said he wanted to go, but that wasn't a good option. The guy could barely keep up on the hike yesterday. He'd slow them. "Better if we split up. Cover more ground running on separate trails."

The guy's eyebrows went up on the word *running*. He

was older, late forties, with a Homer Simpson belly. Not in the best shape for trail running.

With a mumbled "Good point," he turned away, walking toward the entrance to another trail, cupping his hands to his mouth, calling for Cole.

Three hours after they'd set out, Honor was beginning to worry. She'd contacted the others via cell, and no one had found Cole yet. She and Laz had stopped running an hour ago. The trails in this part of the rain forest were rocky, so they could twist an ankle if they weren't careful. But that wasn't why they'd stopped. They'd stopped to backtrack.

Nearly at the Valley of Desolation, the ripe sulfur fields near the Boiling Lake, they'd realized there was no way he could've outpaced them.

That meant he'd gone into the woods somewhere, and most likely that somewhere was along the wooded trail. Now they searched for signs as they hiked back along the trail. Not easy with the rain that had started thirty minutes ago, slicking everything.

Any moment, those clouds would open up and pour buckets. She cursed herself for not trying to track him earlier. She'd been focused on looking out ahead, thinking she'd see him. Now, she watched the ground for signs of his travel. Wait. What was that? She bent and picked up a green-and-gold Loco for Cocoa candy bar wrapper.

It had landed near a boyish boot print. The print led into the woods. Stepping off the rocky, water-softened trail, she saw the boot. It was hidden beneath ferns inside the dense foliage.

Body tense, mind skittish, she walked toward it. An awful, thudding dread pounded in her temples.

The boot was slick with rain that hadn't managed to wash off the blood. Standing, she turned to Laz. Her mouth dry and her voice drier. "Is this the boot he had on?"

He grabbed it and turned it. "Yeah."

Stomach dropping fast and heavy enough to dent earth, she spun from him, whisked through the forest calling Cole's name. Could he have fallen, hit his head, lost his shoe? Was he stumbling around in shock? "As long as the rain doesn't get worse, I think I can track him."

"You got the lead."

With Laz following, she made her way through the woods, scanning the trees, waterlogged footprints, broken ferns.

A crack of thunder. Oh no. The sky opened up and poured. The rain pounded the large-leafed trees, loud enough it seemed a train approached. Their pace slowed. Eventually, she stopped, turned, put up a hand. Laz slid a bit, leaned down. "What's up?"

"Something is off here." The direction… They stood at the top of a rough hill. Below was an area that was thick, choked with vines and brush and not easily accessible. But there was no doubt in her mind. They were headed back toward the hotel. But that wasn't what worried her.

She pulled her rain-slicker hood tight around her head. "He wasn't alone. He was with a man judging by the length of the shoe print."

At that news, Laz reached into his waistband to check something. A gun? Laz had a gun with him. It shouldn't sur- prise her. He'd tried to get her to carry one. She'd refused.

Her respect for weapons was such, she wouldn't carry a gun without extensive training.

And maybe not even then. Laz had insisted she carry mace in her guide backpack, but she was even hesitant to use that less lethal weapon.

She looked up into his hazel eyes and saw them cool. With a flash as brilliant and stunning as the lightning in the sky, Laz became someone totally different.

Tony. This was Tony. This was who he'd been before coming here. His body was spring-loaded, expectant, and ready.

He peered through the curtain of rain, wiped water uselessly from his eyes, repositioned his baseball cap. "I got your back."

Water rushed past her feet, soaked her shoes. She began to walk. Thick vines hung from the trees here, creating hunter green curtains, a cocoon around the tree trunk.

It took a moment to see the opening in the center of these thick, hairy green vines. She pointed. With a signal from Laz, she stepped aside and let him enter.

Stepping after him, she entered the cave-like space. Professional and poised, Laz searched the space, making sure there were no other openings, no one else hidden somewhere behind the enormous tree trunk. He nodded toward the ground for her, and she spotted the boy.

She ran forward, knelt beside Cole. She rolled the boy onto his back. His eyes were wide open and staring. Shock.

Laz joined her by Cole's side and checked for a pulse. "I'll carry him out of here. Can you lead us back?"

She raised an eyebrow. "Of course. But I don't think we should go back the way we came."

"You know another way?"

"We aren't too far from the hotel. There isn't a path, but...I bet if I followed that second set of footprints, it would lead us back there."

He seemed to think about it. "Let's take it slow. Cautiously. You lead. I'll carry Cole."

CHAPTER 30

THE RAIN HAD STOPPED, BUT THE DRIP OF WATER SLIDING off leaves continued, along with the croaking of frogs. Piggybacking a ninety-pound kid through thick jungle, over rocky stones slick with rain, wasn't easy. Laz watched how Honor walked. Silent. Smooth. He tried to mimic her natural awareness and stealth.

She expertly guided him, warned of dips and places he needed to watch. When he was a kid, Leland had told him stories about trackers with skills like hers. That kind of innate balance could be honed until she could move as silently as a ghost over Bubble Wrap.

Fuck. He was doing it again. Analyzing the world and people on how well they'd do in the League. Gotta let that shit go.

Could he? Right now, it felt like a defense mechanism. A way he could see skills that might help Honor. This experience with Cole had his every hackle raised.

Had Cole been going to meet someone? If so, who and why? Why would this person lead him back almost to the hotel? Why not just meet him closer to the hotel? Why would the kid keep going, stumbling forward though he'd lost his shoe?

"You okay?"

He lifted his head from watching Honor's feet, the catlike walk—proud and silent and graceful. "Yeah. Why?"

"You looked like you're chewing lemons."

Chewing something a lot sourer, fear for her, Laz nodded ahead toward the hotel. A group of people rushed toward them. Honor had used her cell the moment they'd gotten a signal.

With a shift of his shoulders, he adjusted Cole on his back. The kid uttered a frightened noise that faded into the murmurs of shock.

They stepped from the woods into the yellow porch lights, and Cole's dad rushed to them, took his son. Laz stretched his back.

Don seemed genuinely upset, patting Cole's hair, cooing to him, and basically doing what any frantic father would do when his kid had gone missing.

For his part, Cole didn't seem to notice, not even when emergency services took over.

Papito came over and put a hand, damp with sweat and rain, on Laz's shoulder. "You did good. Both of you. Now can you turn off the alarm on Honor's room?"

Laz heard it then, the alarm he'd set. *Fuck.*

By the time Laz got into the room, cleared it, and turned off the alarm, his ears rang. The room had been ransacked. Sitting on the chair by her desk, he used his cell to access the security cameras and checked the footage. He didn't recognize the man in the video. Guy had some situational awareness. Hunched, wore a hat, kept his head down. He paused the playback. Something, nothing he could put his finger on, seemed familiar.

Honor started searching the room. Papers were out of

place and the mattress moved, as if someone had looked under it. "How did anyone have time to make this mess with the alarm going off?"

Laz held up his cell phone. "This guy look familiar?"

She came over and he ran the footage. She shook her head.

"Well, whoever he is, he knew something about security. Not a lot. This equipment isn't stellar, but he knew enough to disable the first alarm."

"First?"

"Yeah, I had a secondary alarm linked to your mom's laptop. This guy got greedy, opened the laptop, set it off."

Her hands filled with papers she'd picked up off the floor, Honor said, "Whoever he was, he was looking for something in these files, not just the computer stuff. Do you think he got what he wanted?"

That was the question, wasn't it? He picked up the paper closest to the laptop, scanning it. Something caught his eye, but before he could tell Honor, he jumped, realizing she stood next to him, reading the paper over his shoulder. Quiet like the wind, this one.

Seeing him jump, she sat on the arm of the chair and rubbed his shoulder as if to make it better. Adorable.

"What's this about?" Laz said, pointing to the password, TomCaneIsDEAD1972.

"That's the name of a male lead in a movie Mom starred in."

"Did the character die?"

Her eyebrows rose. "No. But all her passwords are pretty random." She pointed to one, 101bluefrogseatingsugar.

He wasn't convinced. "What was the name of the movie?"

"*Built to Last.*"

He opened the laptop, did a quick search. He clicked on the movie and then on the actor Lenox "Lex" Walker's bio. He read. His stomach sank. "It's not the character who's dead. It's the actor who played him. Lex Walker. Did you know him?"

"Yes." Honor put a hand to her forehead. "Yeah. Sorry. I didn't put it together. Actually forgot he costarred in that movie. It didn't do well. But I think he and my mom kept in touch."

He looked up at her. "He died three months before your mother."

Her eyes narrowed. "You don't think...could he be the star, the one she said was willing to talk on camera, expose a big name using movies to get close to kids ?"

"I'm leaning toward yes. And this looks big. Something that got them both killed."

She shook her head. "But he died on set. Stunt accident. It was a big deal. Accusations against the industry, production company. Multiple lawsuits. I'm sure there was an investigation."

"Good. That means there'd be details. Clues, other than what your mom left here."

"You think the password might have also been a clue? But why would Mom..." Honor let out a small, pained cry. "Are you saying she did this on purpose, left this clue for the police or me, in case...she died, was killed or hurt?"

Fuck. "Maybe."

She put her head in her hands. "I let her down. I...was so stupid, so sheltered. I..."

Laz gathered her to him, pulling her from the arm of the

chair onto his lap. "Don't. It's not your fault. And we're on it now, right? We'll figure it out."

She lifted her head with a sudden jolt. He saw her eyes then, saw the question she wanted to ask but wouldn't.

He'd said *we'll*. Fuck.

He swallowed. Nodded. "I swear it, Honor. I fucking swear it."

CHAPTER 31

HONOR FOUND HERSELF IN THE CHOCOLATE KITCHEN—
a pristine area in the back of the Cocoa Chalet—before
even the sun or Laz had risen. It was not yet four a.m., but
she needed to make chocolate for the store by the pier. And
for her own peace of mind.

Doing the soothing work of creating the little treasures
was about the only thing that could've gotten her out of her
own head, her guilt. Not to mention out of bed with Laz.

That man was quickly becoming everything good to her.

Under the bright lights of the specially crafted kitchen,
she pulled out her ingredients and tools with a clashing of
pots and clinking of containers. Last night had changed her
world. Finding out her mother may have feared for her life,
feared and never told her, feared and left clues just in case…
It was devastating.

But Laz had helped. The way he'd held her. It felt like
the world, the threat and guilt, was outside them. And his
promise last night, to stick with her, stay with her through
this… It meant so much. It tethered her to the ground,
made her feel surer of herself.

With a sigh, she turned on the steel chocolate tempering
machine, adjusted the temperature. While it warmed, she
began breaking up the raw cocoa. The machine beeped, and
she put the cocoa into the well, measuring and adding the
ingredients for the bars.

Sometime later, she startled when the sound of someone moving into the small kitchen broke into her awareness.

"You seem so happy making chocolates."

His deep voice shivered its way down her body. She looked up as he moved across the kitchen. A wave of joy and heat rushed through her. And before she could think about the sanity of such a proclamation said, "You and chocolate are my two favorite things."

Standing feet from her, his eyes lit at her words, but he didn't respond in kind. She felt embarrassed and quickly filled the silence. "I love making chocolate."

"Love, huh?"

Her face heated more, and she smiled. "What's not to love?"

She dipped a spoon into the heated well and drew out a creamy, dark spoonful. She fed it to him.

"Mmm," he said, closing his eyes, savoring it. "You're right." He opened his eyes. "There's nothing here not to love."

For a moment, they looked at each other, and all the falseness, the playfulness faded away. But then it felt awkward, and she looked away. He filled the silence with, "Never tasted anything like it. Nutty with a hint of liquor."

She began to take off her apron. "Yes. But the trick is to get it to stabilize. I need to work on the recipe some more."

She sighed and turned off the machine, and grabbed his hand. "You look so serious."

He bent and kissed her lightly then, because there was no such thing as a light kiss between them, deeper. Her body ignited, flushed with hot want.

He whispered, "I hate the idea of leaving you, but I'm

going to have to after this is over. I don't want any confusion on that point."

Not her favorite idea either. Rising onto her toes, she cradled his face in her hands. "You're here right now."

Pressing her body against the entire length of him, she kissed him. He moaned into her mouth, and heat rumbled through her body. Maybe he was her most favorite thing. She pulled back, her body urgent with need. Did he see it there? Did he—

"Honor?"

She pulled at the button on his cargo shorts and asked him, her voice low, "Is there a place you need to be right now?"

He answered, as she knew he would. "Inside you."

Hot wind blew in through the open windows as they made their way down the mountain. He wished he could stay with her today. But she had to get to the chocolate store by the pier. He had to be on tour with Junior and the new guides today.

Laz couldn't help but admire how sure and steady Honor's hands were as she drove through the twisty mountain roads.

On impulse, he reached out and put his hand on the console between them. Without a second hesitation, she dropped her hand on top. They twined fingers together.

He lifted her hand, kissed her knuckles. Even her hands smelled good. "So Cole and his dad took off?"

"Yes. By private plane this morning. His father wanted him re-examined back home." Honor turned her head. "Did you hear that?"

The car slowed. She must've taken her foot off the gas. They drifted for a moment, down a narrow, winding road flanked by lush greenery. He listened, tried to hear what she'd heard. Did he hear something?

He undid his seat belt, turned in his seat, looked into the back. The seat belt warning started to beep. A blur of movement. Something shot out from under Honor's seat onto the back seat, launched as if from a cannon.

Snake.

Laz jumped back. Instinctively lifted his foot, crashed back against the dash. The snake shot toward him. Fangs, sharp as knives, sunk deep into the heel of his boot.

Fuck. Pushing off the dash, he slammed his heel onto the floor of the back seat. The snake's tail whipped. He kept pressure on the head.

"Here." Calm, serious, Honor opened the back door, handed him a flat, stainless-steel slab of metal with a plastic grip. He grabbed it, looked around, realized she'd pulled over and stopped the car.

He bent, and using the sharp, flat edge like a guillotine— kind of what it looked like—he pushed down with all his weight. The steel bit into the snake's neck. He leaned into it, and it snapped down, severing the head.

He took off his shoe. The head and stub of body kept moving against the heel. He looked at her. "It's a viper. A fer-de-lance. Seen one on a mission in Costa Rica. Deadly."

Silent, she stared at the severed snake head stuck to his boot.

Eyes wide, face pale, she grabbed at her own arms, self-hugged. "There are no poisonous snakes on the island."

CHAPTER 32

HONOR STOOD WITH LAZ OUTSIDE THE CAR, HIM WITH
one shoe off, staring at the snake head attached to his boot.

Using the shaving knife she'd gotten from the back, Laz
pried the snake from his boot. He flicked it onto the side of
the road. "As soon as it stops moving," Laz said, "I'll put it
into my backpack."

"You want to keep it?" Someone had put a deadly snake
in her car.

"Evidence. This wasn't the action of a career criminal. Or
someone who had enough money to pay a career criminal."

Honor had zero idea how a dead snake could be evidence, but she wasn't exactly a professional when it came
to assassination by reptile. Well, she was more experienced
today than she had been yesterday.

Honor broke into a full-body shudder. Done putting his
boot back on, Laz put his arms on her shoulders, turned her,
put his arms around her. She began to cry. "Someone tried
to kill us."

No, not us. They couldn't have known Laz would be in
the car with her. And the snake had been under her seat. If
it had shot forward instead of into the back seat, she'd be
dead. "Me. Someone tried to kill me with a snake. Where
did they even get one? I've heard of snakes accidentally
coming in with freight at the pier, but the authorities are so
strict about finding and eliminating them."

Laz whispered, "How well do you know Junior?"

She pushed away from him with a startled shove to his chest. "Junior?"

Sour moisture rolled across her tongue, and her eyes teared. Her stomach tightened as if someone had punched her. "You think Junior did this?"

"He was the one who put the faulty beaner on Bud. He had access to the pier. Not everyone does. And he wasn't there when we went looking for Cole."

Could Junior have been the one to break into her room? Could he have something to do with those who'd killed her mother? And what did any of this have to do with the offer on her property? "No. If I can't trust him, I can't trust anyone."

"It might not be him. There are others. Gray sure had access to the pier. And she's spoken with José."

José and Gray and Junior? Who could she trust? Nothing was as she'd thought. No one was who she thought. Not her family. Not her life. Not Laz.

She looked anew at Laz. The man who'd just saved her life. "What 'mission' in Costa Rica? What does that mean?"

His lips slammed together, sending a chill down her body. What did she know of him, this stranger she'd saved on the beach? Shaking, she took a step away. When he stepped toward her, she held up her hands.

"It's okay, Honor." He reached out to her. "You're shaking. Adrenaline backlash. Let me hold you."

She shook her head. "Is this real? Are we real? I don't even know your name."

He cursed, ran a hand through his hair. "I know you're confused. Questioning everything. Take a breath here. Remember our first training session when I told you fear can be a gift, a way to discern trouble?"

She nodded, watched how he moved, watched where his hands went. Did he have a gun?

"Well, there's also a kind of fear that holds us back, lies to us, robs of us safety when we are safe. The trick is to learn the difference between the two. The imposter fear and the instinctive gut-level-warning fear. So let me ask you, right now, without thinking too hard on it, what does your gut say about me?"

The truth came instantly to her gut, heart, head, and then lips. "It says I can trust you."

Something like relief or gratitude crossed his face. He took the heels of his hands and rubbed them hard against his eyes. When he lifted them off, his hazel eyes were glossy with moisture. "Hundred percent. Never in doubt. Got it?"

She did, but she wanted more. All of it rushed in at once. The adrenaline backlash, the fear, grief, anger, and sadness. Everything she'd experienced in the last five minutes, the last week. She began to sob.

"Honor," his voice cracked on her name. "Please let me hold you. Please."

Needing to feel grounded, she reached for him and he took her into his arms. He held her shaking body as tightly as she needed to be held, tethering her to the reality of his embrace.

She buried her face in his chest, breathing in soap and salt. "I need to know who you are. I can't take this anymore. I feel like I've lost everything. Like I have no safe place to land. Please, give me a safe place to land. Give me some truth that I can hold onto, that I can believe in. Give me you. Please."

CHAPTER 33

LAZ HAD THOUGHT HE'D KNOWN WHAT FEAR WAS, HAD thought he'd had a pretty good system for dealing with it. A way of blanking his mind and getting down to business.

But he'd never felt fear like this, a battering against his chest, a wood splitter, piercing his throat. He could betray his family, tell the secret that he'd never told another.

Not like Gracie, whose guy had already known so much about the family. And not like Justice, whose love interest Momma had brought into the fold. His person was a world away from them, someone he could keep ignorant by keeping his mouth closed.

Or he could deny her. Even as she stood there, shaking, trusting him despite, all the doubts. Deny her when she'd put her faith in him.

He stared into her eyes, opened his mouth—unsure even as he did so whether the words that would come out next would be an apology or the truth. His phone buzzed in his pocket. A Taser to his abdomen would've caused less of a shock.

Only one person had this number. That person knew never to text. Never. Already aware that he'd need to ditch this phone, never use it again, he pulled it out, flipped it open, and read the one-word text: "RUN!"

Cold washed over his body. The heart that had been hammering dropped a beat and then picked up double time. His brain went still, blank.

A car whooshed down the road. He watched it pass harmlessly by. They couldn't stand out here and discuss this. Okay. Order of importance. Stay calm. Break it down. "You need to start carrying a gun. And I need to check your car before we get back inside."

Her face fell. Her pain and confusion gave a sharp kick to his heart. And then he saw something else, a dropping away, a paying attention that let go of the hurt to see something deeper.

Shit.

"What did the text message say?"

"Leave it, Honor."

"No. You were going to tell me. I could see. And then the text."

He rubbed at his face. "It was a warning. The people after me are close."

Her eyes widened. "I'll take you to your boat."

"Like hell you will. I'm not leaving."

"You promised if you were ever in more danger—"

"I promised we would do this. We. And as for who is in more danger, right now, that's still you."

"I have enough information now that I can go to the police. This snake is evidence."

That was an exaggeration, of course, but he understood her desire to protect him. It pissed him off.

He opened his mouth to tell her she didn't have a choice. Closed it. How to explain to her it was only his *mind* in danger, not his life? It was *her* life. But if his family came for him, they'd take him away. No question. She'd be left without him. And he without his memory.

There had to be a third choice.

Shoulders tight, she marched to the trunk and flung his backpack at him.

He snatched the backpack from the air and stood there. He had another choice here. One that would let him run and keep Honor safe. This case, the mystery of it, was right up Momma's alley.

If he collected the information they had already and sent it to her, with a plea for her to take on the case…would she?

He thought she would. "A couple more days, Honor. I can get the mystery of this sorted enough to keep you safe, enough to organize this case, enough to get you help. Okay?"

Straightening from her search, she met his eyes with an intensity that said the answer was no, but he met her gaze back with equal intensity. He would not leave now. He wouldn't.

The line of her shoulders relaxed. "One more day. Promise?"

Promise? Fuck. "Yeah."

In silence, a silence in which he knew they both felt cheated—might be the definition of compromise there—they went back to work. He took out the bug detector, ran it over the sides, seats, front, and back of the car. No bugs. No tracking devices. And no more fucking vipers.

When he was done, he put his equipment away, took out thick gloves, and put the snake and then the head into a leather pouch he'd taken from his backpack.

"I hate to ask this, Honor," he said as he held up the leather pouch, "but can I store this in a cool place?"

Finished with her own inspection of the bags and containers in the trunk, Honor's eyes widened. She shook her head. "You can't mean with my chocolate?"

Biting back the smile at the absolute horror on her face—she'd reacted less watching him pry a snake head from his boot heel—he clarified. "Can you shift the chocolate into the two containers so I can have the third? I want to ship this to someone. I think we need to get more people on this team."

She considered him a minute. Considered him with eyes that delivered the same jolt to his body as a bolt of lightning from the sky. Pure, silver-hot energy. "Who?"

He released his jaw. Considered. Gave in. "My brother."

A hand came up to her chest, rubbed a circle into her Loco for Cocoa T-shirt. "You have a brother?"

"Yeah."

"Just one?"

He shrugged. "Last I checked."

For a moment, he thought she'd ask more questions, questions he couldn't answer, questions that meant they were about to spend their last day together fighting, but she stopped.

Her face softened, accepting that he couldn't tell her. She let out a breath. "You know I...I lo—" She bit her lip, shook her head. Tears welled in her eyes. "Appreciate your help."

He didn't press, didn't ask, even though it was obvious to both of them that that hadn't been what she was going to say. And that *appreciate your help* meant something entirely different.

His throat grew tight with the words that suddenly wanted to jump out, rush forward. That wouldn't be fair to her. Not when he'd be gone tomorrow. "I really appreciate your help too, Honor. From the bottom of my heart. I appreciate it."

CHAPTER 34

IF SOMEONE HAD TOLD JUSTICE PARISH EIGHT MONTHS ago that she'd be in Dominica hunting down one of her own siblings—let alone her best friend, her brother—she would've gently explained the dire error in that statement. With a fist to their head.

And yet here she searched, broiling under a sun that seemed punishment for her not-dead brother choosing to live on a Caribbean island.

The lapping of waves against Tony's boat lifted and lowered it within the makeshift pier. Nice-looking boat. Sleek and white and expensive. Someone was living the good life. Fucker. She wanted to punch him in his alive face, watch blood flow out of his alive nose.

Shaking her head, she walked away. This anger was only clouding her judgment. Now why did that sound familiar? Oh, maybe because that was what Tony had repeatedly accused her of during the Brothers Grim mission.

Waving off a seagull that dive-bombed her head, she adjusted the bag of stuff she'd taken from Tony's boat and walked from the pier, across the sand, over to the stone parking area. Originally, this was some kind of fishing area, but some industrious person had taken advantage of the relative isolation to make some money.

There were a few cars parked here. And though most of the boats were anchored fishing boats, there were some paying customers. Maybe Gracie and Dusty had had more luck finding Tony.

A good-looking blond, with broad shoulders and a slim waist, hot enough to turn coal to diamonds, walked toward her. Her heart did a little dance in her chest. *Well, hello there, handsome.*

A wide, appreciative grin broke across Sandesh's face. "Whatever you're thinking, the answer is yes."

She smiled back. Her partner in all things, Sandesh was trying hard to make this easier on her. It helped. Well, it helped to know someone cared, but it didn't actually make anything easier.

They turned and walked toward the rental—a bland, dark-blue sedan.

His solidness was so close and reliable, she had to resist leaning into him, smelling him, feeling him. Not for the first time, she wished they were doing something, anything, other than hunting down her lunatic of a brother. "Do you think he's abandoned the boat, gotten another one, or taken a different way off the island?"

Sandesh considered, eyes narrowing. "Maybe. But abandoning a boat can get you unwanted attention and is a lot riskier than selling. And according to the guy running this place, Lazarus Graves still owns the boat and is still paying the slip rental fee."

Justice snorted. Lazarus Graves. Yeah, it was funny, but fuck that noise. He shouldn't be out there still being funny, being anything but miserable after what he'd done. "He's such an ass."

Sandesh put his hand against the small of her back. "Couldn't agree more."

Dude didn't even crack a smile. Out of all of them, Dusty and Sandesh—who'd bonded during a mission to rescue Gracie from a black site—had no humor about this quest.

Sandesh was deadly serious about getting his hands on Tony. Laz. Whatever. He said that anyone who did that to her, caused her that kind of pain, didn't deserve sympathy. To Sandesh, there was no reason good enough for what he'd done. Dusty felt the same way.

And she had to admit, the absolute onslaught of grief had been…awful. As real as if he'd punched a knife into her chest. It had been physical, a deep hurt.

But it wasn't just about that anymore. Not for her. It was about the family. And the unraveling of the unity that had been unbreakable for forty years.

Sandesh's cell rang. He took it from the pocket of his cargo pants, looked at the screen. "It's Dusty."

Sandesh hit the Answer button and told Dusty to "Hold on a sec."

Avoiding a guy trying to sell them live bait, they finished walking the couple of steps to the car, and each slung themselves into a front seat of the sedan. Sandesh driver side.

Since Syria, it was their unspoken agreement. She liked to have her gun hand free.

Slamming her door shut, she dropped her stolen loot into the back seat and leaned toward Sandesh. He put his cell on speaker and turned the engine and air on. "You're on speaker."

"We got him," Dusty said. "He's at the pier. Getting into some kind of touring truck. Belongs to a place called Loco for Cocoa."

Justice's heart jumped double Dutch in her chest.

He was here?

192 DIANA MUÑOZ STEWART

They had him.

Finally.

But why hadn't he run? What was he doing with a tour company? She'd have to have the League run the company.

She exchanged a look with Sandesh that told her he had some of the same questions. He nodded to let her know she had the lead. Good. Meant she wouldn't have to talk over him. "Is he armed?"

"Gracie says he is. She's the one who spotted him. I'd gone—"

"Put her on," Justice interrupted.

"Yes, ma'am."

There was a moment of jostling, and Justice knew, without them telling her, that Dusty and Gracie were sharing earbuds. She'd seen them do it before. How they each compensated for the other's height. Made her neck hurt, but they didn't seem to mind.

"Hey," Gracie said. "He looks good. Tan. Healthy."

Justice avoided looking at Sandesh's narrowing gaze. She didn't want him to see how much that mattered to her. "What do you think, G?" she said. "Follow?"

"No. He'll spot us. Besides, we did a little research. After making a stop at their hotel, the Loco for Cocoa tour ends up back here. Dusty and I are going to make all the arrangements to grab him tonight."

Justice swallowed over the dryness in her throat. "Okay. Sandesh and I—"

"There's more. A woman dropped Tony off. I'm sending you her deets. Can you find out what she knows? We can't afford to leave loose ends."

Woman? "Are you saying he has a girlfriend?"

CHAPTER 35

AFTER HONOR DROPPED LAZ OFF AT THE PIER—HE'D ship the snake and question Junior on tour this afternoon— she returned to her store. Hers was the only car in front of the small, cocoa bean–shaped building.

She opened the store with a jingle from the bells over the door, retrieved the coolers of chocolate, and carried them inside. A pyramid display of bright-green boxes tied with yellow, black, and white ribbon, a glass case filled with bars and truffles. It felt good to be back here.

Behind the glass cases, there were multiple countertops and boxes and shipping materials. Stacks of printed-out orders and shipping labels waited in the printer tray.

Reaching out to her mother's crowd—the elites in Hollywood—kept paying off. Normally, she would feel bad about imposing on them, but at her mother's funeral, Ford had reached out to offer help with "anything she needed," and it had started a ball rolling that kept surprising her.

Honor moved some boxes off the wrapping station to create a space for her chocolate on the counter. Something wriggled across the table. Oh no.

She pulled back the green wrapping paper. Insects and tiny white ant larva writhed across the counter. She screamed, dropped the material, jumped back. The entire top of her workstation was covered in ants and ant larva.

What the hell? How did they get in? This place was so tight, she needed a special vent system to bring in fresh air.

Her workstation had been turned into an ant nest. In three days? Was that possible?

The jingling of bells caused Honor to look up. Two men entered the store. She didn't recognize them but instantly felt a thread of unease.

They were dressed in short-sleeved button-down shirts and khakis. Their eyes found and focused on her.

She turned to them, hoping to block sight of the insects. "Can I help you, gentlemen?"

One of the men laughed, a sluggish sound that bordered on drunk. The other crossed the room. He held up a badge roped around his neck. "We are part of the health inspector's office. Surprise inspection."

Honor's heart sank to her feet. She'd been set up.

The "health inspectors" left a large orange sign, a neon orange sign, taped to the storefront window, covering the beautiful and empty display boxes. Humiliating. She wanted to hide or scream. Instead, she turned the Closed sign, locked the door, and began to clean up the mess.

She became so focused on the task at hand that the knock on the door made her jump. The morning had gotten well and truly away from her. She turned. A woman stood there, wearing all black—on a hot day. She looked...dangerous.

What had Laz said before they'd parted? Keep situational awareness. Store your chocolate, do your orders, don't open your store, don't talk to anyone you don't know. Call me if someone shows up at the store that makes you nervous.

And all of that seemed easy enough when she wasn't

face-to-face with an actual human being knocking on her door. She'd tell her she was closed, get her to leave. Feeling rude, she opened the door a small bit.

"I'm sorry." Honor nodded toward the glaring orange sign. "We're closed. A bit of technical difficulty."

Is that what you called sabotage and threats to one's life?

The woman's earthy complexion and pin-straight black hair suggested Native American heritage. She wore expensive aviator glasses that reflected the mess that was now Honor's hair. "Oh. Can't I just pop in real quick? I'm hungry, have lots of money to spend, and always leave an online review."

Honor's brow wrinkled. So not interested in dealing with someone who thought the entire world could be wrapped around their wishes and money and opinion.

"Yes. Well, I'm sorry." Honor waved around the store, the mess, the ants. "We're both out of luck."

The woman's mouth twitched. Was she trying not to smile? Annoying. Honor began to shut the door, but the woman slipped her foot in, blocking it. Honor's heart began to pound.

The woman pointed at the sign. "What happened?"

She thought about telling her it was none of her business, but the last thing she needed was this woman posting a bad review. "Someone sabotaged my store. With ants."

The woman smirked. "Ants like sugar. You sure they didn't just climb in?"

"And create a whole colony, including larva, on my wrapping table in days? No. It was sabotage. Trust me. Not everyone around here wants me to be a success."

The woman removed her glasses, unmasking the kind of mysterious dark eyes that seemed to know much and give away little. Again, the danger warning flashed through Honor's mind. She pressed against the door.

The woman didn't budge. "That sucks. What was your name again?"

She needed to get rid of this woman. "It's Honor Silva. You can read about me, my store, and even order chocolate online." She reached into her pocket, pulled out her wallet—she'd stopped wearing a purse when she'd became a tour guide—and handed her one of her business cards. "I promise it is much better than this experience would lead you to believe."

The woman took it, then held out her other hand. "I don't doubt it."

Honor shook her hand. Firm grip. Slightly aggressive. Or was she imagining that? "I appreciate your interest in our store. Have a nice rest of your day."

"Oh, I intend to. Problem though. I'm looking to rent a room, preferably someplace in the mountains, near the state park."

The last thing Honor wanted was to have this intimidating woman at the hotel. But since the door had a sign that read, "Ask about a room at the Loco for Cocoa outside Trois Pittons National Park!" she had to be diplomatic. Honor pointed to the business card. "If you go online, you can find a room at our hotel. Sorry, we are currently booked."

Not really. But hopefully the pushy woman took her at her word and wouldn't go online to check for vacancies.

"That's too bad." The woman pumped her eyebrows at her, held up her wrist, showing off a beautiful woven leather bracelet. "Just married. My husband and I are touring the islands."

Oh, touring the islands on her honeymoon. That was so sweet. And something she would never do with Laz. "That's a beautiful bracelet."

She met the woman's eyes and, for a distressing moment, felt as if she might cry. Tears pricked at her eyes.

The woman's look softened. "Boy trouble?"

Paranoid or not, she wasn't about to share that with this woman. In fact, she would do the opposite. Lie. "Not anymore. It's over. If you don't mind." She looked down at the woman's intruding foot.

The woman retreated with a "Nice meeting you. Good luck with your shop."

Honor pushed the door closed and said goodbye. Good riddance. This day had to get better.

On the side of the mountain road she'd been heading back down to Loco for Cocoa in order to meet the tour, Honor watched as smoke poured from the hood of her car. This day.

She took out her cell and dialed Papito's preset. He answered right away. "*Mi hija*?"

Her phone beeped that it was running out of battery. Perfect. "Papito, my car broke down. Can you come get me?"

He hesitated. Honor could hear the sound of people in the background. Was the tour there already? It shouldn't be there yet. "I'll send someone. I'm tied up with guests right now."

Guests? Send someone? There was only one other person available to send. José. This day officially sucked. "Thanks, Papito. Appreciate it."

She gave him her exact location, or tried to. The phone winked off. This day. Well, José would see her on his way down.

Only one thing to do now. Tying up her hair, she opened her trunk and broke into the stash of chocolate she'd been taking back to the hotel.

Plopping into the front seat, door open, legs out, useless phone tossed aside, she opened the plain white container, lifted out a precious morsel, and bit into the smooth, dark piece of heaven.

Mmm.

Head back, eyes closed, she let the chocolate trigger her endorphins and work on her serotonin. She let the magic of all that secret goodness make everything better and then reached for another truffle.

Not for nothing—as Laz would say—better than it melting out here, along with her.

Fifteen minutes later, she was a lot happier, a lot fuller, and was pleasantly surprised when Papito's orange and white Chevy came lurching up the road toward her. So quick.

And José wasn't driving. It was Ford. He must've borrowed the truck to go into town. He'd done so a few times before.

He pulled over behind her car and waved as he got out.

His slick looks, preppy pink shorts, and white button-down were so out of character with his social awkwardness. It endeared him to her.

"Let me get that, Honor," he said, picking up one of the coolers and hustling back to the truck before she could say anything.

She grabbed the other one, which bounced against her thighs as she walked. "Thanks for picking me up. I'm so sorry that you had to do this."

Taking the last cooler from her and placing it on the back seat, Ford brushed off her concern. "I was on my way back from the post office when Papito called." He shut the door, looked back at her car. "Your car overheated, huh?"

She hadn't told Papito that. "How did you know?"

Ford gestured at the open hood. "Actually, I just assumed. Old car. Heat. Driving up a mountain."

Duh. Must not turn into a paranoid freak.

Honor grabbed her backpack as Ford opened the passenger door. "I'm glad we can get a chance to talk before I leave."

Though she had had a day for the bad-day record books, an easy smile broke across her face. "Me too."

CHAPTER 36

INSIDE THE CHEERFUL THOUGH RAGTAG BLUE AND yellow café, sipping coffee way too dark and bitter, Laz checked the secure site, an online portal on the Dark Web where he exchanged messages with Rome, from a computer purchased a half hour ago.

Bob Marley flowed through the speakers, promising every little thing was going to be all right. Laz seriously doubted that.

The Wi-Fi here sucked. As slow and relaxed as this damn optimistic song. Fuck. This anonymizer would take twenty minutes to download. Come on.

As the computer continued to slow walk the download, he made a list of things he'd have to get together for Momma. Even as he scribbled pin-straight letters on the napkin—his father's tutelage had done that much for him—his mind kept returning to Junior.

Sure, a snake at the pier wasn't exactly solid evidence, but there was also something odd about his interaction with Junior this morning. He'd been too upset about Laz bailing on him.

The tour truck had left the pier and was moving away from Roseau when Laz's instinct had hit him full on in the gut. Everything in him said he needed to get out of that truck. He hit the top of the truck and told Junior to pull over. Junior had thought Laz needed to pee, but when he found out he was planning to head back to town, he'd flipped out.

It had been overkill, the nerves, the anger. Junior had

three tour guides and eight guests. He sure as shit didn't need Laz.

Heck, if worse came to worst, Junior could head to the hotel early. Papito would make everything better. He always did.

So why was he so upset? Something was up there. But Laz didn't have time to delve into that right now. That itch on the back of his neck, the one that had sent him scurrying from the truck, had increased. Which was why he'd gone straight to the closest electronics store and cash-purchased a laptop and a no-frills, cheap-ass burner phone.

Download complete. Finally. Laz slid the computer across the blue tablecloth so the server had room to put the basket of eggs, creamy sliced potatoes, and sausage on the table. The guy waited, watched.

Cripes. Laz dipped a white plastic fork into the scrambled eggs, took a bite, made noise about how good it was—though it was too warm, too bland. He thanked the guy, who seemed satisfied with Laz's performance.

Mouth full of mush, Laz started the process of accessing the secure site, something his cheap phone definitely couldn't handle. Fifteen minutes later and he was where he needed to be. His jaw tensed. An email from Rome, sent before the text. Kid must've realized Laz hadn't gotten the secure email, taken a chance and sent the text.

Laz opened the message. "They're in Dominica. Run."

Fuck. Smart of him not to put the word Dominica in a text, but where here? In Roseau? Marigot? Portsmouth? Rome didn't say. But Laz was a hundred percent certain he hadn't been followed today. He'd gotten off the truck miles from the pier and had run back.

Nothing else in the message. But there was a message from earlier, flagged as important. He opened that one. *Fuck.* Rome had found out who'd made the offer on the farm. *Ford Fairchild.*

And not just that. Ford had a police record. Holy shit. Twenty years ago, Ford had broken into Natalie Silva's house in New Mexico. Natalie had refused to press charges. Said it was a mistake.

Except, she'd been the one who'd called the police to report someone was in her house.

His heart began to push the throttle on his blood pressure. There was more. Ford had a connection to Cole's dad, Don Toltz. Don worked for an accounting firm that represented Carson Winthrop, Ford's uncle, and a mega-wealthy movie financier.

Rome had gone the extra mile and investigated Winthrop. BINGO. Winthrop had financed all of Natalie's movies in Dominica. And four films done by Lex Walker, including the one whose set he was killed on.

Could Winthrop be the man Natalie Silva had been trying to bring down? Magic 8-Ball said chances were good. Winthrop could be responsible for her death and the death of Lex Walker.

So what did all of this have to do with Ford offering Honor money for her place?

The film. Natalie's last film. It had to be somewhere at the hotel. They wanted to buy it to search for it? Or to burn the whole thing down? Fuck. That was a stretch.

Didn't fucking matter right now anyways. He needed to find Honor and get her someplace safe. And not while worrying about his sisters. New plan. He emailed a message to

Rome. "Have Momma call off her dogs. Tell her I'm coming in. I've got a case. A big name case. Maybe biggest the League has ever taken on." If Winthrop was involved, that wasn't an exaggeration. "I'm willing to make a deal. Share the information."

Was it too late? Would Momma accept a deal with him that didn't involve fucking with his head? He hoped the kid checked the secure site soon.

Had to rely on Rome here. Any call he made to Momma, Rome, or his sisters would only alert them to where he was. And they weren't the sort to wait for him to turn himself in.

Tossing a big tip on the table, stowing his laptop, swinging up his backpack, he left the cafe. Out on the street, he started a drawn-out surveillance detection route to make sure he wasn't followed.

He needed to get back to Honor, tell her about Ford, convince her to leave with him. He'd get Momma to take on this case once he docked somewhere else.

Could Justice be at the boat? Yeah. He needed a new boat.

Having copied her number into his new no-frills phone, Laz texted Honor—leave store, meet me at Tito's apartment, take the long way—and walked down the sidewalk, doing a drawn-out surveillance detection route to make sure he wasn't followed.

He wasn't, but he pulled out his pepper spray—a slim, tan cylinder with a matching band. Using his teeth, he tugged the flesh colored strap, so the spray lay tight, nearly invisible against his palm.

No answer from Honor. He called. It went right to voicemail. Fuck. Could his family have her? Could Ford have gotten her?

His mind a raging bull, a wild animal in need of a red target, the moment he was sure, he wasn't followed, he threw caution to the wind, out the window, and over the bridge and ran to Honor's store.

He cut through a parking lot behind a service station. Nearly there. Never been so happy to see the cocoa bean–shaped building. He slowed, walked.

"Nice tan, Tone."

Fuck.

Justice.

CHAPTER 37

FORD DROVE SO SLOWLY UP THE MOUNTAIN HE WAS practically at a standstill. Instead of finding it annoying or even endearing, it made Honor suspicious. Was he doing this on purpose?

She didn't normally judge close family friends this way, but she had good reason. Someone had sprung a surprise health inspection on her. Someone had persuaded her guides to abandon her at a critical time. Someone had killed Tito.

And someone, most likely someone she knew, had planted a snake in her car.

Could that someone have made it so her car would break down? Could Ford have done that? Could he have done that and then arranged it so he'd be available to pick her up?

Maybe.

He'd said he wanted to talk to her, but then why was he gripping the steering wheel, peering intently out the front window, leaning forward almost hunched?

Laz had taught her to pay attention to body language. Right now, Ford's body language screamed at her. He was nervous. Anxious. And that yes, he drove slowly on purpose.

Honor reached into her pocket for her cell phone, remembered it had no charge, and began to panic. No cell.

And no weapon. She'd left the gun Laz had given her in her glove compartment. But, wait, she had mace in her touring backpack.

"Honor, you know I've enjoyed being here these last few

weeks," Ford said, wringing his hands around the steering wheel.

She pulled her backpack into her lap, inched next to the door. It wasn't locked. That was a positive. And they were going slow enough that she could jump out.

She relaxed a little bit. Not much. "We've enjoyed having you. I'm sorry you have to leave."

He let out a burst of air as unexpected and intense as his next sentence. "I fell in love with your mother when I was fifteen."

A moment passed before she could gather up words. "I had no idea."

Not the best response.

His face flushed with splotches of red. "It's not something I'm proud of. The way I obsessed over her."

Obsessed? That word struck a chord of warning. Her mother had had many stalkers over the years. Some dangerous. Though she hadn't learned that until she was grown. Her mother would've done better giving Honor the truth, instead of always trying to shield her. "I'm sorry, Ford. If it helps, you weren't the only young man to fall in love with my mother."

Like the tick of a muscle, annoyance flashed and then was gone from his face. "This wasn't some distant infatuation. I knew her."

"I didn't mean to suggest your feelings weren't real."

He slowed the car and pulled over, allowing a car behind them to pass.

Should she jump out, run? No. She wanted to hear what he had to say. As Ford started back up the mountain, she reached into her backpack and wrapped her hand around the mace.

"I met your mother during the filming of *Stranded*. I was shy, awkward, and quiet. She treated me with respect and kindness. She asked my opinion. She genuinely seemed interested in me.

"I thought it was love. It took me a very long time, a lot of therapy, and if I were honest, almost two decades to get completely over her."

Her hand grew slick against the mace. "Did she know?"

A wild bark of laughter. "She knew. During the filming of the sequel, I fell on my knees, begged her to give us a chance."

The second movie. He must have been twenty-five. "What did she say?"

"She was horrified. She told me to get therapy. Even offered to pay for it."

Honor thought back on that second film. She remembered spending time with Ford. He'd doted on her. Probably in the hopes of impressing her mother. "I'm so sorry, Ford. That's awful."

"Thanks. But I'm not telling you for sympathy. I'm telling you, so that you realize you can waste a life, decades, caught up in an illusion."

Was this about Laz? Did Ford suspect he wasn't who he said? "I don't understand."

"Are you happy here?"

Her internal alarm screaming, Honor gripped the door handle and the mace. "I don't know what's going on here, but you need to explain what this is about. I've had my life threatened recently, and I am not in the mood to trust anyone."

He turned his head and looked at her for a beat, maybe a beat too long on the windy road, because when he looked back, he had to overcorrect, and she lurched sideways. "I want you to take that offer on your property."

She didn't bother asking how he knew about the offer. José had made it common knowledge around Loco for Cocoa. But she wondered why he didn't ask about what she'd just said, the threats on her life. "Why do you care if I take that offer?"

"I don't want you to waste time on a dream that isn't yours. And you seem to enjoy the tours, but not as much as selling or making your chocolates."

He'd noticed that? He'd been paying close attention. "I appreciate your advice, but I've rejected the offer."

"You can still take it."

How does he know? "I'm not interested in selling."

"Honor, I'm trying to help you. You don't understand what you're up against."

"What are you trying to tell me, Ford?"

He winced, swallowed. "Just take the money. Go. Forget this place. Go make chocolate somewhere else."

"I've made my choice to stay, stick it out despite the financial issues."

He turned into the drive that led to the hotel. His mouth thinned into a firm, determined line. He drove past José's station, looked over, then back to the road. "Honor, if you don't take that offer, you're seriously going to regret it."

She worked her mouth for a moment. His tone had been sad, resigned, but his words... "Is that a threat?"

"What? No." Ford sat up straighter. "What the hell is going on?"

Mind whirling, it took her a moment to register what he was talking about. There were three police cars in front of the hotel.

CHAPTER 38

As he faced his sisters, Laz's legs and gut turned liquid. He ordered them to steady, along with his heart—which had both fists up, pounding the heavy bag of his ribs.

He hadn't been followed. Justice and Gracie had been waiting. Which meant they'd found out about Honor. Found out enough that they'd pegged here, not his boat, as the best ambush spot.

Dressed for an op, black tactical pants and a T-shirt loose over her concealed carry, Justice no doubt had a second weapon stashed in her hiking boot.

Beyond her was Gracie. Ops attire, her long red hair hung down to her shoulders. Concealed carry both of them. For sure.

Heart taxing for takeoff, a throat full of run-while-you-can choking him, he walked toward them. He'd been less terrified in his life. Hard to remember when.

Though he drew close, neither moved a hair. They didn't reach for their guns, tell him to stop, assess the area or him for a possible hidden threat. Sandesh and Dusty were here.

And that made things more difficult, but also helped. The backup had made both his sisters feel comfortable not drawing a weapon, not asking him to put up his hands. Probably figured that even behind buildings, raised hands would draw attention.

Mistake.

He stopped feet before his wide-eyed, tight-mouthed sisters. "Tell your boys to back off. We need to talk."

Justice nodded, twitched her lip in a half smile, well, grimace, and spoke into the hidden mic, "Give me a sec before you shoot the fucker."

Tony's heart rate went from double to triple time. Shoulder blades began to itch. She hadn't been joking. They had guns drawn on him.

He drew in a breath deep enough to absorb the blow. He had no doubt Justice was getting ready to hit him. Her eyes were filled with equal parts hurt and rage.

As were Gracie's. But Gracie was more likely to knee his balls, and as a Muay Thai fighter she had the skill to do permanent damage. He angled his body away from her.

Justice came at him. Took everything in him not to fall into a defensive posture, to keep his hands down, to wait for the blows. But he had to show them, he wouldn't fight.

He'd let Justice exhaust herself. And then, no cost was too great for Honor, he'd beg for their help. Getting them to help her, take her someplace safe was the most important thing.

With a guttural cry, Justice fisted his shirt, drew him close enough to head butt, lowered her head into his shoulder, and sobbed. She flat out balled with her breath hitching and her tears soaking his shirt.

Fuck.

He couldn't move. Could breathe. Why couldn't she have hit him? Despite his feet being rooted to the spot, his arms started to come around her.

A calm, furious voice spoke behind him. "Don't fucking move."

Sandesh. And not messing around. He kept his arms down, hand cupped to hide the pepper spray. His throat grew tight. His heart abused his chest.

Memories and tears flooded from him. He and Justice hanging out, talking, shooting the shit in the campus garden. Memories of him, Justice, Gracie, and the rest of their unit playing seek-and-find—different from hide-and-seek in complexity and the ground covered. Running the campus, leaving clues meant to lead as much as mislead. That was his family. No game was simple. What had been simple was this. Them.

Nothing was supposed to come before loyalty to family. Nothing. But it had gotten blurry when one of them looked to be headed toward her doom.

He wanted to tell her that, but how could he? Right or wrong, he'd betrayed her. He'd lied. He'd taken his sister's loyalty, their oath of loyalty, and spit on it. And she sobbed into his shoulder like she would never stop, like he had broken her.

And that hurt. It tore him apart inside.

The salt of her tears soaked into the fabric of his T-shirt. He had to say something. Even though he knew, knew it like he knew her, that it would break the spell.

"I'm sorry, J. I'm so fucking sorry."

Her head flew up. She pushed against him, shoved him back, then slapped him with an open hand across his face.

The sting of her open palm was heat and pain and relief. Do it again. Anything. As long as it made her feel better.

She balled up her fists, looked like she'd take a good and proper swing, but she didn't. She gazed around, made sure no one was around. "It's not okay. It's not. You killed us. You did this."

Her grief gutted him, brought him back to that place, the place he'd been when he first came to the Mantua Home. When he'd first arrived and seen a bunch of women and girls who, like his mother, had been hurt, abused, ignored by the world, by their families, by men. He'd let his mother die. And from the moment he'd stepped into that home, the moment he'd learned what the League did, why they did it, he knew, deep down, he wasn't worthy of being rescued.

He'd let his father get away with murder.

"Didn't mean to hurt you, J. Not you either, G."

Gracie shook her head at him. Her eyes were slick with tears, her fists clenched. Her face was red with anger and sadness. Guilt gripped his throat, squeezed. Gracie looked so fuckin' vulnerable. So hurt.

"Security footage spotted you outside my club, you know." Gracie said. "Why come back? Why risk it?"

He'd been worried about her. Knew she'd replay her last words to him—she'd called him a traitor—and he'd just wanted to see if she was okay. But you can't see broken from the outside. And he didn't have time to get into this.

"There's a case here. Big one." Tony shifted a little, tried to loosen the circle around him. "The woman who owns this shop, Honor. She's in trouble."

"You're in trouble," Dusty said from somewhere behind and to his right. "Or don't you realize what's about to happen to you."

His mouth flooded with saliva. His stomach churned. "I know. M-erase. But, for the record, this isn't what I did to you, Dusty."

Even as easy going as Dusty was, all Southern charm, he

THE COST OF HONOR

couldn't keep the anger from his voice. "Oh, I know. What you did was experimental. Something you'd need permission to do to a field mouse."

Time was ticking away. "Look, I get that you're pissed. And if after what I have to tell Momma she still wants to take my memories—"

"No need for if," Sandesh said. "Although I'd like you to keep the ones of her tears, the ones where you felt, and you fucking had to feel it, how much you hurt her."

Tony swallowed. They were here to take him. They weren't going to listen to shit he had to say.

His only chance to get away was to inflict pain. Quick. Aggressive. Determined. Shouldn't have let them surround him. Trying to get a sense of where Dusty stood exactly, he shifted. This time Dusty said, "What's in your hand?"

Ready or not. Sandesh wouldn't shoot. Right?

"Ease your hand open," Dusty said.

Fear skittered across Tony's stomach like a crab. He slowly raised his arms like he was surrendering. "It's…"

He kicked back, fast and hard. His heel popped into Dusty's groin.

Dusty hit the ground. Tony pivoted, fired pepper spray into Sandesh's eyes. Sandesh cursed, lowered his gun, wiped his eyes.

Tony spun to run. Justice hit him with a punch to his throat. He rolled out, choking, trying to catch his breath. Gracie came up on his other side, slammed him with a knee to his side, nearly busted his kidney, that hurt.

He backed away, held up the pepper spray to keep the petite redhead from getting in another shot.

"You won't shoot," Gracie said, closing.

He blasted her. She cried out. And Dusty shot from the ground like the Terminator. Big. Hard as steel. No stopping him.

Aware of the big guy coming, Tony used what he knew of Justice, her fighting style and lurched at her. As expected, she charged to meet him.

He stepped to the side, tripped her down onto asphalt. Using her as a roadblock of sorts to slow Dusty.

Dusty jumped over Justice, caught Tony around the middle and tossed him to the ground. Umph. Pepper spray arm slammed into the ground with a crack and zing that shot into his elbow. His arm went numb.

Dusty dropped on him. His fist slammed, one, two, three times into Tony's head. He fought back, got in a few good hits, but the guy was pissed, seeing red. A madman.

The hits came hard and fast until for a second everything went black. When he opened his eyes, he was still on the ground, feet all around him.

He groaned, rolled. Blood poured from his nose. One eye was swollen shut. *Have to warn Honor about Ford.* Swinging his arms forward, dragging himself a few feet, swinging the other, he moved toward the store.

Sensed more than saw the four of them—catching their breaths—trailing him. They spoke about him, his useless struggle, like giving a play-by-play of a sports team.

"He's headed for the store." Sandesh.

"Girl left a while ago." Dusty.

Fuck. He swung his right arm, hauled himself forward.

"I'd feel bad for him," Justice said, "Except soon he won't remember this."

"Give me the needle." Gracie.

Movement. He swung an arm faster, hit glass, grunted, dragged. There was a sting, right in his ass cheek. And then the world dimmed and went black.

CHAPTER 39

HONOR OPENED THE TRUCK DOOR, FORCING FORD TO jerk to a stop. She jumped out and raced over to the scene.

Even if she hadn't just had that disturbing conversation—a conversation where Ford suggested she was in trouble, or had he been threatening her?—she would've had a hard time making sense of this.

The tour truck had smashed into a tree. There was an ambulance. Guests from the tour and the hotel milled about, but some were being tended near the ambulance. Junior was in the back of a police cruiser, handcuffed. Papito was talking with a police officer. Where was Laz?

"He is just a boy, Lonny," Papito said, addressing the officer.

Honor felt awkward interrupting but couldn't help herself. "What's going on here?"

Officer Lonny, a dark-skinned man with sympathetic eyes, explained. "The driver of your tour truck, a José Clemente, also known as Junior, went off the rails. Instead of taking the guests on a tour of the rain forest, he drove them here and crashed into that tree."

"Two of the guests were mildly injured," Papito added.

"We've interviewed the rest," Lonny said, "and are making arrangements to drive them back to their ship."

"Junior? But why arrest him? It was an accident, right?"

He shook his head at her. "No accident. According to the guests, he drove directly into it. And you know how much these tours mean to island business. This is very serious."

She knew that. And she knew how much they meant to her business. If someone sued...

"Is it okay if I speak with my cousin?" She didn't remind him he was her cousin in name only.

Lonny, writing in a notebook, flicked his head in a can't-stop-you-if-I-don't-see-you gesture. She didn't ask twice.

Avoiding the other officers, Honor crept over to the police car that held Junior. The door was closed, windows open. Sweating, Junior sat with his hands cuffed behind him. She bent to talk to him, putting her hand on the side of the cruiser, then snatching it back. Hot.

"Junior. Are you okay?"

His eyes stayed glued to the rubber floor mat. "I drove into a tree."

"On accident?"

He sniffed, sucked in mucus.

"Junior?"

He let out a breath, looked up. "On purpose. I did it on purpose."

Her heart skidded to an abrupt halt. "Why?"

"Don't you get it? The world is bad. People are bad. Even people you think are good. Like your boyfriend. He took off. Guess we won't be seeing him again." He shook his head. "You should go too. Take the money. Run."

Laz had left? What money? Oh, he meant the offer on the business. Cold washed down Honor's body. This wasn't about the hotel. "Is this about my mother's last documentary?"

Junior's head shot up and around. "Run, Honor. Get out."

The terror in his voice transferred to her, froze her mind and vocal cords.

"What are you doing? No talking to the prisoner." A different officer, not Lonny, came over to the car and crowded her from behind.

Honor shifted her left shoulder, so it seemed she'd leave, but whispered, "Did you put a snake in my car?"

A cloud of grief, a tangible darkness bowed his head. Junior nodded.

Honor's stomach sank to her feet. He had? "Why?"

"Step away from the vehicle." The officer grabbed her arm. He wasn't messing around.

Because Junior's pain was so sharp, so tangible she felt a need to ease it as she was dragged away. "It'll be okay, Junior," she said.

Tears falling onto his cargo pants, Junior shook his lowered head. "Not going to be okay. Never was."

CHAPTER 40

TONY WOKE UP WITH A SPASM THAT MADE HIS BODY jerk against the straps tying him down. His head throbbed. Could barely see through one eye. Where was he?

Strapped to a captain's chair, one of four arranged around a table, there were curved walls, glossy brown molding and through the portal window he sat next to came the *thwump, thwump* of blades.

He was on one of Parish Industries luxury copters. They were flying him home to have his brain fucked with.

Honor was alone.

He worked moisture back into his mouth. "Hey." Not enough moisture. It came out as a rasp. He tried again, louder. "Hey. J? G? Turn us around. I need to get back."

Dusty and Sandesh walked over, stood to his left. He had to wiggle in his seat to get a look at their pissed-off faces. Good to see Dusty had a cut on the corner of his eye. At least he'd managed one good punch.

Sandesh said, "You're in no position to be giving orders."

Dusty gave him an evaluative look. "That eye's got to hurt."

Hurt like hell. So did his neck. "Let me talk to Justice. Let me talk to Gracie. This isn't your business. Let me talk to my family."

Sandesh moved forward and in two seconds had Tony's jaw squeezed in his big fucking hand. "Justice is my business. My family."

"Sandesh, let go."

Justice. Her voice was always so strong, so sure, but it sounded remarkably small when she'd said that. Sandesh let go. But not before using his viselike grip to nearly shatter Tony's jaw.

Tony swished his jaw around, wishing he could do the same to his neck. The duct tape he strongly suspected taped his forehead to this chair pinched with every breath.

"What do you want?" Justice said as she and Gracie pushed past the men. Tony's courage shattered. Gracie's eyes ringed in red. Justice had a scrape along her jaw. They both looked so hurt, so angry, and distrustful.

They had reason to be.

He'd made a mistake. A monument of mistakes. But right now he had one chance to get them to turn this copter around before Honor got hurt.

How long had they been in the air? How long had he been out?

Focus. He could do this. But it wouldn't be by stating his case, explaining why he'd gone against the League. He couldn't bring up League rules and how he'd thought he was doing the right thing. That would drag up a freaking court case.

And he sure couldn't appeal to them as his family or just as his sisters. No. Emotions would be bad right now. Bad for him. Bad for Honor.

He had to appeal to them as operatives. He said, "Natalie Silva, aka, Kiki Hart, yes the famous actress, was murdered by none other than Carson Winthrop."

Justice inhaled a sharp breath, scooted past the table, and sat down in the seat across from him. "Carson Winthrop?

The same guy accused twice of lewd acts with minors. Both times in California. Both times the charges were dropped. That Carson Winthrop?"

He'd counted on J knowing that scumbag. "That's the one. Natalie made a documentary with a big-name star, Lenox 'Lex' Walker," no reason to tell them this part was a well-informed hypothesis, "who provided testimony that Winthrop used movies he financed to get close to and abuse child actors."

Grace sat down next to Justice. She'd pulled out her cell and was typing on it. She looked up. "He's dead. This guy Lex."

Dusty sat on the arm of Gracie's chair. "You saying Winthrop killed Lex too?"

He had them now. "Yeah. I am."

Sandesh made a sound in his throat. Justice looked up at him, nodded. Sandesh put one knee on the seat next to Tony, pulled out a knife, cut the binds holding his head to the chair. Good news, not duct tape.

Sandesh sat down next to him. "Keep talking," he said.

Tony rolled his head around. "Natalie's daughter, Honor Silva, is in danger. She—"

"The woman from the chocolate store," Justice said. "Your girlfriend?"

Shit. Ignore that question. "She owns all her mother's prior films." Had to avoid the details he didn't understand, like why someone offered her so much money for her property. "Recently, she's had her life and her business threatened. I believe it's because the documentary is on her property."

"Does she have it?" Sandesh said.

"She has all her mom's old files and films. I believe it's

hidden in them somewhere. Or maybe there is information, clues in the files as to where it's hidden."

"Winthrop is after her?" Gracie said.

Fuck. Yes. Where was Honor? How far was he from her?

Quieting his panic, he explained. "His nephew, Ford Fairchild, is on the island. I believe he poses an imminent threat to Honor. Her life is in danger."

Justice crossed her legs, right foot on left knee. "You really like this girl, huh?"

That question, the way she asked it, not an accident. Nearly identical to the one he'd once asked her about Sandesh. He'd asked because he'd been jealous. Because, at the time, he'd thought he was in love with Justice. A fact he'd also blurted out right before he fake-died.

She was asking to feel him out, see how he'd changed, or why. How to explain this without sounding pathetic? Not for nothing, he was pathetic. "You know for a long time, I thought it was you, J. I thought you were my perfect match."

Sandesh snorted a, "No kidding."

He closed his eyes, counted the breaths before he spoke. "I just didn't know, didn't get it. Before Honor, I'd never been in love. Never had that moment where I looked into someone's eyes and saw…"

Tears. Fucking tears. Goddamn it. He shook his head. It was all he could do to brush them away.

Sandesh shifted next to him. Yeah, it was fucking awkward for everyone.

How long would it take to turn this bird around?

Justice reached into her boot, pulled out a knife. With a few quick slices, she freed him, tossing aside strips of rope.

He moaned with relief, sat forward, shrugged his shoulders. He rocked his head around on his neck. "Thanks."

Rising, Gracie went over and got a water bottle from the fridge and offered it to him. He took it, drank.

Gracie sat back down. "We can't turn around. Not without approval from Momma."

Justice said, "Best bet for getting Momma's approval would be to agree to M-erasure."

Tony felt his entire body melt and tense at the same time. *No f'ing way.* "You've both gone against her orders before."

"Well, that was before all the shit you set in motion," Justice said.

"The League is in turmoil because of your stunt and your letter," Gracie said.

Fuck. Didn't have time for this. "Then let me call Honor. Please. I'm begging. Her life is in danger. And she's sitting out there fucking waiting on me."

Gracie and Justice exchanged a look. With a nod from Justice, Gracie pulled one of the helicopter's phones from its molded place near a window.

"Make your call," Justice said.

"On speakerphone," Gracie added.

CHAPTER 41

HONOR PARKED PAPITO'S TRUCK AND GOT OUT. THE AREA where Laz's boat was moored was quiet this late at night.

And dark. Would've been better to have a flashlight, but she hadn't thought ahead. The moment the police had left, she'd gone to find Laz.

The light on her phone barely lit the unsteady, rocking makeshift planks as she came upon Laz's boat. She hadn't noticed before, but she did now. The boat was named *Another Brick in the Wall*.

Had Laz named it? She jumped up onto the boat with some difficulty as there was no ladder. "Hello? Laz?"

Using her phone, she scanned the doorway. It was open. A panel appeared by the door with the words, *System breached. Reset?*

Having no idea what that meant, she climbed down. The boat rocked under her. The flashlight on her phone did little for the dense darkness down here. She groped along the sides of the wall, pressed, slapped, and swept her hands along the wall. Where was the switch?

Something clicked. The lights blinked on revealing a square couch attached to the wall, a small table before it, gleaming wood walls and ceiling, and recessed lighting. There was a small galley to her right. And a hallway with two doors beyond this cozy area. She crept forward.

One of the two doors led to a bathroom. The other was a cabin. Shiny mahogany wood paneling and shelving.

Inside, the room had been searched. It wasn't torn apart or vandalized, but the doors on the cabinets under the bed were all open. She knew Laz well enough that she knew he was neater than this place suggested. And, yes, maybe he'd just been pretending to be neat in order to impress her, but that wasn't the person she knew either. He seemed genuinely neat.

She began to search the room. There had to be something here that would tell her where he'd gone. Or who he really was.

An hour later, sweating, frustrated, she listened as someone moved across the deck. Could it be Laz?

Probably, but…she looked around the disheveled cabin for a weapon.

Her cell rang. She glanced. Unknown number. It could be Laz. He'd told her he was going to get another burner phone. She accepted the call.

"Honor?"

So good to hear his voice, she nearly sobbed. "Where are you? Are you okay? I've been searching for hours."

"Honor. Listen. You need to hide. Go someplace safe. I'm—"

Whoever was upstairs began talking. Men. Sounded like two of them. Her heart in her throat, hands shaking. "Someone's here. On your boat. Two men. I hear them talking."

Laz's voice changed instantly. Gone was the sweet, caring, concerned man. Present was the cold, calculated, listen-to-me-and-don't-fuck-around man. Present was Tony. "Honor, what room are you in?"

"Bedroom."

"There is a gun under—"

Someone spoke. A woman. "We took all the weapons off your boat."

He cursed.

He had speakerphone on? Who was the woman?

"Okay. Listen. Grab the bilge pump off the wall. Stand on the footlocker by the door. The pump is heavy. Steel. Hit the first fucker through with all your worth. You don't hit to defend yourself. You hit to kill. Got it?"

Oh, God. *Kill?* "They're coming down."

"Go after the next guy. Quick. Brutal. Find his weak spot. Use what I taught you."

"I...I—"

"You got this, Honor. You got it. Now, drop the phone. Leave it on. Go get 'em."

The instructions were delivered with a calm surety that almost made her think she could do it. She dropped the phone on the bunk.

Fingers feeling as limp and padded as corn dogs, palms sweaty, heart surging, she silently moved across the room and removed the steel bilge pump, which looked remarkably like a bike pump.

She gripped it in her hands, climbed atop the footlocker beside the door, and lifted both arms.

Her mouth became so dry her tongue felt hard-boiled. She couldn't swallow past it. Could barely breath past it.

A man came into the room holding a knife. Terror. A moment of frozen terror. Seeing or sensing her, he spun and brought his large knife forward. That released her. With a scream of pure rage, she drove the bilge pump down and into his skull.

A loud crack as the solid resistance of his skull gave way. Her stomach flipped, twisted, turned sour.

His eyes slipped back into his head like he'd just given standing a second thought. The man melted to the ground. A moment of relief and then arms grabbed her middle, dragged her backward. She screamed in denial, in fear, in rage. Spreading her arms out, she braced herself in the doorjamb, struggled.

A moment later she was in a choke hold. Without even thinking about it, her right hand struck back and her fingers jammed into his eye. He cursed, arched back, lifted her, tried to drag her through the doorway.

She kicked, flailed, tried to scream, then calmed. He was short. Short enough she could…Reaching down, she grabbed his balls, and yanked like pulling taffy. She heard something tear.

His scream was iconic. A scream that made every hair on her neck rise. He released her, dropped to the ground.

She ran, slamming against the hallway's walls as she went.

Heart shrieking like a banshee in her chest, sweat soaking her eyes, Honor's every movement seemed slow and thick. Expecting at any moment another man would appear, she lunged through the cabin and up the steps.

Outside, she jumped from the boat, landed on the makeshift dock, and sprinted away.

CHAPTER 42

HONOR'S SCREAM HIT TONY LIKE A FAST BALL TO THE ribs. A crack of awareness, a sharp stab of pain in his side, and a floundering, groping struggle for air.

He stood inside the luxury jet, stone still on the outside. Heart racing. Blood boiling. His ears so tuned to the sounds coming through the helicopter's speakers he couldn't move. He'd given Honor what he could, advice. And now? She fought for her life.

A thunk. Something breaking? A fierce, aggressive scream. Honor. A bloodcurdling scream. Male.

That was his girl.

As Dusty used another line to place a call to the police in Roseau, Tony's body filled with an anguish so shocking, it tore through him like a thousand volts of electric current. Painful. Pitiless. Paralyzing. The hot and heavy pressure, transported him back in time, back to that terrified and helpless kid in a cage, unable to do anything while the person he loved was hurt.

When the Dominica police department was patched through, Dusty told them where the boat was moored and that a woman was being attacked there.

The thuds and cries from the speakers had moved away, gotten distant, then stopped.

Silence. Everyone stared at Tony. Their eyes held deep pity. What was it Justice had said to him when Sandesh had been taken? *"Sorry is for someone who has no choice but to learn to deal with something. I have a choice."*

Did he? Was his only option to leave Honor to fight her way through her troubles? Even if she...Even when she made it to safety, what then? Would she go back to the hotel and into the waiting arms of whoever had sent those men. Ford?

His mind raced through options. He had one thing to offer. One. He turned to Justice. "Call Momma. Tell her I'll do it. I'll agree to M-erasure. Just turn this fucking thing around. Now."

Normally a luxury helicopter ride to a Caribbean island didn't make Tony's stomach turn. But it wasn't the ride that had his gut rolling over. It was his fear for Honor. This thing couldn't fly fast enough.

As soon as Momma had given the approval, the pilot had turned the copter around and the group had gotten to work. Setting up an operations center at the back of the copter. Computers were open. Layouts discussed. Plans made.

Unable to stay seated, Tony—now in black pants and shirt, thanks to Justice stealing some from his boat earlier—stood by the table, watching Gracie's fingers fly over her keyboard. Watching Sandesh and Justice go over the print-out of the hotel.

He felt useless.

Now that they'd agreed on a plan, the mood was tense. As tense as a group of people can be when they're flying to try and save the life of a woman who, even now, might be...

He couldn't think that. Why wasn't she answering her cell? Why wasn't anyone answering at the hotel?

Fuck.

She'd gotten away. She had to have. According to the police in Dominica, who gotten over to the boat fairly quick, by the time they'd arrived no one was there. But there were signs of a struggle. Had Honor gotten out? Gotten away? What happened to the men?

Could they have hurt her? Taken her? Tossed her body overboard?

He rubbed at his chest. No. He'd feel it. He'd feel it if she weren't on this planet anymore. Fairy-tale stuff or no, he'd fucking feel it.

But where was she? And were they doing the right thing, going to the hotel? Maybe they should go to Roseau. Time was ticking. Choosing wrong, could damn or save Honor. Which one. Which fucking one?

"We're doing the right thing," Sandesh said.

Tony's heard jerked in his direction. He realized then that the entire table stared at him. Nothing for it. No place to hide. Didn't really want to. Not anymore. "What makes you so sure?"

Justice leaned forward. Matter of fact. "Those guys were too injured to get rid of a body before the police showed up."

"Listen to her," Dusty said. "Makes sense. Your girl took those two men out, left them too injured to follow. Cops came. Honor ran back to the hotel. That's where we go."

Rubbing a hand across his face, he looked down at Gracie, typing furiously into a computer. "Please tell me you got a connection."

Twirling a Jolly Rancher with her tongue, Gracie shook her head. "I...The password isn't working." She trailed off, continued typing. "You sure that's the one?"

"That's it," Tony said, slamming a fist into the palm of his hand. He was two seconds from tearing shit apart. This feeling…fucking helpless.

"Got it," Gracie said.

He looked at her. His throat so filled with tension it felt like steel rods had replaced the muscles in his neck, jaw.

Gracie continued to type. "Dusty, sent you the link. Can you make it go live?"

"Yes, ma'am." From beside her, Dusty hit a series of buttons on the control panel embedded in the table. A screen dropped.

It took a minute for the screen to pop to life, but when it did, Justice let out a startled, "Holy shit. No one found them."

"Told you I hid them well," Tony said, sitting back in his seat to get a closer look at the first images of the hotel.

"You got every doorway," Sandesh said. "Good. Can we get this streamed live to our NVGs, Gracie?"

"Yep. When we go in, the image will appear in the corner of our night vision goggles, so we can see what we're walking into."

The images taken from the cameras Tony had hidden at the hotel cycled, giving an incredible insight into the layout. Where was she? Where…

Tony laser-focused on every image, taking in every detail in a flash. "What the hell," he said, leaning closer to the screen as an image floated past. "Grab it, G."

"Got it," she said. The cycling images stopped and one image, the back patio, came into focus.

"We need to call the police," Dusty said and looked away.

Tony shook his head. He swallowed the sick in his

throat. "The hotel is an hour from the closest police. We're thirty minutes. And we're better equipped to deal with this without getting innocents killed."

"Where is Honor?" Sandesh said.

"There," Justice said.

Tony watched in horror as Honor, crossbow in hand, crept from the bushes and opened fire, on a group of people that included her grandfather.

Oh, baby. Tony hit the intercom on the table and told the pilot to "Fucking fly faster."

CHAPTER 43

Normally, it only took an hour for Honor to get back to the chalet, but she'd pulled over when her body had started to shake so hard her car began to veer across the road.

Even now, she felt twitchy. Her stomach heaved as she parked in a spot near the fermenting station. Exhausted. Numb.

She climbed out of the car. Once inside, she'd get to her room and sleep. No. Not sleep. She had to call Laz. Tony. *Where was Tony? Was he safe?*

Good God, how had she forgotten about him? *It's shock*, a little voice said in her head. Shock? Reaching up, she rubbed at a swollen lump on her head. The size of a monkey's fist.

The drag of her feet competed with the croaks of frogs as she pulled herself up the front steps.

Eyes watering with exhaustion, head as heavy as an eighty-pound melon, she staggered into the hotel. So quiet.

She needed to get to her room, get cleaned up, and sleep. Not sleep. Call Laz. Uh, Tony. Stupid, woozy brain.

A sharp pained cry sent electric gooseflesh across her skin. That wasn't a bird. Another cry. A human. A human in pain. Papito? Where was Papito?

Her own pain forgotten, fingers trembling, she grabbed her crossbow from the trophy case. She filled the quiver attached to the bow. Weapon in hand, her mind cleared. Adrenaline had returned.

Carrying the weapon in the ready position, she made her way through the hotel and toward the sounds of someone being beaten. She stalked through room after empty room. No guests?

At the patio doors, she stole forward. Nose pressed to the glass, she looked out. Fire cast a ghastly orange glow around a ghastly sight.

A bloodied Ford dangled between two men, her newest tour guides. The ones Papito had hired. Their skin tone said they barely saw the sun, but they were big, strong.

A third man punched the staggered Ford over and over. She knew him. He was the man from the tour. The one who had almost died. Bud.

Bud was beating Ford? Why? Doesn't matter. *Call the police.*

Feet easing back, she turned and ran through the hall to the front desk. She picked up the phone. No dial tone?

Of course not, a little voice said in her head, *this was planned.* Hotel empty. No communication available.

She put the phone down. What was she going to do? Her heart hammered. Her mind reeled.

Ford screamed. Chills rolled down her body. The hair on her neck rose. Dear God, they were killing him. Sweat slicked her hand, making the stock of her bow slippery.

If only she had a gun.

The crossbow will have to do.

Or a phone.

You left it on the boat.

She could run.

It will take over an hour in the dark to get to the nearest village—longer—and an hour more for the police to arrive. Too long.

Throat dry, heart hammering, she took the safety off her weapon, crept back and out the side door.

The thick, meaty sounds of flesh being struck and Ford's sharp, pained cries filled the usually serene night. Quick and quiet, she moved across the brick path, ducking under the trees and stalking through the mud.

As silent as the Moon across the sky, she inched forward until she could see the whole of the patio. There were others here. In addition to the two new tour guides and Bud, there were three other people. Her muscles froze and blood ran cold.

Oh no. No.

Papito stood and watched as the men hurt Ford. A stab of hot pain ripped open her chest. Her heart bled as she took in her grandfather, standing beside Mia, her expression as serene as if she watched a yoga pose.

In the chair before Papito and Mia sat José. He was tied up. His eyes stared blankly ahead. Whatever his fate, that blank look said, he'd already accepted it. Years ago.

Behind José stood one of the men from the boat. He had a bandage over half his head.

How had he gotten back here before her?

You fell asleep in the car. That's right. She'd forgotten. She'd gotten so woozy. She'd pulled off the road. Slept. Oh, God.

She couldn't do this. She was injured.

There is only you.

Papito bent over, placed a palm against José's face. "Where is Natalie's last film?"

José closed his eyes, shook his head.

Papito got on one knee. "After all I have done for you. I saved your life."

José's eyes popped open. He began to laugh even as tears streaked his face. "I'm no longer that boy, the one you stole from the streets, the one who believed you did things for others. Believed that you were helping me when you helped yourself to me. I see now. Everything you do, you do for yourself. It is abuse."

"*Pfft.*" Papito waved a dismissive hand. "Abuse? This is just a matter of social conditioning. Rules are changeable. They are not the same for everyone. When Natalie discovered what the producer and financier of her films were doing, I realized this. Even when she put the information online. No one cared. That's when I understood. It wasn't my behavior that had to change, just my status."

Honor pressed her lips together to keep from vomiting. Bile filled her mouth. José had been right. She'd only seen what she wanted to see.

Papito looked over at Bud. "Try the other one again."

After a confirming glance cast in Mia's direction, Bud grabbed a fistful of Ford's hair, lifted his head, drove a fist into his face. "Who has the film?"

Ford coughed blood. His head sagged. His knees buckled. "He took it. Laz."

"Bullshit," Papito said, spinning from José to Ford. "I know it was you. You were Natalie's informant. You gave her the proof against your uncle that she put in that film. You are the reason she is dead."

He shook his head. "I never… If I'd had proof, I'd have given it to the police. If I had the film now, I'd give it to the authorities. Natalie…she didn't trust them, trust anyone. She should have."

"Tell her that when you see her," Papito spat.

Tears and sweat traced jagged paths down Ford's bloodied face and swollen eyes, but he glared at Papito. "Tell her yourself. You think he'll let you live? After you blackmailed him, after you lost the film?"

A stunned, worried look flashed across Papito's face. He turned to Mia. As she nodded, her mouth turned down in a that's-accurate frown.

"I did not lose the film," Papito protested. "Tito stole it from me! Ford and Jose know where it is!"

Papito...all this time.

As Honor accepted the truth, shock dropped away and a deep, focused calm washed over her. Through the trees, with a stealth as natural as it was necessary, she made her way behind the group. Drawing back on the string, the weight of the bows powerful tension pulling at her as her hand brushed her cheek, she aimed at one of the men holding Ford and shot.

He pitched forward with a cry, taking Ford down with him. She nocked and let fly another arrow. It missed, passing through Bud's legs. He let out a "Fuck me."

People scattered.

Papito and Mia dove for cover. The other man who'd been holding Ford, a guy wearing a red baseball hat, got to his feet, took a gun from his waistband, and shot into the woods. Missed. There was no way any of them could see her. No way any of them could hear her. That didn't stop them.

Pulling out his own gun, Bud followed Red Hat into the trees.

She moved as quietly as wind. Behind her, the men crashed through the brush, stumbled in the dark.

Walking from her hiding spot, she raised her weapon. The last man, the one with a bandaged head, saw her and raised his gun just as her arrow punched through his stomach.

The force of the arrow knocked him to the ground.

Gunshots rang out. Bud had returned, shooting. Her body jerked as someone smashed into her. She hit the ground, slid against the stones.

José? Bent from the weight of the cast-iron chair he was strapped to, José had thrown himself in front of her, taken the bullets. Blood gushed from his wounds as he fell, eyes growing blank.

No! Honor picked up her crossbow, fired shot after rapid shot. Bud dove into the bushes as an arrow skimmed his arm.

"Honor."

At the sound of Ford's voice, Honor helped him to his feet. He stumbled ahead of her while she shot into the trees to keep Bud and Red Hat down.

Her heart booming in her chest, they made it to the cover of the Cocoa Chalet and then into the tree line.

It was dark in the woods. The moist fronds and lilting ferns made it slippery, but Honor would've had no problem keeping her feet if not for Ford stumbling at her side. Crossbow tucked against her, she carried him with the other arm.

Only the fact that her pursuers would need to get flashlights to find their way in the dark saved her and Ford.

They crossed a stream, keeping to the rocks. On the other side, she dragged him up the embankment and deeper into the woods. The jungle chorus of tree crickets decorated the night with their relentless calls. Until the crash of Ford's weakened body silenced them.

Leaning to her right, taking more of Ford's weight, using the crossbow almost as a walking stick, she cursed when she looked back to see flashlights.

CHAPTER 44

IT WAS IMPOSSIBLE TO SHOOT HER CROSSBOW WHILE dragging Ford, so Honor used the only skill that could help them escape their pursuers. She felt the trail, felt her way through these woods. She'd only taken this way through the brush once, when looking for Cole, but for her, it was enough. It became so dark that she relied on that skill like she never had before.

Slowly the lights following grew distant. Sometime later, she found the opening, the tree that Cole had hidden within.

Inside the dark, moist confinement under the vine-camouflaged tree, Honor helped Ford to the ground. He curled on his side, holding his ribs. He'd been shot.

Sweat poured down her body, dampening the shirt she quickly removed and began to tear into strips. "I'm going to bind your wound. You're well hidden here. Once you're stable, I'm going to make my way out of here, sneak away, and get us help."

"I'm sorry. I should have told you."

She definitely could've used whatever information he had. "These men. Who are they?"

He wiped at his eyes. Sweat or tears, she couldn't tell. "I'm your dad."

Her hands stilled in the middle of tying the strips together. Her body chilled. "No. You're not more than fifteen years..." Could her mother have...? *No.* "Are you saying you were the donor?"

He shook his head.

Liar. "You were obsessed with my mom. You're making this up. She would never have taken advantage of a boy that young. She made documentaries about this kind of abuse, about…"

Resting his head against the brown dirt, he shook it back and forth. "She didn't know. My uncle provided me a false passport. Big for my age. Everyone thought I was nineteen."

Ford was her father?

Every speech her mother had given, every fiery word and passionate call for action suddenly seemed damning. Finished tying the strips together, she sat back. Dumbfounded.

"The first ten years…knowing about you." He sucked in a breath. "The pain…"

He trailed off and she wasn't sure if he meant the pain he was experiencing now or then. Or maybe both.

"After the second movie, Natalie reached out. Got me into therapy. Helped. Not something we talk about, not for a young teen getting laid by a star. I mean, that's considered every boy's dream. But I wasn't emotionally equipped." He flinched, hissed at her fingers began again to work the bandage around his wound.

Honor tried to think of how he must've felt. A child in so many ways, he'd followed his sexual instinct to sleep with a woman, and after, he'd thought he'd found the secret to the universe. Love and lust and all things Hollywood in one package. What adults called lies and delusion. Of course, he didn't just move on. Of course, he didn't just put a notch on his belt. He was a father at fifteen. And though it wasn't her fault, she couldn't help the ill feeling. "I'm sorry. She was a hypocrite. A liar."

"No." He tried to sit up, fell back. "Honor, your mother... found out and was stunned. Horrified. She quit making movies."

That's why her mother had quit making movies shortly after that second film?

"Years later, she began to question. How did I get a false passport? Were there other boys? She began to investigate and make documentaries. Stumbled upon Carson Winthrop's cabal. Global. Intellectuals, financiers, string pullers, leaders, call themselves pederasts. Lovers of children. They help protect each other. Keep everything quiet, out of the press, out of the courts."

Sour sick rose through Honor's throat, rolled across her tongue. They were putting spin on pedophilia.

"Her work inspired me to fight back too. Against my uncle. My boss. And the head of this group. Began feeding her information."

"You were a double agent, of sorts?"

He barked a sick, sad laugh. "I tried... Told her about..."

"Lex Walker?"

He sucked in air. Released. "Not just me... Her documentary...laid out. Proof. Names. The money trail. Winthrop came down hard. Had Lex killed."

That explained Lex's death. And her mother's. Her mother had stumbled upon a group operating outside all laws, people with money and power and reach.

"You brought clues to where your mother's film was here. Hidden clues were inside her files. It took him nearly two years to put everything together, but Papito found it. Once he had the film, he used it to blackmail my uncle."

Honor looked away, into the dark. As the separate facts fell together in her mind, she was able to fill in the missing pieces, like a puzzle on *Wheel of Fortune*. Papito had manipulated her for her money. When she'd first come here after her mother's death, he'd played off her sense of duty to family, played off what he acted like was her mother's neglect of this place. He'd gotten his way, but that hadn't been enough.

Now she understood why they'd been beating Ford. "Who stole the film from Papito?"

"Junior took it. Mia—Winthrop sent her—thought it was…Tito. Killed him for it."

But Junior was in jail. "Who has it now?"

A twig broke in the forest. Leaves crunched. People were moving through the dark. They must have night vision goggles to be as quiet as they were. Could they see in here?

In answer a series of gunshots lit up the night. Honor's crossbow was hit from her hands.

She dropped down, found it. Broken. More gunshots. She jumped away. Ford cried out.

Honor bent and grabbed his arm, tried to drag him deeper into the growth. His weight, dead weight, pulled her back.

Dead.

Crying out, she dropped his arm, flung herself away, huddled back against the tree trunk.

CHAPTER 45

HER MIND SCREAMING *RUN, RUN, RUN,* HONOR SCUTTLED closer to the tree trunk. Something big scurried over her shoulder and she brushed it away. No matter how much she blinked, the darkness of the forest was so complete, she was blind.

The smell of lighter fluid hit her nose a moment before the *whoosh* and then the orange glow of fire.

She watched in terror as the flames spread along the vines. Panicked, she tried to squeeze through the brush, angling her shoulders. Her hair snagged in vines and branches. It was too dense.

The fire reached higher as someone squeezed out more lighter fluid. This brush was too wet to catch. They were trying to smoke her out. Make it so she couldn't breathe.

The smoke made her cough, sent tears streaming from her eyes. Her only way out was through fire—and into a group of men with guns, waiting for her.

She was trapped. Honor leaned back, her fingers scraping the dirt. Wait. Was that wetness? She tunneled her fingers into the earth, then began to dig in earnest, hit mud. Nails caked, she dug faster, deeper, until she found water. Splashing water and mud across her face, she kept one eye on the embers drifting down from the flames overhead.

When she was a child, her mother had taken her to an inspirational seminar. She hadn't been allowed to participate, but she'd watched as the instructor worked the group up into a frenzy and made them walk across hot coals.

She'd been so amazed by it all, but her mother's boyfriend—what's his name—told her, "It's the sweat. It creates a barrier between your feet and the fire. You don't need much."

She hoped that he hadn't been wrong. She prayed it as she drenched herself in water and mud.

A crackle of burning wood overhead, and she realized the fire was somehow catching. The sap. Oh, she'd forgotten. These trees were highly flammable. Locals used them for fuel.

Something squeaked near her. Without thinking, she reached out and grabbed the rat. It struggled in her grasp, tried to bite her, but she held its mouth closed. "We're getting out of here."

Covered in mud, smoke blinding her eyes and burning her throat, a rat in one hand, Honor took her two remaining arrows from her quiver, held them in her hand, at her shoulder, like a javelin.

Taking in one last desperate breath, laced with fire and mold and the fearful smell of rat shit on her hands, she exhaled. *Not for nothing.* A sense of "so be it" washed over her as she crouched and bolted through the fire.

It seemed to go on forever. The fire grabbed at her, tore with sharp, angry, red claws. She protected the rat with her arm, carried it like a football.

Blinded, she broke through and ran straight into someone. He *umph*ed, grabbed her. Blinking rapidly as her eyes adjusted, she blindly shoved the rat at him.

The man cursed, let her go, as the rat scrambled onto his face and red hat with his claws.

She turned, saw a figure raise a gun. "Stop," he said.

She slammed the burning arrows into his neck. He fell back. The arrows had pierced through his neck, the ends of the arrows on fire, lit the stunned and sorrowful look on his face. Papito.

Her eyes blinking, blinking with pain and tears, she lurched away. Someone tackled her, drove her to the ground with a "Try to go for my balls now, bitch."

The other man from the boat.

Whip-fast, she elbowed him in the face. One. Two. Three times. Each hit accompanied by a sickening sound. The first a crack. The second a mushy thwuck. The third a small whimper.

His grip loosened. She rolled, threw him off, picked up his weapon, and scrambled away on arms and legs.

Someone was shooting at her. The first shot missed. The second shot hit her in the side. Spun her around, knocked her to the ground.

Weapon raised, Mia stalked forward from the trees. "You're proving much harder to kill than your mo…"

His words were cut off by a loud, sudden wind, but Honor had heard enough.

With the gun she'd stolen tucked close to her side, Honor waited for Bud to get closer. She had to make this shot. She would. She had not let Junior down, Ford, her mother, she had not lost Laz, to die while this man who had killed her mother lived.

The wind increased, along with a thrumming that told Honor, as clearly as Bud's head being tilted toward the sky, his reinforcements had arrived. Helicopter. She rolled and shot. Bud ducked and ran.

Suddenly the woods were filled with ropes, people sliding down them.

Hands trembling, she wobbled her feet, and shot at them. The recoil threw her back to the ground, knocking the weapon from her hand.

Sweat poured from her skin. Mud slid into her eyes. She began to crawl away.

She couldn't die. She couldn't. Laz. She'd never see him again. And despite everything she'd lost, it was his loss that mattered most, that hurt most.

A man with a green helmet grabbed her. She kicked, fought, but she was weakened, hurt, bleeding. He quickly got her under control, scooped her up, drew her against him, held her tight.

Eyes watering, muddy, head pounding, she stared at the face under the helmet, heard his familiar voice. "Fuck. She's been shot. Beam me up. She needs medical attention."

Tony?

Honor felt darkness wash over her, but she fought it back. *Him?* She clung to awareness, clung to him. But the blackness rode over her again. And she wasn't sure if she spoke the words or if she'd just thought them. "I love you, Tony."

CHAPTER 46

"FLY PAST THE HOUSE," TONY SAID, SEEING THE FIRE. SHE was there. He knew it.

Harness on, it took him only a minute to move to the jump door. Below, he saw Honor run from the center of fire, like a Phoenix, reborn and mad as hell.

She shoved something at one man who fell back, punched two arrows into the neck of another. She ran, spun, and fell to the ground. Someone came out of the treeline. The word came down as soon as the hover was secure. Tony dropped.

He landed nearly on top of her, but she scrambled away. "Honor, Honor, it's me. Stop struggling."

She didn't hear him. She was panicking.

He gently wrestled her under control, cradled her to his chest. They'd made it. They'd fucking made it in time.

His team was all around, keeping off the bad guys, most of whom were dead or had fled into the woods anyway.

If they'd been a minute slower. If she'd been an ounce less fierce, less determined. Couldn't think that way. Couldn't. They'd made it. Worth whatever they did to his memory. Worth it.

Making sure the harness around her was secure, that she was turned into him, held by him, he gripped her. Wetness. Blood? "Fuck. She's been shot."

He told his sister to bring him up and into the helicopter

with his heart in his throat. Honor looked at him then, looked and saw not a threat but him. Her eyes, reflecting the moon, widened.

He saw the moment she recognized him, saw him and not a threat. Not for nothing, those eyes were beautiful. Even mud caked and tearing.

He smiled at her. "Stay with me now. With me."

Her lips moved, mouthed, "I love you, Tony."

His heart tore open. He held her closer, tipped up his head, guided her into the helo. When he was inside, he scooted into his jump seat, kept her close, even as they were untethered and Sandesh, who had experience as an EMT, examined her.

"Let go," Sandesh said.

And he tried, he really fucking tried, but what came out was, "Go screw yourself."

She loved him. This woman. That shouldn't make his stomach hurt, but it did. It made him angry too. Furious as fuck. Because they would take that truth, that memory. The League would demand one more thing, one more sacrifice for him to prove his loyalty.

He stroked her damp, burnt hair and cleared the mud from her face. He kissed her forehead, her cheek, and he told her over and over, though she couldn't hear him, wouldn't remember, that he loved her. He did love her. And the prospect of losing this, losing her...It ached. Like something ripped his insides out.

Working on her wound, Sandesh said, "It's not bad. But this would be easier if you'd put her down."

"No."

Mumbling to himself, Sandesh went back to work on the wound.

He knew he should let him work, but if he let Honor go, he'd have one less minute with her. He needed this, wanted every second until he was forced to let go.

I love you, Tony.

He wished he could've told her. Those words meant everything to him. Everything. But the last thing he'd do now, knowing what would happen to him, was to give her something just to have it taken away.

CHAPTER 47

TONY WAS AT THE MERCY OF THE LEAGUE. THE MOMENT they'd landed, internal security had boarded—along with medical staff—and had taken a still unconscious Honor.

Tony was driven home in the limo with Dusty, Sandesh, Justice, and Gracie.

They'd informed him, Honor would be in the best of hands, have the best of care for her wounds, and be in one of the best rooms at the Mantua Home.

And no doubt that was true. But her care was all about keeping him in line, making him willingly submit to the procedure. They were going to M-erase him. Before that, they'd treat him like a criminal, walk him through the front doors of the Mantua home. His perp walk. His walk of shame.

The limo pulled through the Mantua Academy gates and up and over a speedbump that looked like it could take out a semi.

He had no doubt equipment inside had scanned the car. Good feature.

Fall foliage decorated the trees that lined hills, walkways, and the numerous buildings of the elite boarding school. Thanks to a stunt he'd pulled to try to get his family's attention. Looked like he had their attention now.

God, he'd missed this place. Missed the purpose of it, the feeling of doing something that mattered.

The limo pulled to a stop in front of what the kids called, The Big House. Bigger than a palace, beneath this huge place were expansive secret levels filled with the technology and training center for the League of Warrior Women.

The chauffeur opened the limo door.

Tony wiped his sweaty palms on his pants, climbed out, crossed the cobbled drive, and went up the stone stairs to his home. The front door opened to reveal a grand staircase and a grander family. His heart did a backflip in his chest.

Momma and Leland stood by the enormous front stairs. Momma's face covered in a gray silk veil. Leland wearing a matching tie.

And everywhere else stood his people. They were in the doorway to the gym. On the steps. Standing in the hall. He met the eyes of all of them, one at a time. He wanted to appear contrite, but there was a stubbornness in his spine right now that he hadn't expected.

He wasn't going down like that. He wasn't going down as the guy who'd done wrong.

The clapping starting from the gym. It took him a moment to realize it was Dari—black hair with a blue stripe—and the leader of the Troublemaker's Guild. Was she clapping for him?

Rome, Jules, Cee, and their unit—the Vampire Academy—began to clap and hoot too. The older units were quiet and angry-looking. The little kids just looked confused.

Momma spun on those cheering, so fast her veil lifted, revealing for a flash the damaged skin underneath. The room quieted.

So this was what Justice and Gracie had meant. What he'd done to the League. He'd split them down the middle. Two factions. Those that supported what he'd done and why he had done it. And those who didn't. No wonder Momma was so pissed at him. He was an unintentional leader of the rebellion.

Shit. His chances of walking out of here with his memories...zero.

Speaking of remembering, who the hell was that tall, black-haired kid? He stared at the guy who hovered beside Cee. Those eyes. So green. So familiar. There was something about him, a tickle of a memory. Tony's heart stopped. Dead. Fell over. Crushed.

No fucking way. "Tyler? Ty, is that you?"

The kid smirked, nodded. Tony hadn't expected the emotion that rushed over him like a freakin' storm. But there it was. Ty. They'd made a place for him, here, at the home. They'd gotten him back. The League really was changing. He swallowed. The kid had been a toddler when he'd been taken, but... "Do you remember me?"

What was he saying? There was no way—

Ty turned his head. "Did you used to hold me upside down by my feet?"

Fuck. That did it. That fucking did it. He walked over and grabbed Ty in a bear hug. He scared the hell out of him, but he didn't care. Kid was tall. Taller than him. But skinny. Wiry. He could be trained. Yeah. Definitely.

"Let go of my son."

Gracie.

He let go, stepped away. His sister stood in the hall, her fair face growing pink. Probably the last thing she wanted was for her son to have more pain, more memories of the time he lost with the family. Too late. That was the price paid for what had happened.

She'd given up her son years ago to save him and her

then boyfriend from the League. Looks like she'd realized what a mistake that had been. No way around it. He looked at his sister and smiled. "He's back."

Gracie made a choking sound. Tear sprung to her eyes. She nodded.

"I'm glad, G. I'm so fucking happy for you."

"Well, that's just great," Leland said. His gravel voice sounded like it had been dipped in ice water and chilled overnight. At the North Pole. "Now that you've said your hellos. There's a chair with your name on it downstairs."

CHAPTER 48

INSIDE HIS MOTHER'S GAUDY UNDERGROUND OFFICE, hands clasped behind his back, Tony stood in front of his mother's kitschy desk feeling like an errant student hauled before the disapproving principal.

A principal whose face he couldn't read. Through the silver slit that showed her eyes, brown and observant, there was no sense of her emotions. Standing behind her like a consigliere, Leland's face was blank.

The only other people in the room were his sisters, Gracie and Justice, holding onto enough resentment and anger to condemn him.

Gracie stood beside Justice, who sat on the edge of Momma's desk, glaring at him. "Why'd you do it? Why tell Rome and the younger units that you planned on faking your death? Why get them involved? Why pit them against the League?"

Keeping his own face impassive, Tony remained at attention, hands clasped behind his back, feet spread wide. He'd never expressly told any of the younger units his objection to Justice's mission. Before Mexico, Romeo had gotten hold of a copy of the letter Tony had written to Momma and drawn his own conclusion. He finally let his eyes meet Justice's critical gaze. "You don't know me at all."

"Really?" Gracie said. "How long have you been talking to Romeo on the side?"

Crud. They knew about the cell communications. He groped for something to say.

Justice cocked a grin. "Seems like the only thing you do more half-assed than dying is telling the truth."

Tony ran a hand over his face. "I didn't tell Rome what I was going to do. He read the letter I wrote to Momma, we were talking about it, and I said something that accidentally clued him in to my plans. After that...well, he had skills I needed."

"What skills?" Leland asked.

Not going to answer that. "I wanted to have someone here know that I wasn't dead. I figured when I'd gone deep enough under and things had cooled down, he could let you all know. But I didn't go out of my way to align the younger units against Momma. They read the letter, same as you. It's just they drew different conclusions about me saving Justice's life—"

Justice sprang at him like a lion after an impala, slammed a hand to his chest. "You saved nothing. You have no idea how my mission would've gone if you hadn't been playing games with me."

Like hell he didn't. "I knew. You were out of control. You needed to be taken off that operation. You made one stupid mistake after another. Everyone knew it. You think I was the only one who wanted to stop you?"

"Bridget doesn't count. She hates all violence."

"She counts. And so does Gracie. And so does Dada." He pointed toward Momma. "All of us went to Momma. All of us told her that she needed to take you off the operation."

A moment of doubt flashed across Justice's face, but she

THE COST OF HONOR

was never one to doubt herself for long. "I guess I proved you wrong."

"You proved us right. That mission was fucked from the get-go. No way the Brothers Grim needed to be taken out by you in the same place, at the same time. No fucking way."

"If you took out one—"

"The other would be notified. Bullshit. We had enough intel and agents to do them simultaneously."

"No."

"Yes. You wanted to kill them both. You did. And Momma went along with it. Even though the plan was fucked. The execution was fucked. And it was my job to run around trying to put my finger in every fucking hole you put in the dam."

Momma clapped her hands together. "Enough."

The room went silent. Tony hadn't expected her to step into this. It wasn't like Momma. She let all the heat go out of a room, out of a conversation, out of an argument before she got involved.

Momma grasped at the many bracelets that decorated her arm. "Justice's mission did not have a singular goal—taking out the Brothers' organization. Her case was the one time, the one opportunity where the family would be able to win against those that had harmed one of ours." She touched her veil and her jewelry jangled. "Not even I had that chance. The man who scarred me never paid for his crime. It was about healing Justice. Perhaps all of us. Did you not see that?"

Of course he saw that. She'd wanted Justice to stand over the dead bodies of the men who'd hurt her. "Oh, I get it. But isn't that why we have rules, rules that say safety supersedes revenge, to prevent us from doing exactly that?"

"My desire was to see Justice prevail, to have her nightmare end with the destruction of her pain, those who'd caused it. And by doing this give a piece of victory back to all our girls. Perhaps that clouded my judgment."

Tony felt the world shift under him. He waited for it. Disbelief and hope warring for equal control of his spinning thoughts.

"But that is of no consequence now. Now, we must make the choice that saves the family. The League. The only question is" her eyes met his, "do you still willingly agree to do what is right? To relinquish a memory, be absolved of a sin, to make up for your betrayal, your attack on this family?"

With Honor upstairs, sick and dependent on this family to keep her safe from the likes of Winthrop, she wasn't really offering him a choice. Just the illusion of a choice.

But he would add some stipulations, because this, this sacrifice, would finally make him worthy of the League. "As long as I get to be on the mission to take down Winthrop. As long as Honor is kept safe, never has her memory fucked with. As long as this is the last time anyone in this fucking family has to go through this. And as long as, from now on, everyone follows the fucking rules."

CHAPTER 49

TONY WAS STRAPPED TO THE CHAIR. ELECTRODES dropped from a mechanical helmet connected to the ceiling were attached to his head, fingers, and torso. Wires flowed to a machine with a large screen filled with graphs and lines of information.

The M-erasure room, unnaturally cold with white, sterile walls, buzzed with electricity. Being in this Dr. Jekyll's nightmare terrified him even more, and he'd been pretty damn terrified before coming in here. He supposed it needed to be cold for all the computers and technical mind-fucking crap.

Tony's older sister Zuri walked into the M-erasure room with a briskness that made his blood pound in time to the *click, click, click* of her heels. This was not a woman to mess with. Her dark skin glowed with her determination and vitality. Her long, braided black hair flowed behind her as if trying to keep up with the scientist's brisk pace.

Her brown eyes, intelligent and intense, skimmed over him as she made her way to the panel of equipment. He would think her unaffected, but the line of her shoulders, draped in a doctor's lab coat, tightened, as did the set of her mouth.

She was anxious? Go figure. "Hey, Z," he said.

She flinched and adjusted her black A-line skirt under her lab coat. "Hey, Tone. How have you bean today?"

That accent. *Bean* not *been*. And her voice. She had one

of the most beautiful voices. Like amber honey, sweet and rich, with a mild Kenyan accent. That accent gave certain words a properly pronounced feel. Where Tony mashed syllables, her tongue embraced them.

Ah, you know, been better. Less hunted. Less worried. Less strapped to a chair, waiting to have my brain zapped. "Good. You?"

She pushed a button on the table of equipment, a large block with wires, sensors, and electric dials. "I have never"—the word sounded like *nevah*—"been so torn. On the one hand, I see the need." Her eyes pinned him with accusation…and then softened.

"And on the otha', I see the boy who would sit and let me read *The Lord of the Rings* to him, gently correcting my English."

"I just liked the way you talked, Z." A beat of silence, a beat too long for his frustrated, anxious nerves. "What about Bridge? Did you feel conflicted when you did her?"

Zuri shrugged. "Do you mean the first time?"

He jerked forward in the chair. The straps tugged him back. "Jesus. There was more than one?" Girl must have Swiss cheese for a brain.

"Three years ago, Bridget asked me to remove the memory of her addiction."

Bridget had been purposefully addicted to drugs in Laos. Fuck. He'd never known she struggled with that. "But all that meditation. She's so calm. She's—"

"You misunderstand. She wanted me to see if we could devise a treatment for other addicts."

God, he loved Bridget. "So you fucked with her head twice?"

Zuri frowned. "I did not *fuck*, as you say, with her head. I disrupted the place where her attachment to an emotional idea existed. Her brain then altered her memories."

"Dumb it down, Z."

She stopped fiddling with stuff. "Your mind is not a book, written and done. It is more a computer file, capable of being pulled out and altered. Using a chemical and electrical process, I can disrupt one memory while inserting another."

Sounded painful. "Okay. So that's how you rewrite stuff?"

"Again, I do little. You see, our perception of the world is already flawed, incomplete. Our mind, supported by belief and conditioning, fills in the blanks of our senses. Changing a key idea or feeling, just one tweaked memory, forces the mind to make sense of conflicting memories. Your own brain rewrites your memories. It's amazing really, how well our minds can trick us."

Creepy. "Z, I've never been more afraid of you in my life."

Her brow creased. "Why—"

"So if you just take my fear that J was going to get hurt, my brain will alter everything to fit?"

"Yes. Basically."

"So you won't be taking Honor from me? Dominica?"

Zuri recoiled. "No. Nevah. I would fight anyone who would try to take that from you."

All the muscles in Tony's body turned to liquid. One memory. Not really even a memory, an attachment, a fear. And she'd done this before. Bridget was okay. "Is Bridge the only one? Or have you done other people in the family?"

Zuri pulled a flashlight from the pocket of her lab coat and examined his eyes. "Momma."

"You altered Momma's memory?"

"She wouldn't let me touch Bridget until she'd tried it herself."

"What'd she want altered?"

"She couldn't decide. She asked Leland to choose."

"Did he?"

She pocketed her flashlight. "Yes. It worked out quite well. She had no idea that you were Leland's nephew. Until you put it into that letter."

After Zuri snapped the shield over his face, no matter how he blinked, Tony couldn't see a thing.

He could hear Momma and Zuri working. They were good together, practiced, professional. Leland was the only other person in the room.

"I am injecting the medicine," Zuri said. And a strong hand gripped his. Not Zuri's. Not Momma's. Leland's.

The machine began to buzz, the medication rushing first with intense pain and then warmth coursing through his body. Tony felt himself sinking, down and down and down. Out of his body and into a place of total blackness. And there was a soft, coaxing, cajoling voice that spoke to him through the darkness. It asked questions about Mexico. He answered, and the memories floated in front of him, visually there but not part of him.

He watched as he entered Walid's compound, watched

as the alarm went off, as the whole plan backfired. Fuck. This was bad. He'd promised himself when he came to the Mantua Home he'd never let this happen again. One for all. All for one. He had to save her. The buzzing increased, scattering his thoughts.

The voice spoke, told him it was okay, Justice could and would take care of herself.

And he thought the voice was right. She could take care of herself. And the vision he had, the dream of stopping it, of conspiring, none of that had ever happened.

He let it all go. And it felt good. It felt good not to have the responsibility. It felt good to watch the movie rewrite itself, changing everything. It felt so fucking good that he let the soft, calm voice wash over him, reinvent history. Tears fell from his eyes. This was better, so much better than the fucking guilt.

The movie played before him, and he watched as he left his sisters with a hug, sailed off with their blessing, and the voice said, "You sail to an island. To Dominica. A vacation, one you took even from your identity. They called you Laz. You met someone. Tell me about her. Where were you when you first met? First kissed?"

No. No fucking way. He resisted. "I don't remember." A shock ripped through his head. He screamed. That fucking hurt.

The voice again, soft and gentle. If he answered the voice, the pain would not come back. The voice was comfort. The voice was sincere. The voice would make everything better.

The voice said, "This is very important. Tell me about Honor, about being Laz."

"Go fuck yourself."

Another hot shock. He screamed. He thrashed. The pain burst through his head like a storm. And he ran.

Crouched under the utility sink in the back of the three-bay mechanic's garage, Laz hid.

His father continued to bellow, kick empty gas cans and tools out of the way of his angry stride.

The crashes echoed around a garage covered with car parts and tools and equipment. Not a place for a six-year-old with no shoes or shirt to play, but the smell of exhaust fumes and oil were as familiar as the rented apartment upstairs.

Laz spent a lot of time at the window upstairs, staring at the club across the four-lane highway. Women and men moved back and forth from the club to the dark motel next door.

His father had told Laz that his mother was there. And if he looked long enough, he was sure to spot her.

This wasn't true. His mother was dead. But pretending she wasn't, pretending he looked for her, pretending his father hadn't killed her, was a game they played.

It made his father happy. He'd laugh whenever he saw Laz gazing out the window. Sometimes he'd even pat him on the head. Other than that touch, the only physical contact he had with his father involved rage, alcohol, and nowhere to run.

Nowhere to run now.

His father's calloused hand snaked under the sink and around his arm. He dragged him out. The belt whipped across his ass and back before he even got to his feet.

Laz bent and twisted, lost count of the strikes, the number of times his boy body jolted like being hit by an electric current. His father released his arm. He fell to the ground, curled up into a ball.

His father bent close, pulled Laz's long, dark hair, leaned in close enough to whisper-spit in his still ringing ear. "Don't eat my dog's food. Worthless piece of shit. He earns that food."

A moment of intense hatred, a moment so pure and fine, it had a point. The point flared to life in Laz's heart, in his hands, which turned to claws of steel. Like Wolverine.

He leapt from the ground and onto his father. The man fell back, screaming.

Laz stabbed clawed hands over and over through his father's face, a blur of anger.

His father stopped moving. Laz sat back, panting. His father stared up at him. Dead. Hazel eyes. Dark hair. Thirtysomething face. Not his father.

No. Not his father's face. *His* face.

Laz yelled, jolted upright in bed, and remembered. He was safe. In his house, the Mantua Home. No longer a son to that bastard. No longer a victim. And no longer Laz.

CHAPTER 50

In Honor's dream, Laz dangled by fingertips from a mountain. She lay on her stomach, looking over the edge. Dominica sat below them, impossibly far, misted by clouds—as if the mountain had risen to the sky.

Frantic, she reached for Laz. "I'm here. I'm here. Give me your hand."

With a growl, he swung up, stretched for her. Closer they drew until their fingers touched. Arm aching, toes digging into the soil, hips scraping against the rocky ground, face contorted in concentration, she extended. So close.

A helicopter passed overhead. The sound throbbed against her ears. Wind pressed her into the ground, scattered dirt into her face and hair. The whirling current tore Laz's tenuous grip.

He fell. He plummeted down, hand outstretched, pleading with her. His panicked eyes stared at her with a look she'd never seen on his face. Lost.

She screamed and reached for him. He fell toward the hard and unyielding green of earth.

Honor woke with a scream and jerk so violent, she flung herself into a seated position and nearly crashed into the person standing by her bed.

Zuri grasped Honor by her forearms. "It's okay. Okay." She pushed back a little, lowering Honor onto the pillows. "You are safe."

Safe? Her eyes skimmed away from Zuri's angular face and full lips to the bedroom. Light flushed through a series of six-foot-long windows. Blue-and-tan silk drapery pooled onto a lightly stained wood floor. A dresser, an armoire, and a sitting area with a couch and two chairs. This room, like this entire place, was beyond anything she'd ever experienced before. And she hadn't grown up poor.

All signs told her that Zuri's statement was correct. She was safe.

Except this room felt like a prison. So said the fact that the door was locked, and it had already been explained to her that without a chip under her skin, she wouldn't be able to exit.

So what Zuri said, Honor had learned, wasn't true. "Can I see La…Tony today?"

Zuri let out a breath. "As I've explained, he knows you're here. If he wishes to see you, no one would stop him."

Same answer she'd given for the last two days. The answer that told Honor a few things.

One, Tony didn't want to see her. She didn't believe that for a single minute. He'd been afraid of someone, in danger. Her instinct and her dreams told her he still was.

Two, she was definitely a prisoner. Oh, not prisoner, a *guest* in a safe house in the States. They, a secret society of which Laz/Tony was one, were trying to keep her safe from Winthrop. A safety no one else would provide her since she had no proof of any of her claims. Her mother was a disgraced former actress.

And Honor had disappeared from a violent and bloody murder scene. According to Zuri, Honor's only chance of bringing down the men her mother had tried to expose, was to trust the League of Warrior Women.

Sure. Heavy sarcasm, because three, this woman was a liar. Cool accent, melodic voice, big liar.

A chapel bell gonged through the open windows rolling across the idyllic campus Honor could see from her third-floor window. The clear tone expelled the last vestiges of sleep from Honor's mind. Zuri stepped back as Honor swung her legs out of bed, gasped at the pain in her side. As badly as it hurt, the bullet had only grazed her side. "I need to see La…Tony. Now."

Zuri put a hand on her arm. "Let's start small. I can remove the bandages today. Would you'd like to shower?"

Honor's hands were covered in bandages, like heavy white mittens. Second- and third-degree burns from the fire. They hurt. Itched. She didn't have to think twice. She held them up. "I appreciate this. I appreciate all of your medical help. But don't you think something needs to be done about my Junior?"

Junior had been taken from the jail on Dominica. No one knew where he was.

"As I've told you before, this is nothing you need to worry about. I can assure you that something is being done. Facts are being assembled. Plans made. A whole group of highly trained professionals are on the case. Now, hold still."

A whole team. Oh. Well. Sorry to bother you. Liar.

The removal of the bandages startled her. They were healed. Completely healed. The healing skin, pink and sore, didn't match the rest of her, but they worked and looked fine. She could move them, use them, with little pain. Who were these people?

Zuri was ecstatic over their appearance. The salve she'd been putting on Honor was experimental. Honor had given her permission to use it. The woman could sell ice to an Alaskan. "Please hold them up," Zuri said, snapping pictures with her phone. She checked and double-checked each finger. "Good. Make a fist. Excellent."

Great, now she was a hand model. "I really appreciate all you've done, but that's it," Honor said, spinning on her heel and walking away.

The warm lavish shower—like every inch of this room— had every amenity, but even the warmth of the cascading water couldn't stop the haunting memories.

Honor caught her breath, sucking in drops of water. She curled in on herself, dropped to the blue shower tile, and began to sob. Pain gripped her by the neck, shook her so hard everything seemed to break at once. It hurt, not for who she'd thought Pops had been, but for all the hurting people she'd failed to notice.

Tito, José, Ford. Dead. Her mother. All dead. And Junior? Someone had taken him from prison, someone had him. What were they doing for him! She cried, bawled her fists, cursed. She was done, done letting these people keep her prisoner.

CHAPTER 51

DRESSED IN HIS WORKOUT CLOTHES, THE ALL-BLACK uniform that felt like a call to action the moment he put it on, Tony came down the front stairs of the Mantua Home humming a tune despite his pounding headache.

Good to be home. That shit in Mexico—no one to blame since it had been his plan—had been intense, so intense he'd had to take a vacation, get clear of the family for a while. Meet a girl. Get laid.

His head flashed with pain. Fucking headache. Too much drinking. Not enough working out. But he was back now and ready to take on the next case. He double-checked today's agenda on his phone. Spice Girls meeting scheduled LLC @ 9:30 to discuss the Dominica case.

After the headache he had for the last two day, he had to play catch-up with the plans for this mission to expose Winthrop. And redeem his screwup.

He hadn't once thought that the offer on Honor's property could be something to help Honor, to keep her safe from a man who'd actively worked to steal her money. Papito. Manipulating Honor, taking her money hadn't been enough. He'd gotten his hands on her mother's film in order to blackmail Carson Winthrop into giving him money and into killing his granddaughter.

Shit. So much to sort out.

Leave it to him to take a vacation to get away from the job and walk smack into a job, but the actual case had been on the periphery of his focus. He'd been all about the girl. Seemed stupid now. Not just stupid, it seemed completely unlike himself. But that was what vacations were. You pretended to be someone else.

He was clear, done pretending. Time to get back to being himself.

At the bottom of the stairs, he looked across into the gym. He saw the Troublemakers Guild and Vampire Academy sans Romeo waiting by the doors. Still in their pajamas. He took out his cell, checked the time.

"Hey," he said, crossing to them. "It's nearly 7:45 and you guys aren't even in your gym clothes? Did you all eat breakfast before going on a morning run?"

Sure, it was Saturday, but life was getting soft around here. Came back just in time.

They stared at him. Not one word. Okay, he hadn't been gone that long. "Get moving. Got a sparring session with Rome, then a morning meeting, but I'll be back here regular time—even if I have to walk out of my meeting."

Again nothing. And that wasn't like these people. Especially the Troublemakers Guild—Daryl, Kitty, and Jensen. Those three. Shudder.

"Tony?" Cee said.

"Yeah?" Why was Cee crying? What was going on here today? "Do you remember me?"

"What? Yeah, Cee, I fucking remember you. Was gone a couple months. Not years." Shaking his head, he began to turn. What was it Bridget always said? *When something makes you uncomfortable, pay even more attention.*

He turned back to her, to them. "Why'd you ask? What's goin' on?"

He met their eyes in turn. And each, in turn, cast their eyes away. The group shifted, some even backed up. All but Daryl/Dari, who stepped forward. She'd been adopted as a child after her mother—a dissident from Iran—was killed. She'd come into the home with the kind of attitude only someone who had nothing to lose could have.

An elaborate tattoo of a thorny vine with bright flowers wound around the olive skin of her left arm, stretching from her left shoulder to her wrist. A blue streak through her hair, appropriate since she could talk a blue streak. "They took your memory. Altered it."

A kick to the balls would've caused less of a shock. As the words sunk in, a jolt of pain cascaded up his body even as another awareness, a softer, gentle reassurance, emerged. It was okay. He'd given them permission. Fuck. That's right. How did he forget that?

Aftereffects, that gentle voice reminded him. *Tell them it's okay.*

He let out a breath. "Yeah. I know. It had to be done. I'm good with it."

"They messed it up," Cee said. "Something's wrong."

Alarm spiked again through his body. "What do you mean they messed it up?"

Cee slapped her hands against her sides. "I heard Momma talking with Zuri. She said your resistance caused an emotional break."

"Resistance is futile," Dari said.

Not fucking funny. What was going on? "Okay, well, that's none of your business." Apparently not his either. "Now get your shit together. Stop staring at me. It is what it is. We all know the rules. We all play by the rules."

He stopped only because he felt the weight of those words, felt them down to the soles of his shoes. This meant something. And inside, he was split in two, both for and against that sentence. He felt the tear in his chest, as if two people had dug fingers into either side of his rib cage and were pulling.

He rubbed his ribs and walked away, leaving them to gasp and whisper about whether or not he was in his right fucking mind.

Truth. He wasn't sure. Because now that they mentioned it, he realized something was different. His memory of Dominica, of Honor in Dominica. It was like a layer of the memories were missing. Not the actual event, but the emotion attached to the events. He remembered feeling everything, but now he felt nothing.

It's okay. Temporary. No need to panic. Nothing to panic about.

So why did his chest hurt?

The smell in the underground gym—an enormous space with state-of-the-art equipment, including an obstacle course *American Ninja Warrior* would be proud to sport—might be Tony's favorite in the whole world. Well, that and chocolate.

Chocolate?

But even being back here, along with the feel of being active and totally in the moment, in flow with his body, couldn't keep him from a little brotherly annoyance.

"You're not keeping your head in the game, Rome,"

Tony said, offering the kid up from his prone position on the sparring mat.

Pale skin slicked with sweat, amber-brown eyes bouncing around the room, Romeo took the offered hand with a mumbled "Sorry."

Tony pulled him to his feet. With a brisk rub of one hand through his dark hair, Romeo did the thing that was really starting to get on Tony's nerves—he avoided eye contact.

"Seriously, Rome, you're killing me with this. What's with you?"

He shook his head. "Nothing. It's just…" He looked away and then whispered, "This fucking sucks."

Tony handed the kid the cleaning fluid and a rag. Loser cleaned up. "Look, whatever this is, you have to let it go. I agreed…" Rome leaned in closer. "I could tell you what they took. I would."

No fucking way. "No. No more screwing with my fucking head."

"What about Honor?" Rome said. "You don't even remember—"

"Tony?"

He turned at the sound of that unexpected voice. Holy shit. "Victor?"

Dressed in all-black League workout gear, looking tanned and toned, a lot healthier than the last time he'd seen him— shot up by bad guys—Victor rushed over and gave him a hug.

Releasing him, Victor swatted him on the head. "*Pendejo.*"

Tony rubbed the spot. "What the fuck?"

Folding jacked arms across his chest, stretching his black tank, emphasizing a scar running along his collarbone,

Victor said, "Gave you the best night of your life. And you never called."

Tony narrowed his eyes. "Dude, you shouldn't fuck with someone who's had their memory altered."

Victor laughed. "Just checking, amigo. They said you were the same with a small blip in the radar. Seems about right."

"It's not right," Romeo said. And when Tony and Victor looked at him, he added, "He's different."

Tony pointed at the mat. "Clean up."

The kid dropped down and began to clean their sweat from the mat, but his pronouncement, "He's different," had struck a gong of anxiety that rippled through Tony's awareness. Had they done it? The thing he'd always worried that the League would do—make him into the man they wanted at the expense of the man he was?

He shook that disturbing thought away. "Why you here?"

Victor held up his wrist. "Got myself a permanent invite."

What? Now he knew something was fucked up. "Didn't think you'd be the type of person who'd want anything to do with the League."

"I'm the type of person who likes to be prepared. Right now, your family is using my charity as cover. I'd like seeing what the League is all about. Also, this is a test run. See if we can't help each other in other ways. I've got a couple Ex Ops who might fit in here."

"You think your guys will be given an in into the League?" Tony couldn't keep the astonishment off his face or out of his tone.

Victor frowned. "That's what Momma told me. And I'm in for your next op. Winthrop."

What. The. Fuck? Momma had allowed Ty back. Dusty into the League. Given Victor clearance, bringing him in on ops, and talking about creating access to the League for some of Victor's ex-Special Forces buddies?

What the hell had caused these changes? It couldn't have anything to do with whatever memory they'd taken from him, right?

CHAPTER 52

AFTER HER SHOWER, HONOR DRESSED IN BLACK PANTS and matching shirt. They had a lot of clothes for her here—all her size—but she preferred these. It was passive-aggressive, but a prisoner needed a prison uniform.

She came out of the bedroom area of her suite to find Zuri in the sitting area, on a blue patterned couch, cleaning up her medical equipment. Good, she was leaving.

Couldn't well break out of here with Zuri hanging around. And they barely left her alone.

She longed for alone time, to hand roast cocoa beans, blend her chocolate, invent a new flavor, and sculpt those flavors into a beautiful work of art.

Today, it would be something dark and sweet and painful. Something that might leave you with a hangover. Something with tequila. Something so visual, when you saw the small chocolate sculpture, glazed with colors—like red and jade—you saw beauty and brokenness.

But making chocolate was her old life. A life where her pleasures came at the expense of other people. Tito. José. Ford. Her mother. Junior. Now, she was a different woman.

As much as what happened had hurt her, it hurt so much she couldn't imagine a time where she could breathe without pain, it had made her stronger. Determined.

Determined enough to break free from this room, find the man she loved, and demand to be part of finding Junior. And bringing Winthrop to justice.

She made her way through the main living area, moving past Zuri. Without a word, Honor whisked out onto the balcony. Hands on the railing, she let the early morning sun warm her damp hair and damper spirits.

The spire of a chapel nestled between white, brick, and steel-and-glass buildings. A beautiful campus. The Mantua Academy. Ironic that it was a place of learning, intellectual freedom, since she didn't even have access to the internet.

Leaving the balcony, she found Zuri finished packing up, Honor tried again. "Can I see Tony now?"

Zuri sighed. "Is there anything else I can bring you?"

Small on answers. Big on bringing her stuff. Which was all part of her plan. "Do you think you could have someone bring me supplies to make chocolate? A tempering machine would be great. Now that my hands are back, I might as well work. That's what I do. I'm a chocolatier."

Zuri frowned. "I'm sorry. I hadn't thought." She looked at Honor's hands, looked at them as if they somehow belonged to her. Possessive. "Be careful with your hands. That remarkable result of my salve." She bit her lip. "I'm not sure you understand…" She shook herself. "Sorry. Sure. I'll have the things sent up."

Gee. Thanks. Honor smiled at her. "You're the best."

CHAPTER 53

SITTING AT A CONFERENCE TABLE IN THE MANTUA HOME library, Justice could not stop wringing her hands. She felt like a cartoon supervillain. The stress of this moment, of sitting in this library—a whimsical place that looked like a fairy tale had exploded—across the table from Tony, seeing him himself and yet missing something so important, was eating her up inside.

"Stop staring at me, J," Tony said. "You're giving me the creeps."

Her lips turned up despite wringing her hands. She looked away, straight into Sandesh's blue eyes.

A small line creased the bridge of his nose. He mouthed, "This sucks."

She nodded. It did. A few days ago, it had seemed they'd only be taking Tony's memories of his betrayal, all the negative emotions of that betrayal, restoring who he'd been, but today…well, it seemed like he was less of himself.

That wasn't exactly true. He wasn't less of the man Justice knew. It wasn't that he wasn't who he'd been before meeting Honor. He was exactly like his old self. Flip. Direct. Dedicated. Walled off.

But the intensity, the openness, the…passion that she'd seen from him on the plane in Dominica was muted. Not just muted. Gone completely. And that felt more than wrong. That felt criminal.

And she knew she wasn't the only one to feel it. Everyone

in the library, at this table—Dusty, Gracie, Momma, Leland, Zuri, Romeo, Victor, and Sandesh—avoided eye contact with Tony.

"So the snake had no venom," Tony said, reading through the notes Romeo had provided to everyone. He flipped to the next page. "And this thing with Bud...you're suggesting when Bud almost fell off the cliff that was Junior helping Honor too? How'd you figure that out?"

Romeo wiped at his forehead. Kid was doing great, despite sweating bullets. Smart of Momma to involve him in the case, bring him back into the fold, and by extension his unit, Vampire Academy. "I double and triple checked. Even image searched from a photo someone had posted online. That guy Bud wasn't listed on the cruise ships passenger list. Not even under a different name."

Justice sat forward. Seemed like the slowest getaway car ever, but kind of brilliant. "So he'd gotten onto the ship illegally. Probably paid someone to sneak him onboard and planned to get off at the next port after he killed Honor?"

Dusty said, "He was there to kill Honor and this kid, Junior, a prince among men, tried to stop him?"

"Exactly," Romeo said. "Bud was there to verify the film, take it, and kill Honor. Winthrop, and this is deep speculation on our part, would've transferred money to an offshore account for Papito, aka Ramone Silva."

Typing on the laptop in front of her, Gracie looked up. "Papito also had an insurance policy on Honor. Two million. Not your typical policy on a chocolatier."

Sandesh raised an eyebrow. "Papito would've gotten insurance money for Honor's death, kept the hotel, which it looks like he planned on burning, and rights to Kiki

Hart's images to sell to whoever, and all that money from Winthrop."

"Sounds like Papito was a greedy bastard," Justice said.

"And that was his best quality," Tony said.

Tony looked directly at her, grinned. Justice looked away. Not the kind of thing he'd normally joke about, not if he still felt something for Honor.

What had they done? *Crap.* She fidgeted as guilt tightened her chest. They'd fucked him up. She was going to lose her shit. She'd never wanted this.

Sandesh's warm hand found hers under the table, squeezed. He didn't say a word. And she blessed him, every gorgeous inch, because if there was one thing she couldn't stand right now, it would be someone telling her this was okay. It clearly was not.

A simultaneous beep had everyone reaching for their tablets at the same time. The first thing Justice noticed, what they all must have noticed since it was in big red letters at the top of the page was, MISSION TO FREE JOSÉ CLEMENTE. Internal security had found Junior.

Gracie let out a breath, a soft sigh, the end of which was lost as the home alarm started to blare.

CHAPTER 54

HAVING NO IDEA WHEN SOMEONE FROM THE STAFF would come, Honor finished with the lump in her bed. Looked good. It resembled her sleeping form. She'd even found a dark, hairy jacket—too trendy for her—in the armoire. She'd used it to make it seem like a tuft of hair stuck out. Not bad.

Finished with that, she hid behind a loveseat in a reading nook close to the room's front door.

Forty minutes later, the door beeped and clicked. A twentysomething with blond hair and a maid's uniform entered. She pushed a wheeled metallic cart filled with some of the best chocolate-making supplies in the business. She didn't call out to Honor but went quietly about her business, taking the items off the cart and putting them into the kitchen.

When the woman was done, she pushed her cart up to the door and reached her hand up. Just like when Zuri left or anyone from the staff left, there was a click and a beep. The girl pulled the door, bent across the cart as she wheeled it out the door. Now.

Honor came out as silent as a butterfly. She mimicked the woman perfectly. It helped that the woman didn't turn around. She expected the door to close and lock on its own.

Honor followed her out into the hall. The door clicked closed, then began to beep. The woman spun so quickly, Honor was nearly caught, but she managed to mimic the woman's movements, just like when she was a kid. She kept hidden behind her as the woman went back to the door, waved her wrist over a pad by the doorway. A mechanical voice issued from the pad and said, "Verify that two people have exited the room. Authorization necessary."

The woman did a full 360, with Honor following every move. She shrugged. "It's a trolley, daft machine," the woman said with a rather strong Scottish accent. Waving her wrist over the pad, she said, "Come on, home security, got work here."

"Getting a visual," a voice said, and the pad blinked to life, showing the woman in the hall, the entire corridor, and Honor.

The woman whirled on her with a scream. An alarm sounded.

Honor ran. She waited for the chase. Kept looking ahead and behind for people. But no one followed. What the heck? She'd expected to be chased down, like in the woods. She'd expected to fight. She'd expected pain and anger and...

The alarm cut off.

A female voice came over a speaker. "Hello, Honor. This is Martha with home security. No one will hurt you. Stop there. Someone will meet you, show you around."

No thanks. She wasn't going back into witness protection. Sheesh, this place was huge. But she'd been taken through here before. And even as drugged and out of it as she'd been, she knew her way to the front door. She ran down another hall, turned down another, found the staircase, and ran down.

Her side ached. Blood soaked through her shirt. Again the voice came. This time, the woman seemed concerned.

"If you'd like to run around, that's fine. But you are injured. Wouldn't it be better to allow us to show you around?"

Honor reached the front door, grabbed the handle with swollen fingers, and pulled. It didn't budge. A mechanical voice said, "Exterior doors locked. Authorization required."

She dropped the handle, dropped her shoulders. No way out of here.

Feeling stupid, not sure if the voice could hear her, she said, "I want to talk to Tony."

"That can be arranged."

Honor spun. She'd thought she was ninja quiet, but this woman... Wait. She recognized her. The Native American woman who'd come to her shop. Honor pointed an accusing and puffy red finger at her. "You. You came to my shop. You were there looking for Tony?"

"Actually," the woman said, "at that point, I already knew where he was. I was there to feel you out, see what you knew about us, the family."

"The family?"

The woman's brow creased. She said, almost a whisper, "He really didn't tell you?"

"What are you talking about? Who are you?"

The dark-eyed woman walked forward, like stalking prey was her way of life. Honor tensed. The woman stopped. "You don't need to be afraid. I'm Justice Parish. Tony's sister."

Honor shook her head. "Sister? I thought he only had one brother."

Someone snorted and stepped from behind Justice. A fair-skinned redhead. The woman waved at her. "He does have only one brother. But he has twenty-six sisters. I'm Gracie Parish."

Honor's mouth dropped open. Her eyes jumped from Gracie to Justice to the gym at her right. The doors to the gym were closed, but faces peered out from the glass. Kids and teens a wondrous variety of skin tones were gathered there. Staring at her.

"You're..." She swallowed but didn't say it. The Parish family. What she knew of them, she knew distantly through social media and tabloids. Which, to her mind anyway, meant she didn't know them at all. Wait. She did know one of them, very well. Tony Parish. That was Laz's real name.

Pain, physical from her wounds and emotional from her heart, surged through her. A knot made up of fear, pain, and stress formed in the back of her throat. "It's okay," Gracie said. "I know all of this is confusing. Trust me though, we're here to help. That's what we do." Behind her, there was a click. Honor jumped, moved away from the front door. Two men entered, both muscular, both handsome, both terrifying.

She spun back to the women. "Where's Tony?"

Gracie inclined her head. "He's downstairs." She pointed to the men who'd entered. "The big guy is mine. His name is Dusty."

The big guy said, "Warms my heart. Pleased to meet you, Honor." He had a nice voice. Southern. Congenial.

"And Sandesh, the handsome guy, is mine," Justice said, earning her a swat from Gracie.

Sandesh nodded hello to her and then said, "Nice to meet you, Honor. I think you're going to want to come with us, learn more about what's going on here. We want to help you and your cousin, Junior."

Honor's heart sped up. "You know where Junior is?"

"We'd like you to join us," Justice answered. "We found Junior."

Honor had a security detail. Well, that was the way she saw it. They were all cordial, but they were flanking her. Like this house wasn't intimidating enough.

She'd never seen anything like it. And she'd grown up with money. Well, before her mother had spent it all on documentaries. Nothing like this. Not just the rich wallpaper, high ceilings, but the intricate and delicate nature of every crafted detail.

Justice stopped by an elevator and pushed a button. The door opened. Sandesh and Dusty went inside. Justice waved to indicate Honor should go.

She did. Only because they told her they were taking her to Momma's office. And Tony was there.

Justice and Gracie followed her. They all spread their feet wide. *What was going on?* There was a change, a subtle shift in the tremor under the floor. Just a moment, but she prepared before the elevator dropped. Oh crap. She transferred her weight to compensate.

The big man, Dusty, clung to the sides, and the others in the square steel box—Sandesh, Justice, and Gracie—had shifted arms for balance. No wonder. This was a terrifying elevator.

But she'd managed to look unmoved. Which, judging by the looks she was getting, was important.

They reevaluated her. She felt it, like the shift under her feet. Something in their eyes, their estimation of her, changed.

"Is there a problem?" she asked.

"You just became a legend," Dusty said, righting himself as the elevator came to a full stop.

Justice said, "You didn't move."

"That made me swallow my candy," Gracie said.

The elevator doors slid open. And this time, as the four of them took up positions around her, she saw them take the job a little more seriously.

They walked down a sterile hallway. The blank emptiness of it made Honor miss the beauty of her hotel, her candy shop, her ignorance.

That was wrong. She didn't want to be ignorant.

She'd rather what she had. Anger. Determination. And, yes, fear. But the kind of fear that made her want to do something. The kind of fear that demanded she do something to help Junior.

They came to a door. Justice didn't knock. She swung it open and entered.

Following behind her, Honor entered, drawing in a breath laced with roses. She held it as her eyes scanned the unfamiliar room and the people inside. A tall man. A short woman with a niqab. Zuri. And…him.

CHAPTER 55

TONY FOLLOWED MOMMA, LELAND, AND ZURI INTO Momma's lower-level office, a warm place filled with color and kitschy decorations from around the world. Decorations that represented something from each of her children.

Momma motioned toward the couches set up in a conversation area. He sat. Momma and Leland sat across from him. Zuri next to him. She smelled like lavender and coffee. Probably because she held a cup of coffee.

Leland shifted, seemed anxious. What was that about? "Tony, we—"

Momma put a hand on Leland's knee. He stilled and they exchanged a quick glance. It was a very familiar gesture, one that told a lot about them as a couple. And they were a couple. Tony had known that since the first moment he'd seen them together.

He recalled it now. Early morning in Philly. He'd slowly made his way back there after running away from his dad. He'd crawled out from his usual spot behind the dumpster and made his way to the kitchen. This restaurant was the only place that put their spoiled food out in the morning. Which meant no rats got in it. Not right away anyway.

And they had regular trash cans. He'd been careful to vary his route there, make sure no one followed, no one discovered this treasure trove. He'd been shown this place by a homeless woman who'd gotten into a home-work program.

That too had been Momma and Leland. They'd set

everything up. They wanted him brought into the family but didn't want ties to Leland. Not after Leland had gone through the trouble of killing Tony's dad. Looking back, he should've known.

The back door to the restaurant was open, but no one in the kitchen ever noticed him, stopped him. The sound of workers and plates and cooking drifted out as he lifted off the lid. His stomach growled. The food was always in a white bag, always seemed fresh. He picked it out and tore into the egg and sausage sandwich.

"Did you just eat trash?"

He spun around. A little girl. Dark hair, dark eyes, and a horrified look on her face. He swallowed, hid the bag behind himself, then felt bad.

He held it out to her. "You hungry?"

A normal seven-year-old would probably have told him he was gross and run away. Especially one whose family was in the restaurant, eating breakfast. But Justice, his Justice, had shrugged, walked closer, taken the bag.

She'd looked inside. "Thanks."

He'd watched her eat the doughnut, longing on his face. That could've been lunch.

She'd smiled at him. "You really want this doughnut." She had laughed, took off a piece, and shared.

He'd fallen in love with her then. A second before a man and woman came out the back of the restaurant. Leland and Momma. Tony had been instantly wary of him. So tall. Straight of spine and direct of gaze.

And Momma had seemed so mysterious. Much shorter with a veil over her face. For a moment, their gazes had fallen on him, with pity and something else.

"We told you not to go out back," Leland had said. "Why must you always disobey us?"

Justice's face had scrunched up, like she was actually thinking on why that was. Of course, they had planned on her doing exactly that. What they hadn't planned on, couldn't have, was what happened next. Justice had grabbed his hand. "I decided what I want for my birthday."

Momma and Leland had exchanged a glance. Something in that exchange had told Tony everything he had to know. They were a couple. They loved each other. That was over twenty years ago. But they still looked at each other the same way.

Momma lifted her hand from Leland's thigh. "Zuri has a theory on what has been happening to you since the procedure."

Procedure. She couldn't bring herself to call it what it was. An experimental mind fucking. "You talking about the fact that I can't seem to conjure one emotion about anything that happened after Mexico?"

Momma nodded. Leland frowned. Zuri shifted sideways, toward him and said, "In order for memories to be reconsolidated properly, the subject must, to some extent, follow suggestion and willingly alter them. You resisted. That resistance caused a conflict. Your brain can't correct the conflict, so it has chosen to protect you. That protection is a type of amnesia, an emotion-induced retrograde amnesia. It's actually quite common in trauma. The fault lies in the amygdala. I believe I can correct it."

"No."

Zuri startled. "Hear me out. It's not as much medical as emotional tweaking. We simply need to spark the feeling that went along with the original memory. One session. Hypnosis—"

He shook his head. "No, Z. No fucking way." He stood from his seat. "That's enough. I'm calling enough. I might not be worthy of the League, but I sure as shit don't deserve this."

Did he? He'd assumed they'd altered his memory to save him from whatever awful shit had gone down in Mexico. Something he definitely didn't want. But was that the truth?

"Do you really feel you're not worthy of the League?" Momma said.

"Don't you? I mean, I screwed up. I...I knew he was hurting her. I didn't do anything to help."

"You were a child," Leland said, something in his posture giving the slightest bit to the weight of grief. For him or for his mother, he couldn't know.

Fuck. He was done lying about this. He'd seen his father kill his mother. He'd kept quiet.

"He killed her, Leland. If I'd have said something to anyone all those years he was abusing her. If I had opened my fucking mouth.

"And you know what's worse? I saw him do it. I fucking saw my father kill my mother. And I stayed quiet. For years. First person I ever told was Honor. Funny that, since I can't recall feeling the emotion of telling her, not like I feel the shame of it here. Keeping quiet was the most dishonorable thing I've ever done. And the reason I can never be worthy of all of you."

The room went as quiet as a ship sunk in the deepest, least travelled, coldest part of the ocean. That cold spread through him. Now they knew. Not worthy of them. Not worthy of the League.

Momma drew in a deep breath. Probably didn't want to hear whatever she was about to say, but his ears tuned into that breath, focused on the flutter of her veil, and...

The door swung open. Justice entered, along with Gracie, Sandesh, Dusty, and...

Honor.

Shit.

Her eyes swung to him, widened. Goose bumps washed down his body. Or the memory of goose bumps. Of looking into her eyes, of wanting her to kiss him. Fuck. He remembered that he'd felt something, but the memory was empty of feeling now.

He stood there, dumbfounded, as she rushed to him, threw her arms around him, and kissed him.

Hadn't intended to kiss her back, hadn't intended for his lips to lock on hers, for his arms to draw her closer, for that sound to roll through his throat, for his tongue to roll into her mouth.

Heat and desire unlocked, and for a moment, a flash, he felt everything. The kiss went on for a long time. He only knew this by the fact that when they stopped, drew back from the kiss, the room was empty. In every other way, he'd lost track of time.

Fuck. He was a jerk. An idiot. "I'm sorry." He stepped back. He felt that, felt the emptiness of her touch leaving him, of the space created. Everything in him wanted to kiss her senseless, kiss her until the heat melted them, until no space existed between them. Because *that* he knew he'd feel.

But it would mean something more to her than it would to me. He wasn't that big of an asshole. "I should've come to your room. Explained things. I've been a coward."

A sound like heartbreak and disbelief escaped Honor. It tore a hole in him as brutal and instant as lead through his gut. "So you could've come to my room? They weren't keeping you away?"

CHAPTER 56

HONOR COULD FEEL THE CHANGE IN TONY, SEE IT, HEAR it. A thousand unmistakable cues. The way his body had felt against her, needy but not rejoicing. The way his eyes swept her face with a lack of warmth. The tone of his voice. Worried. Awkward. The step back he took from her. The way his eyes darted away when she asked him why he didn't come to her room. "Tony? What's going on?"

He drew a breath in through clenched teeth, a troubled hiss. "Yeah. That's the thing. I'm not exactly the guy you met in Dominica."

"What happened to you?"

He did look at her then. "Why would you think something happened to me? Why not I'm just different in a different space?"

She took a step closer, and when he tried to step back again, she grabbed the front of his black T-shirt with both hands, held him there. "The fact that you can ask that makes me very nervous. I know you. Not everything about you, but the stuff that matters. What did they do to you?"

He squared his shoulders. "If by them you mean my family, you should back off from that."

"No. I just spent days locked in a room so secure, the staff opens the doors with chips embedded in their wrists. With a woman who has multiple degrees, who healed third-degree burns in days. In a home that has a level to it that is far below ground. Judging by the drop of the elevator. I'm scared right now. My whole world has changed overnight and not for the better."

His eyes softened. He shook himself. "You come from a different world, different place, different rules, so this is going to sound crazy."

Crazy she could handle. It was the lies, the not knowing that she couldn't put up with anymore. She wanted to know everything he'd hidden from her. "Crazier than the fact that you're a member of a secret society of vigilantes called The League of Warrior Women?"

"It's not just a secret society of vigilantes. It's a global powerhouse of intellectuals and scientists, assassins and teachers, leaders, tech wizards, and spies intent on making the world a better, more fair place. This complex group operates outside the law, because often the powers that be don't have the interests of the most vulnerable populations in mind. And when you take on a mission that big, that far-reaching the individual sometimes needs to sacrifice. That's what I did, sacrifice. My sister Zuri—" He rubbed a hand in a circular motion over his chest. "—has developed a way to alter the memory of past experiences. Change them. Mind-altering stuff really."

"You mean she knows how to fuck with your mind?"

He nodded. "In a nutshell. Yeah. Z changed a memory of mine. Something that I needed to get rid of. Something painful. I agreed to it. And that part went fine, but then something else went wrong. Not sure exactly what. Basically, everything that happened since the moment I arrived on Dominica is an emotional blur."

Unable to control the surge of pain, she dropped her hands from his shirt with a small, pained cry. She remembered something he had told her when they first met in the hospital. She'd asked him, *"If you feel bad, why did you leave?"* And his answer. *"It was that or lose my mind."*

Oh. He'd been being literal. They'd taken him from her.

"Why would you agree to have your memory altered?" That didn't sound like him.

He snorted. "That I don't remember. But the family motto is all for one and one for all, so I'm guessing it had something to do with them."

"But you remember me?"

"I do."

She didn't bother to try and hide or control her tears. "So it's just the emotions, you feel differently?"

He shifted toward her, backed away. "Don't cry. It might just be a glitch. But everything that happened after that mission is muted. Like I have a visual but not an emotional sense of it."

As if she could stop the tears. She took another step back, looked at her feet, at the sneakers they had given her. Black. Exactly the same as everyone. Even his. They'd changed his head, but… She looked back up at him. "But the head and the heart are two different things."

"I used to think that too."

"Can they fix you?"

"I'm not undergoing any procedures. But Zuri says it's like any kind of amnesia. It might just come back. Something can jar it loose. She says the emotion is there, locked inside me. I just need the right experience to unlock it."

"Like the Cowardly Lion needed the right experience to unlock his courage."

"Kind of."

"Can I help?"

"Think we just have to wait and see. You understand that, right?"

Understand? No. She did not understand. She'd lost everything. Her family. Her business. Him. She shook her head. The man he had been would've done anything, anything, to get back to her.

His face grew concerned, like he did feel something. Not something for someone he loved, but something for a fellow human being. It hurt worse than if he'd showed her nothing. He said, "You're welcome here. Safe. And…" He closed his eyes, as if preparing to plunge into a cold pool. "I'd like to get to know you. Again."

CHAPTER 57

HONOR WAS FREE TO ROAM THE HOUSE, FREE TO WALK around with Tony. Well, she had a chip that monitored her and told these people exactly where she was, but right now that seemed the least important thing. The most important thing?

Jarring Tony's memory. Not just that, but connecting with him. She couldn't stand the distance between them. After Leland and Momma had returned and explained the rules to her, told her they'd be meeting to discuss her rescuing Junior.

Before then, Tony was to show her around.

A bit awkward. Mostly, because she was planning something reckless. Something that would surely crack open his heart.

Desire. Warmth had pooled between her legs. Her sex had begun to pulse. And a need as sensitive and demanding as the urge to breathe had poured into her. Now. Now. Now. It screamed at her, into her.

It would work. It had to.

Her wrist still sore from where Leland had inserted the chip, she'd sent Tony a look. His eyebrows rose.

"Is there any place down here where we can be alone? No cameras? No monitors?"

She'd thought he'd resist, but a smile rolled across his face. And her legs near dropped out from under her.

Now…Grabbing her hand, he tugged her along, back

the opposite way of where the rooms where, to a secluded hallway.

This was bad. She knew it. Crazy. At the end of the corridor was a steel door. Tony put his wrist up and it beeped. He directed her to do the same, explaining, "Only two doors. This one. And one at the top. No cameras inside."

A moment later, they entered a stone tower with a spiral steel staircase, like something you might stick a missile inside.

"For all its high-tech," Tony said. "The League has some archaic areas." He pointed up. "These stairs go up to the garage. We used to have to run it as teens. Long ways up. Gracie, back when she cursed, called it a shit-ton-of-stairs stairway."

She craned her head as they walked. She liked hearing this. "How many stairs?"

"386."

"That is a shit-ton-of-stairs."

He nodded. "You wanted to talk alone. This is the place. No cameras. No recording devices. You can only get in and out with a chip, so it's pretty secure. Whaddya wanna talk about?"

As if. Wordless, she dragged him up two landings. The silo resounded with their quick footsteps as they jogged up the metal treads. It smelled like concrete and water and compressed dirt.

She didn't care about the where. Only that it was now.

The tingling want caused even the feel of her G-string fabric against her moist slick clit to cause her to bite her tongue.

Only a few minutes, a few minutes of him was all she needed. To connect with him, to remember him, to create a memory of her that could not be taken.

"Here," she breathed, tugging him into an alcove carved off the stairs. Like the rest of the silo, it was cement.

He pulled her into it, into him. The feel of his hard-on pressed against her body sent a chorus of "Hallelujah" soaring through her.

"Wait," she pulled back from him, tugged off her pants and underwear.

He moaned. "Don't know what I've done right in my life, but I'm about to start going to church."

His eyes glued to her. She wrapped a leg around him, crushed her wetness against him, rocked herself against his need and the coarseness of his jeans. "Now. I need you now."

Her voice sounded desperate, as desperate as she felt. With a grunt that seemed all he could manage, he unbuttoned his jeans, dropped them. Scooping one hand under her, he lifted her, pressed her against the wall, and pushed himself inside her.

Even before his first full thrust, she'd begun to feel the pressure of her orgasm. And as he moved into her, holding her protectively against the wall, rocking all of his hot strength deep, so deep inside … She cried out. This. Him. Yes.

The sound of her pleasure, drove him wild, and he pumped into her with a furious, bucking pace. Kissing her as deeply and hotly as he penetrated her.

Unable to do anything, but hold on, she kissed him back, dizzy with the sensations spiraling through her body.

He rode her so deeply, filled her so completely that she began to come before she knew what was happening.

What was happening?

She cried out as the coil of energy, tight and throbbing,

broke over her and she clung to him, clung to his shoulders. His rhythm frantic, she was helpless against the pace, the waves of pleasure. Unable to recognize anything outside of that place where they connected and the tremors rocked her body.

He never slowed. With each driving thrust he brought her senses alive again. The energy jostled and tripped every joyous nerve, searing his stroking flesh against hers. "Yes, yes," she begged, writhing. "Again. I'm close."

The pressure tightened, squeezed, so good, so close.

The wild rhythm of his body slapping against hers echoed through the stairwell. She didn't care. Nothing but this feeling mattered. She came again, unable to contain her cries as her core squeezed and pulsed around all that fine, male hardness.

A moment later, he joined her, with a "Fuck" and a "Never want to stop."

Even after he was spent, he kept rocking into her, and Honor was certain all it would take would be a few moments more of this for him to grow hard again, for them to go again.

With a touch of her hand against his face, she slowed him. He blinked, grinned like he'd been caught with his hand in the cookie jar, lowered her. His heavy breaths echoed in the stairwell. She kissed his neck. "How do you feel?"

His breath loud in her ears. "Uh—"

"Do you feel anything?"

"Uh—"

"Just say it."

"I feel satisfied." He shrugged. "And a little embarrassed."

She punched him.

CHAPTER 58

THE BRIEFING ROOM LOOKED REMARKABLY LIKE A classroom—cascading rows of desks, a podium at the front, and a huge screen. It seemed like a lifetime since Tony had conducted a mission briefing here.

There were almost thirty people in the room, including his unit and their significants—Dusty and Sandesh. There was a group from internal security and seven other family members, including Momma and Leland, and The Troublemakers Guild. But none of them really had him off his game.

She did.

Shouldn't have slept with her. Should've checked on her, talked to her before this. Hadn't been able to do it, look this woman in those beautiful eyes and tell her that he felt nothing for her. Not when she was recovering. He'd wanted to give her time.

Fine. All right. He was a coward.

Tony crossed in front of the projected image on the large screen at the front of the room. "This is Kiki Hart—"

"It's Natalie Silva," Honor said from her seat in the front row. Momma sat next to her, a niqab covering her face, shoulders back. She looked remarkably unsuited to sitting at that desk.

"Sorry," he said, meaning it. She'd been through hell. Bruised eyes, cut up, red, swollen hands. And that was just the outside stuff. "Natalie Silva, from here on out known as Superhero Silva, made documentaries on the abuse within

THE COST OF HONOR

Hollywood. Specifically trying to take on one Carson Winthrop. Production company owner. Film producer. Financier. Slippery fucker."

"Super slippery," Leland said. "He's been accused twice of lewd acts with minors. Both times the charges were dropped. The victims paid off."

Momma shifted in her chair, put a hand on her side as if her hip hurt. "Carson Winthrop is a big donor to political parties and one of the wealthiest men in the world. No one looks into what he does, because they are too busy seeing how they can get into his pockets."

Momma cleared her throat. "In addition to all this, he is a huge player in the shadow economy—laundering money."

"If we have so much on this guy," Romeo said, "why haven't we gone after him before?"

Momma's hands traced and retraced the edge of the desk in front of her. Her bracelets jangled. "I thought him too powerful, too protected." She stopped and glanced over at Honor. "But our Superhero Silva took him on, despite how he tried to shame and debase her."

"Do we suspect…" Sandesh, seated next to Justice, looked down at his tablet, read, "José Clemente, aka Junior, is with Winthrop, on…an island?"

"That's the best guess," Tony said. "His bail was paid. He was released and disappeared."

Tony flipped the image on the screen to the island, pointed to Gracie. She had a laptop open in front of her and had been clicking away as Momma spoke. A Jolly Rancher gripped between her front teeth, she sucked it into her mouth. "The island is outside of Estonia. It's sixty acres… Looks pretty isolated."

"An isolated island? Go figure," Dusty said, jostling her shoulder, making her smile.

Tony stopped for a moment and took in the way they looked at each other. They were good together. Gracie smiled a lot with him. And laughed.

"What about the film?" someone shouted from the cheap seats.

Tony pointed to Kyle from internal. He sat at a large console filled with electronics and a projector in the center of the room. He flipped some dials. The screen behind Tony changed. And his older sister, Shell from Fantastic Five, appeared on the screen. Live.

Brazilian brown skin, playful brown eyes, and dyed red hair, she sat at a desk in a hotel room. "Hello, darlings. I'm here at château witness protection with Don and his son Cole." She held up a thumb drive. "And the evidence that is going to put Carson Winthrop behind bars for a long time."

A rumble of approval and excitement rippled around the room.

"Why is this film so important?" Justice said. "This man has been accused and not just in court. He settles. Sweeps these things under the rug. Superhero Silva gave her life to make films that told the truth. They're on the internet. So how could this film change anything?"

"Good question," Tony said. "And thanks to Shell and her wife Lacy being on the West Coast, we were able to get to Don and get answers."

Shell adjusted her laptop camera to take in the man next to her. Behind them in a sitting area Lacy played a game with Cole. "Let me introduce Don Toltz. He's going to tell you his son Cole's story. Please save your questions for the end."

Don's face was ruddy, embarrassed or angry, it was hard to tell. "I work for my father's accounting firm."

"Speak up," someone from internal said. And Tony gave the guy the stink eye. Fuck, these people could be so insensitive.

Don repeated himself louder and then, "Truth is, I did a lot of the social networking." He shook his head, face going redder. "Not the online kind. The real-life kind. That's how I landed Carson Winthrop to the firm. Years ago. Spent a lot of time on his island over the years, socializing, making friends with him."

A long pause, a pause where it seemed he was swallowing a ball of emotion. His eyes brimmed with tears. "Brought Cole there most times." He looked down. His lower lip thinned. "He hurt my son." A long pause. Don's breathing heavy. Clearing his throat, he continued. "I knew going to the cops…" He shook his head. "Winthrop was too powerful. Seemed like there was nothing I could do. I told my father. And…he didn't believe me. I think he was so blinded by the account."

Tony cringed, looked away. He'd been blinded by his past experiences with his own abusive father. Had labeled Don based on that too. He'd seen him being an overbearing jerk. Never once considered the idea that the guy had the right of that place, knew he'd brought his son there, that he'd put him in danger. But he'd done so to give him back a sense of control. To let him bring down Winthrop too.

"I became obsessed with researching Carson. Saw all of Natalie's documentaries. And then it came to me, how I could get him. I moved to Natalie's neighborhood, introduced myself, and in nearly the next breath told her why I was there."

He looked up, eyes filled with fierceness. "She was... an amazing woman. She took us into her confidence. She was devastated to learn about Cole. Told me about her latest documentary, that she had a big star who was going to expose Winthrop. Said it would finally get people's attention."

He shook his head. "I didn't think it was enough. I told her that I could get financials on Winthrop. I was on the inside, I could get the thing that really brought him down. It took me over a year of work. Natalie helped. That's where the bulk of her money went. With my insights, she paid hackers. We got a lot of dirt. His money laundering. The location of close to two-billion dollars of illegal monies. She put it all in that film. Wove it around Lex's story. And Cole's."

Don's face went as red as a beet. Lowering his head he began to sob, choking out, "It was powerful stuff."

Shell put an arm around him. "It is powerful stuff," she said. "And it will bring him down." She looked up at the camera. "Let's break."

Kyle pressed a button and the screen went blank.

There was a long moment of silence. The room absorbing what had happened. They had the film. They had the means to take down Winthrop.

Honor spoke what everyone had to be thinking. "Having the film, doesn't mean we leave Junior, right? We're still going to rescue him, right?"

We're?

Leland shifted in his seat. Man looked more uncomfortable than Momma. In fact, this was the first time he'd ever seen them in on a mission briefing. Usually they watched and asked questions via speakers from Momma's office. "Of course, we get Junior."

"Great," Justice said. "Always wanted to invade an island."

Tony clicked to the next screen, an aerial of the island. "We have a rundown of the security there from internal. Familiarize yourselves with it. The island has barriers, but also opportunities. Much easier to disrupt the grid. It's all tied into itself. Gracie has agreed to be our special operator, providing on-site jamming, drones, and cyber. The tactical team won't need to be large, not with her support. The Troublemakers Guild will be backup only. But me, Gracie, Victor, and Justice can—"

"Whoa, there, son," Dusty said. "Sandesh and I are along for this ride. Don't count us out now."

"Wouldn't miss it," Sandesh added.

He blinked at them. Uncertain. Tony had never, not once in his entire time at the League, been on an op with more than two guys in the field. "Momma has final say on the team. That's her call."

He looked at Momma. She smiled and said, "I welcome their expertise."

She did?

"Hold on," Honor said, standing up. Tony couldn't help the smile. And this shit was not funny, but damn she was bold, standing up in front of this intimidating bunch. "What about me? You act like I'm not participating in the mission."

He opened his mouth to gently and respectfully tell her that it wasn't a good idea. That she wasn't prepared. That her hands were still recovering. That she didn't have the weapons training. And what came out was, "That's because you sure as shit are not."

The room rumbled with comments like "Whoa" and "He told you" and "Don't take that from him."

These people. Man they loved to turn the volume up on awkward. Probably could've used nicer words.

He had no idea where all this anger was coming from.

Honor put hands on hips. "I'm going. I owe it to my mother. To my father, a man who risked his life, lost his life, to keep me safe. To Junior, who repeatedly tried to scare me away to save me. He even crashed the tour truck hoping it would finally send me away. But that only clued Papito into what was going on. That Junior had aligned with José and Ford to try and protect me. I won't be protected anymore."

Tony rubbed his face, opened his mouth.

"Are you saying," Zuri said, standing from her spot, bunch of Jack-in-the-boxes, "that you wished to be considered for a place in the League of Warrior Women?"

Really? "What the fuck, Z?"

League rule number one, if a woman rescued by the League asked to join, showed any real kind of potential, they were considered.

Honor's head spun from Zuri to him. She caught on quick. "That's exactly what I'm saying. I wish to join."

"What could you provide the mission?" Momma asked.

Heat flushed along his neck and a dull throb started in his head. Momma was seriously considering her? Even if she became a warrior woman, she'd need more training. The League didn't just send lambs to the slaughter. That was another rule. That rule... Fucking headache now.

Honor turned to Momma. "I'm an excellent shot. Olympic level."

Exaggerate much? "You were an alternate on the Olympic *archery* team."

"My skills transfer to other weapons. And I've trained extensively with La—Tony. Those skills helped me rescue Ford Fairchild from the middle of multiple armed men."

Tony couldn't help the annoyed breath.

She stuck out her chin. "And I've been to the island."

She had? "You've been?"

"When I was ten. Before my mother's second movie started filming, I was there with her for a working vacation. My mom worked. I hung out. We were there for a week."

"How much could you remember from that?" Justice said.

Tony was sure she remembered it all.

"I remember every inch perfectly. And I can tell you things about the house you won't otherwise know. I know, for example, that there are three safe rooms."

A ball of intense panic exploded in Tony's chest. He had no idea where it had come from, but the beat kept time with the red headache pulsing in his head. "You're injured." His breathing felt labored. "Your hands."

"I think she should go," Zuri said. "I'll come too. Keep an eye on her hands."

Tony shook his head. He had to stop this. "Honor, do you really want to come on an extraction, against highly trained security, knowing how difficult it will be, knowing you could put the entire team in jeopardy, get someone killed?"

He relaxed back on his heels. She couldn't push it now. Score one for peer pressure.

The room stilled, waited for her to answer. Not Tony. He knew her answer. She shrugged. "It'll be dangerous with or without me."

"What!?"

"I agree with Zuri," Momma said. "I'm going to approve this candidate for the League and for the mission."

Tony saw red. It punched up through his mind and flushed through his body. His head started to pound. This wasn't right. He ground his teeth together. "No," he said. He wouldn't let this happen. Not after...his mom.

"Are you okay?" Honor asked, sliding over to him. "Your nose is bleeding."

He wiped at it. Shit. He was blowing a gasket. "Look, Honor—"

She put up her hand in a stop talking and listen gesture. Softly, so soft he strained to hear, she said, "I can move silently through the house. A home I remember. Junior will recognize and trust me. I know you're confused. But right now, without thinking too much about it, what does your gut say about me? Can you trust me?"

The heat in his face and head diminished. Somehow, he trusted this woman. He'd trust her with his life. Was that a feeling? Maybe. Or maybe it was just observation. "It says I can trust you."

She nodded. "Hundred percent. Never doubt it."

Warmth suffused his body. This had happened before. He remembered it. More importantly, he remembered feeling it. He looked over at Momma. Was it his imagination or did her eyes look smug? What was she up to?

CHAPTER 59

NIGHT. DARKNESS. THE ROLL OF THE OCEAN. NONE OF these things were new or unusual or disconcerting to Honor normally. But normally, she wasn't crouched down, straddling the side of an inflatable boat, skimming silently though the ocean, headed toward a private island off the coast of Estonia. Sea spray soaked her face and hair. No way to protect her eyes, because her gloved hands grasped tightly to the tether rope.

Eight people were on the large inflatable, heavier bodies at the front—meaning Dusty and Sandesh. Tony as coxswain manned the motor. Gracie, Justice, Zuri, and Victor, like her, clung to the sides. With their helmets, dark clothes, camouflaged faces, not to mention the spray of ocean, she could barely see any of them.

The only light came from the coast of Estonia in the distance, rocky cliffs lit with regular life, homes, dinner, family, safety.

This was more than she'd bargained for. Fear, dry throat, and pounding heart made everything slightly disorienting in the moonless, starless night. She'd started out feeling like she'd every reason to be on this mission. Her mother had given her life to this cause.

Not even when Tony had tried to pressure her into not going did she consider she didn't belong. But now as Tony cut the motor, pulling it so the propeller came out of the water, everyone grabbing paddles, with her a second slower…

What was she doing here? This was crazy. She'd under-estimated the organization, this mission. Her place in it. Seriously? How had they thought it was okay for her to come? Training, experience with weapons, experience keeping her panic at bay, her mind focused. She had none of those things.

The Parish family had all those things, and they'd chosen to let her come. She clung to that, telling herself what Momma had said to her as she'd bid them all goodbye. "There is nothing that will happen during this mission that you cannot handle."

She had to believe that. Momma knew things. She was smart. Had connections. Such connections. They'd launched from *Oceanic Voyager*, a marine biology research vessel in the area. Part of Parish Holdings. All but a few of the crew had been given time off, so the Parish "executives" could arrive and "survey" the project.

Seven team members were still on the boat, a tech team from internal that spoke in Honor's earpiece. Honor clung to her quick, calm, professional instructions like they were her own conscience. Not for nothing, as Tony would say.

"You're a hundred yards out," internal said. "All quiet on the island."

That was something. They used a satellite to give real-time information on island activity. From here, the island looked quiet. A few lights twinkling in the distance. The ocean waves pushed against the shore with a gentle *whoosh*. Salt and sea coated her senses.

An experienced kayaker, she drove her paddle down aggressively as they crested up and over waves, nearing the shore. She strained to see the beach. Everyone else could see through their night vision goggles. She'd flipped hers up.

NVGs cut off a sense she hadn't even known she'd had until she'd put the glasses on. A sense of expansiveness, of feeling connected, of—she wasn't even sure what to call it, but the goggles blocked it.

Tony had tried repeatedly to get her to wear them, telling her, "We have eyes in the sky. Small floating drones, size of a bird, that will skim the trees, give us real-time information about what's coming up ahead. If you wear the NVG, that visual will be in the corner of your goggles."

She'd tried, but it made her sick, disoriented.

The boat rocked up one last wave and reached the beach. Dusty and Sandesh jumped from the bow and guided it out of the water. Once the rubber met the resistance of the sand, she flung herself over the side, grabbed the thick handles, and pulled along with everyone else.

Oomph. Weighed a ton. Even with eight people carrying it into the tree line. What was in this thing? Once far enough under the cover of the trees, Victor and Tony began pulling out weapons and tools. The team dressed quickly in protective body armor, then began to stalk forward in silence.

Despite her sure footing, the comfort of moving naturally through the woods, Honor had to fight to keep her terror away. She had to focus on the mission, on Junior, who'd risked himself multiple times to try to save her. *Hold on, Junior. We're coming for you.*

CHAPTER 60

TONY'S ANGER WITH HAVING HONOR HERE MEANT HE focused on her. Her economy of movement. The instinctual application of aggressive stance and protective measures… Did she even recognize how amazing she was? The rest of them had NVGs, and still they moved with caution. Her? She went right for the woods.

Among the trees, she was even better. Sandesh and Justice moved off to do recon on the home and to set J up as sniper. Dusty and Victor took watch on the perimeter. Scouting inside the woods, Honor moved through the trees like she'd grown up here. Zuri hung by her side, giving her instructions that any field operative should already know like the back of her hand.

Shit. He was so angry, he was going to puke.

Crouched in the center of it all, Gracie hid under a light-refracting blanket while she sent out mini drones. Tony watched the images that appeared in his glasses as she flew them through the trees. Things were incredible. Tiny. Light. Near soundless.

"Where'd you say you got these things?" he said, squatting beside the blanketed Gracie.

"A senator's daughter tried to kill me with them. Working with internal, I helped adapt them for mission use."

Kill her? Couldn't leave this family alone for a fucking minute.

He watched though his NVG as Gracie swung the small drone around the property. Hugging the house, she guided it through an open wall of sliding glass doors.

She was great at this. Still. "Don't get careless, G."

"I've been flying it around campus for months. Was only spotted once. By Dari."

"Fucking Troublemakers," he said. "Good thing they're on our team." She laughed.

The interior of the home—milled beams, marble floor, white walls with expensive artwork—ran in a video feed peripherally, a stable view, in the corner of his NVG.

The mini floated up the staircase, turned down one hall, then a second. This was where thermal spectral analysis had told them Junior was. Tony held his breath.

"Got him," Gracie said. "No other reason for a guard."

"Great. Get that thing out of there."

"Nope. I'm staying." She parked the mini inside a plant in the hall. "Get going. I'll get to work on the cameras, sensors."

"Copy that." Tony clicked his mic. "Ready here. What you see, J?"

"Patrol just passed. I've got a visual on your exit point and the guardhouse. I'm setup here. They can't get out without going through me or Sandesh."

"Sounds like they're not getting out," Victor said through the mic.

"Not likely," Tony said. His own voice matter-of-fact, like they broke in and took down a decades-old pedophile ring every day of the week.

Okay. They had experience.

Tony gave the go-ahead for the group—Dusty, Victor, Zuri, and Honor—to drop back from recon toward the house. Avoiding a maintenance road, they cut at an angle through the trees until they closed in on the house. In a lot of ways, it was your typical beach house. Lots of white, Hampton-esque pillars, cedar shingles, large sliding glass doors. And then there were the things that told you it was more. The cameras stationed all over, the sensors, the guards patrolling with AK-47s.

"I've got control of their cameras," Gracie said. "I'll be jamming their tech in five, four, three, two, one." They broke from the woods. It would be a little bit before the guards realized something was up. If Dominica had taught Tony anything, it was that island tech was notoriously unreliable.

They split up. Everyone knew their roles. Dusty and Victor would make sure no one snuck up on them from behind. The rest of them would go into the house, get Junior, get out. Justice would keep the guards inside their barracks if the alarm went. And Sandesh would silently take out anyone who came out before then.

Tony's group, including him, Honor, and Zuri, moved forward. AR-15 at the ready, Tony shouldered the weight of his gear with ease. Adrenaline pumped through his body, and he let his mind ride the focus without giving into anxiety.

He skirted the back patio. Zuri and Honor followed.

They moved to the corner of the house, hugging the wall. Hand gripping his muzzle, he prepared to clear the space. Pivoting off his left foot, he rounded the corner. Guard. He nailed him in the throat with the point of his weapon. The guy jerked back. Tony hit him across the face with the butt of his rifle. Clear.

The others followed. As he moved, he felt rather than

saw them behind him. He could hear Zuri moving. From Honor…nada. Like she floated on a cloud. Damn. That stealth was worth its weight in gold.

They moved toward the entrance, a side door they'd chosen minutes before because it was near where Junior was being held. Kind of felt familiar, being outside a home this elegant while he dripped violence. Home sweet home.

Nearly at the entry point, a guard came out. Guy was going from light to darkness, so his eyes weren't adjusted to begin with. Add to that, he'd put a cigarette in his mouth and flicked his lighter, he'd never see Tony coming. From the shadows, Tony jumped forward, grabbed his arm, twisted, and broke his elbow with a pop. He then used that newly created flexibility to smash the guy's nose with his own palm.

So quick, the guy didn't even have time to moan.

The alarm went off. *How the hell?* Gracie had the cameras. How'd they been spotted? Blast shields slid slowly down over the doors and windows. Tossing a smoke bomb for cover, Tony crouched by the entrance and shot as another guard came out. Shit. Had to get inside before the shields dropped. He'd worry about how to get out later.

CHAPTER 61

HONOR COULDN'T BELIEVE SHE WAS IN A FIREFIGHT. Metal shields slid down over the windows and doors.

Shots were fired from somewhere in the distance. Guards raced out from inside and behind the house. Crouching down, Zuri threw down a smoke bomb for cover, as Victor and Dusty gave the group cover fire. Terrified of being shot, Honor crouched by the side of the house.

Across from her, Tony crouched down too, but only to toss a smoke bomb to cover their movements. Gunfire erupted from the house. Tony shot back at whoever was shooting at them.

Zuri began firing into the house too. This was nuts. There was no way they were getting in this way.

Bullets ricocheted off the lowering metal shields with white hot light. The shields. Soon they wouldn't be able to get in the house.

Wait. Honor knew another way in by the laundry. Hoping, the entry was still there, she turned and raced back along the house. Running in a crouch, leading with her weapon, she spotted the small doggie door and scooted under the shield lowering over it. The metal slid closed with a clang, blocking off the firefight behind her.

Inside the lights had all gone off. Only track lighting.

How was she getting out of here?

After clearing the room, she ran down a small hallway.

The house was still fairly quiet. People must be huddled in their safe rooms.

Gracie's voice popped into her ear. "Follow the bouncing ball left. And don't worry, I disabled the inside cameras. The alarm triggered because they were off so long."

Bouncing ball? Her heart pounding in her throat, Honor saw the mini drone floating. She followed around a corner, but then pulled up short.

"Go back," Gracie said. "Two armed guards ahead."

Honor inched forward.

Go back? But Junior was upstairs, and the stairs were right there. And the guards' backs were turned to her. They were looking at some kind of tablet.

Honor moved with silent and quick strides across the marble foyer. Gracie's hiss tickled her ear as Honor passed so close to the armed guards, she could see the hair on the back of his neck, a loose thread on his shirt. So close she could reach out and touch them. If they turned, they'd spot her. She hit the stairs, as silent as she'd ever been in her life, looking to make sure they didn't turn, didn't alert the many other guards in the house. They didn't.

"You're doing great," Gracie said.

It didn't feel great. It felt like she had the basketball, was driving down the court, and had no idea how to make a basket. Adrenaline pumped through her body. Nearly at the top of the stairs, every detail of the carpet—the small burgundy triangles, outlined in gold—became startlingly clear.

She moved up into a hall. For a moment it seemed, even to her own senses, that she had left the ground. Past room after room, she floated. Sweat dripped along her face, soaked her collar.

As she approached another turn, she heard Junior's cries of pain. Her stomach lurched. She cleared the corner. One guard. Aiming, imagining she gripped her bow, she fired her silenced weapon.

Blood, a fine mist, sprayed from the man's head, and almost simultaneously, he fell. Her stomach nearly gave up its contents. She put all of her emotion away. Became as silent inside as she was outside. A ghost. Unafraid of what was in the dark. Unafraid to make the rash choice. The Cowardly Lion was home. And looking for blood.

Focused on Junior, his screams, she raced to the door, put her hand on the handle, put pressure on it. No go. "G, it's locked."

"Search the guard."

Dropping to her knees, she ran her hand along his pants, his pockets. Nothing.

"What's that around his neck?" Gracie asked.

Junior cried out again. Cold chills gripped her body. *Hold on. I'm here. I am here.*

Gracie was right. There was something around his neck. A security badge. Ripping it off, she turned and swiped it across a pad at the door. It clicked. Gun raised, she entered just as Gracie said, "Don't go in like that!"

CHAPTER 62

WHATEVER GRACIE HAD BEEN MANAGING TO DO WITH the security, it looked like they'd kicked her out. Guards came at a run.

Zuri managed a lock on a guard that sprung out from a side door, immobilizing the joint. His shoulder cracked and tore from the socket. The guy started to bawl. She silenced him.

Tony took on the obstacle in front of him. A series of quick, bone-breaking strikes to a guard's face. Down and out.

His earpiece crackled. "Tone, head south around the house. I'm holding a gate," Gracie said.

He ran. As he did, one after another of the rusted security gates fell into place. He ran faster, racing their fall, racing back across the patio, toward the large sliding glass doors, and the slowly lowering shield. The shield that looked to be fighting itself.

That was it. That was the one.

Please don't let it be bulletproof.

He shot. Glass shattered. And he launched through the falling debris, flying like Superman under the grate. He thought he'd cleared it until he felt the pain.

Fuck. Fuck. His right boot heel. He twisted as much as he could, undid his laces, yanked his crushed heel from his shoe. Leaving his boot, he limped forward. Fuck that hurt.

And he'd lost his earpiece. He pushed it back inside.

"Don't go in like that!"

Gracie? Gunfire. What was going on? He clicked his mic. "Gracie, you got eyes on the prize?"

Silence. His teeth clenched. "What's going on, G?"

"Keep the channel clear."

"G—"

"Shut the fuck up, Tony."

Did Gracie just curse? Holy shit. Honestly, if she *hadn't* cursed, he wouldn't have panicked. But hearing that… Heel pouring blood, he ran on the balls of his feet. He shouldn't have let Honor come. Should have fought Momma harder on this.

Fuck. His fault.

A minute later, Gracie came back on. "Go left. There is a hallway, leads to the front stairs. There'll be two guards at the top of the landing. They're waiting in case Honor exits."

In case Honor exits? He followed her instructions. Scanning, he moved up the stairs.

At the landing, he turned, proceeded up the next set of stairs. Two guards appeared. He shot, hit one. The other sunk to a knee, lifted his weapon. Tony sprang over the railing, jumped back to the lower landing.

Thanks to Gracie's eye in the sky, he didn't need to guess where the guy was. Crouching down, he stuck his rifle through the railing. The guy saw Tony's weapon a second too late. Tony shot. Luck. That's all it was. Tony had been one second faster.

Pop, red spray. Guy down. Tony climbed back over the railing, ran up the steps. Where the fuck was she?

At the open door lay a dead guy. Tony ran down the hall, heard the crack of someone being hit, and moved into the doorway.

And then there was an AK in Tony's face.

He grabbed the barrel, spun into the weapon, hit the guy in the nose, jerked the weapon free, moved into the room—and saw a man shoot Honor.

CHAPTER 63

HONOR HAD JUST ENOUGH TIME TO HEAR GRACIE'S warning, enough time to see Junior tied to a chair—face slick with blood, hair plastered with sweat. The smell of burnt skin and burnt wood and burnt hair thick in her nostrils. And then a fist.

She ducked, rising up with the barrel of her gun pointed. She shot the man under his jaw. Blood, like warm soup, splattered.

She swung her gun toward the second man. The only weapon he had was a device in his hands attached to wires that ran to tongs piercing Junior's skin.

"Honor, two men to your left."

The hit slapped the side of her head, cracked her cheek, sent her floating to the floor in a slow, stunned moment of absolute silence. And then she slammed against the floor with a force that rocketed into her body.

Eyes tearing, Honor's vision swam. Above her, the man who'd hit her considered her like a bug he was about to crush. Weak spot. Fast as a storm, she kicked with brutal, focused force against the man's knee. A crunch of bone and tear of ligaments. The man cried out. Dropped. Honor swung her gun around, shot him directly in the apex of his skull. Then aimed her weapon toward the last man.

Too late.

The man with the box had dropped it, found a gun. He had it aimed at Honor. He shot. The bullet hit her at nearly the same instant she shot, nearly the same instant someone else shot, and their bullets fired at box man—*bam, bam, bam*.

He fell. She looked up. Tony.

Stunned, the impact of the bullets expanding in waves of pain throughout her chest, she couldn't breath, couldn't think.

Tony ran over to her, dropped to her side. "Honor!"

He was crying, pulled at her vest. "Where are you hurt? Fuck."

Catching her breath, Honor put up her hands, met his eyes. "The body armor got them all," she said, though it hurt like hell.

His nose was bleeding. His eyes were wild.

He pulled her up, hugged her tight. Releasing her, his hands cupped her face. His eyes. For a moment, they shone with love. And then, he blanked his face and stepped back. "You okay to move?"

Pain, worse than her inability to suck in enough air, lanced her heart. "Junior."

Together, they went to Junior and began to unhook him. Honor wouldn't let herself shake, lose her mind over this. But poor Junior. Passed out, nose and face a bruised mess. He was not okay to move.

Tony turned to Honor. "I'm going to need to carry him. Can you lead us out?"

She held her rifle at the ready. "Yes."

With Junior in a fireman's carry over Tony's shoulder, Honor stalked down the hallway. As Gracie had informed them, they didn't run into anyone in the hall. They'd taken down everyone on this side of the house. And Justice and

Sandesh had kept any guards from being able to enter before the blasts shields went down. They didn't run into anyone, but when they came down the stairs. She clicked her mic. "Gracie, how do we get out?"

"Stand back," Gracie said. "Far back. Dusty has the rocket launcher aimed at the front door."

Tony groaned as they rushed back up the stairs. It was then that she noticed he was missing a shoe, the back of his foot bled, badly, and he wobbled. At the top, he fell, with Junior swinging on his back like a sack. Honor dropped beside them, and then *BOOM*.

Crashing glass, falling debris, smoke.

Her ears ringing, coughing up a lung, she brushed away dust and debris. Tony rolled to sitting. He repositioned Junior, stood, nearly dropped him. Trembling, Honor got to her own feet.

She only had herself to carry, and her legs shook. She had no idea how Tony managed to get Junior down the steps.

At the end of the stairs, Sandesh took Junior onto his back, keeping one hand across Junior's unconscious body, but in the other hand, he held a gun. He looked at Tony. "You good?"

Tony nodded, though Honor had never seen him so pale. Sandesh adjusted Junior's lax body and said, "Justice is holding down the barracks. No more resistance outside."

Thank God.

"We've got incoming," Gracie said. "A helicopter just landed."

"You have to be fucking kidding me," Honor said at exactly the same time as Tony did. She looked at him, surprised that they'd spoken in sync. He winked at her. Was she imagining it? Or had he looked at her with real tenderness? No time to discuss, they hustled out of the house and toward the beach.

And they hustled out of the house.

CHAPTER 64

As Tony raced back through the woods to collect Gracie and jump into the boat, he kept control of his mind, his emotions—barely.

Seeing Honor on the floor, a gun pointed at her, knowing he was too late, knowing he would be responsible for her death, had broken the wall in his mind. It wasn't just emotion. It wasn't. He remembered what happened in Mexico. What he'd done and why. Red and rage and the emotional memory, the thing he'd hidden from Zuri, the thing he'd tried to save for himself, burst through his mind and body.

The rush of emotion had nearly drowned him. And the heartbreaking thought that he'd remembered her, all of her, his love for her, only to lose her. He'd lost her.

He hadn't been fast enough.

But then...fuck. She had been. She'd been okay. She was okay. He intended to keep her that way.

They ran through the trees. Through his night vision goggles, the green surreal world pitched with his strides, but his eyes stayed on Honor's running form in front of him. *She was alive.*

The only thing that tempered his rage right now was that. And his love for Honor. But he had to hide that from her. This shit wasn't over. And there was no room here for soft explanations, apologies, begging for forgiveness. He should never have agreed to M-erasure. If he wasn't worthy of the League, as he was, then fuck them. Because this woman said he was worthy of her. And that was all that fucking mattered to him.

He was going to tell her. He would tell her all of it. Just let them get the fuck out of here. When they arrived at the inflatable, Gracie had packed up her stuff, explained the radio silence, and was holding a handle of the inflatable.

Everyone ran to their handles. Sandesh laid Junior inside the boat, took his handle. Like a well-oiled machine, one that fears for its ever-loving life, they lifted the boat and bolted for the water.

Not as smooth as when they'd come in, but a hell of a lot faster.

The resistance of the ocean swells pushed against them, but they shoved back, launched into the boat, grabbed paddles. They cleared the waves quickly, got far enough out that Tony could engage the motor. He started it up, swung them around.

The whoop of the blades hit his ears a second before he saw the copter swoop down, lights on, gunner out.

Near simultaneously, from around a corner of the island, a boat full of guards—probably the pissed-off guards Justice had held off—zipped forward.

Justice faced their direction, brought her advanced tactical weapon, an MK14 Nighthawk up. There was no way she'd be able to hit anyone on that boat. Not with them bouncing along. Not with the movement of the other boat. No way.

She shot. The coxswain jerked, fell against the tiller, turned the boat around in circles. Holy shit.

Inside the inflatable, Dusty raised the rocket launcher. Sandesh got under him, let him rest the thing across his shoulder. Ballsy. They aimed at the copter.

The helicopter neared, firing, eating up water. Tony cranked every bit of power from the engine.

Fuck. Was that a mistake? Should he slow to give them calm to aim?

Dusty fired the rocket launcher, nearly tipped out of the boat. Might have if not for the hold Zuri and Victor had on his tactical vest.

The helicopter veered the rocket, and kept coming.

They were dead.

The thought brought him a sense of calm. He looked at Honor. Her face wasn't turned up to the sky, to the helicopter. It was turned to him. He smiled at her. Let the love fill him, his eyes, his body, his blood. He mouthed, "I love you."

And the sky rained down fire.

CHAPTER 65

FIRE DANCED, CRACKLED IN THE DEEPLY DUG FIREPIT they'd made in the sand. Moonlight stretched across the ocean. A warm breeze drifted along the beach of the Parish family's private island.

One hand propping him up on the sand, the other running along the ring on her finger, Tony took in another breath of Honor. Cocoa and salt. She snuggled into his shoulder, kissed his collarbone.

"What did Momma say when you called?"

"The investigation is sending rats scurrying. It's all over the papers. As the daughter of the woman who broke this thing wide open, you're going to have to come out of hiding soon."

She sighed, snuggled closer. "Do you think Cole is ready for that?"

"His father will protect him as much as possible."

"That guy is a hero," Dusty said from across the fire. Tony looked up at him. He sat in an Adirondack chair sunk deep into the sand. Gracie sat on his lap. "Still can't believe his father brought him to the island, put him in danger, to get Superhero Silva's last film, and in order to give him back a sense of control."

"Fooled me," Tony said. Truth was, he'd been blinded by his past experiences with his own abusive father. Had labeled Don based on that too. "I never put together that Cole might've gone into the woods to get the film because his

332 DIANA MUÑOZ STEWART

father had instructed him to do it. Or that his dad had planned the whole, 'Cole's lost' thing to have an excuse to leave once Cole got back, without raising suspicions."

Or that Cole had been running from him and Honor. They were what had spooked him.

"He had to be so cautious," Justice said from under the plaid blanket she shared with Sandesh. Light from the fire played across her jet black hair. "After he realized his son had been abused by Winthrop, the guy he worked for, his firm's biggest client, one of the richest men in the world, he knew he was in danger. And so was his son."

"Lucky he joined forces with Superhero Silva," Sandesh said.

Tony felt Honor smile against his neck.

Gracie sat forward on Dusty's lap. He rubbed a hand across her back, lower. "And that Natalie seized the opportunity Don represented. She recognized telling Cole's story—one more child, one more incident—wouldn't destroy the conspiracy of silence."

"Exactly," Justice said. Her head pillowed on Sandesh's shoulder. Her knees up, tenting the blanket. "Why put out more of the same information already being ignored? But put out something explosive, a famous star like Lex coming out along with Cole and the global financial misdealings. Smart."

It had been smart. Also dangerous. Natalie had taken the leads Don and Ford had given her and passed them onto cyber hackers who she'd paid to delve deep into Winthrop's shady dealings. She'd understood what Papito had come to understand—there are different rules for different people. And the best way to take Winthrop out was to follow the money.

She hadn't lived to see it, but it had worked.

Already judges and media moguls who knew what Winthrop was, what he did, and who worked to protect him were being caught up in the growing scandal. Winthrop's perp walk was about the prettiest thing Tony had even seen. And this a week after he had to stomach seeing the guy held up as the lone survivor of a violent terrorist attack.

"How's Junior doing, Honor?" Zuri asked. Victor was trying to cozy up next to her, and Zuri sent him a not-in-this-lifetime-dude look. Just made the guy smile prettier.

"He's recovering. Your…Momma has seen to all his medical bills and care, physical and emotional. As much as he did, sacrificed, he feels badly that he didn't turn on Papito sooner."

"He's got no reason to feel bad. He did what he could after a lifetime of being under Papito's control." Tony understood just how messed up that was. How a demented adult like Papito, abusive, control freak, could determine how someone acted and thought through conditioned fear.

And though Honor told him not to blame Momma for allowing her on the mission, told him even though they both knew it had been to break the hold of the M-erasure, he still did.

No family is perfect. His even less so. And he'd work that stuff out eventually. For now, this weekend on the family's private island, he was going to let it all go.

"I would have recognized the threat in Mia from day one," Victor said. "Those yogis. Can't trust them."

Laughter rumbled around the group. Good thing Bridget hadn't arrived yet. Mia had also been arrested for her part in everything.

The *whoop, whoop* of a helicopter passed overhead.

"Group two is arriving," Sandesh said.

Beside him, Honor made a small, nervous sound.

"You okay?"

"You mean am I going to be okay meeting your entire family, all bazillion of them?"

He nibbled her ear. "I meant, you okay being the center of attention? The bride walking down the aisle? Haven't changed your mind, have you?"

Lord knew she had reason. His family was crazy. Vigilantes. Mind fuckers. And they had their own culture. A culture that was nowhere near as prim and buttoned up as the normal suburban family.

Honor shook her head. "My mind and my heart are filled with you. To me, we're already joined forever. Our wedding tomorrow is just the ceremony, the celebration of our always connection."

Fuck. He kissed her, deep and possessive. "You're the best thing that ever happened to me. Like a fairy tale come to life. And I love you so much, it hurts in all the best ways."

At that, music blasted down from the main house, breaking up the satisfied comfort of the group on the beach. Justice shifted from the blanket she'd covered herself and Sandesh in. Those two hadn't stopped petting each other under there. Tony didn't want to know.

Justice glared at the house. "The Troublemakers Guild."

Tony saw his opportunity for a little nighttime fireworks. "Go get 'em, J."

Her dark eyes, reflecting the fire, swung to him. She shrugged her shoulders. "I would. Normally. But they did save our lives. Feel like I owe their crazy asses a bit more respect."

"Not just them," Victor said, sounding genuinely affronted. "One of mine was flying the helo. That was some fancy flying that allowed your girl to shoot down the helo full of bad guys. Remember that."

"How could we forget?" Zuri said. "You are constantly reminding us."

"You most of all," Victor said. And to Tony's complete and utter surprise, his sister, the lab rat, who was more comfortable at a target range than with men, smiled at him.

"This is the perfect night," Honor said, capturing his hand. "But I think tomorrow night, the night we share our names, will be better."

"Couldn't agree more, future Mrs. Honora Parish-Silva."

She laughed, brought her hot lips to his.

He kissed her, possessed her lips with his. Deliriously happy knowing that they had all the time in the world. Every moment from here on out would be theirs. And whatever shit had happened in their pasts faded away because of what was in their present. This. They. Them.

ACKNOWLEDGMENTS

Writing the Black Ops Confidential series has been such an incredible and rewarding creative experience. I've been blessed to be able to fulfill my dream of writing about a secret society of vigilantes that scour the globe writing wrongs. But in order for this dream to come true, to make this series the best it could be, and to get this series out into the wider world, I needed the support, talent, and painstaking effort of many smart and creative people. People whose work and friendship I value beyond words.

I've been so lucky on this journey to have had as my advocate and cheerleader my wonderful agent, Michelle Grajkowski. Thank you, Michelle for your hard work, encouragement, guidance and most of all your friendship. If not for Michelle, this series would not have found the perfect home at Sourcebooks.

I am so endlessly grateful to my publisher, Sourcebooks, and to Dominique Raccah for starting the dynamic publishing company that allowed my dream to come true. And for hiring so many wonderful and dedicated people!

One of the amazing and talented women at Sourcebooks, and someone I admire and greatly appreciate, is my energetic and brilliant editor, Cat Clyne. A huge thank-you to Cat for believing in the series, sticking with it, and for making each book the absolute best it could be. I am beyond grateful to have had your intelligence, expertise, insights, and creative talent on my side.

I'm equally grateful to the entire team at Sourcebooks Casablanca and would like to especially acknowledge the hard work of my production editor, Jessica Smith. Jessica has shepherded the second and third books in the Black Ops series to their sparkly finished product. Thank you, Jessica!

And a thousand hugs and kisses and rose petals thrown at the feet of Stef Sloma, Kay Birkner, Kirsten Wenum, and Ashlyn Keil. You guys are the best. I am in awe of your hard work and your tireless dedication. I am so grateful for everything you do at SB from social media, to marketing materials, to promotion, to author packets, educational videos on marketing, and a thousand other things. And you do all of this with such kindness and genuine enthusiasm. I can't express how much all of your efforts and enthusiasm have meant to me through this journey. I just love you guys.

A special thanks to Dawn Adams for the wonderful artwork that she created for the covers on each of the three books in the series. Each cover has been spectacular. It's been a true gift for me as an author to have these beautiful covers visually represent and capture my work.

A big thanks to Lisa Marie Bone for her directional edits. Your insights made a huge difference in how I approached many aspects of this third book in the series. Thank you so very much.

I'd like to give a huge thank-you to Gavin De Becker for his book, *The Gift of Fear*. It was instrumental in helping me to create a character that understood, and could train others to understand, how to recognize and avoid violence.

I'd also like to thank my brother-in-law, Wilson Stewart, for quickly answering my weird and probably disturbing text messages about guns and self-defense issues.

A sincere thank-you to all of the librarians and bookstore owners, big and small, who have taken a chance on this series and stocked it on their real and virtual shelves. Thank you for recommending a series about a badass group of women who take on the bad guys.

And finally, my undying gratitude to all the avid readers who have picked up the Black Ops (Band of Sisters) series and who continue to enthusiastically support the adventures of the League of Warrior Women. I consider it a privilege to be able to make this connection with each and every one of you.

ABOUT THE AUTHOR

Diana Muñoz Stewart is the award-winning romantic suspense author of the Black Ops Confidential series, which includes *I Am Justice*, *The Price of Grace*, and *The Cost of Honor* (Sourcebooks). She lives in eastern Pennsylvania in an often chaotic and always welcoming home that—depending on the day—can include a husband, kids, extended family, friends, and a canine or two.

When not writing, Diana can be found kayaking, doing sprints up her long driveway—harder than it sounds—practicing yoga on her deck, or hiking with the man who's had her heart since they were teens.

Learn more or connect with Diana at:
dianamunozstewart.com.
facebook.com/DMSwrites
@dmunozstewart

See where the Black Ops Confidential
story began! Read on for an excerpt from

I AM
JUSTICE

CHAPTER 1

APPARENTLY, CAMO COULDN'T HIDE YOU FROM EVERY-
thing. Justice yanked free of another thorn in the brush-
choked woods. She squatted at the tree line and focused her
night vision goggles on the rear of the bleak home turned
bleaker business. The battered, white-shingled two-story sat
on the poorest edge of a rural community in Pennsylvania.

Rural as hell. They didn't even have their own police
force and had to rely on staties.

She snapped pictures of the gravel-and-stone backyard
and the rusty propane tank propped on wooden legs like a
miniature submarine dry-docked after fifty years at sea.

The whole "massage parlor" was dingy, dirty, and depressing.

Given the choice, most people steered well clear. Not
Justice. She wanted inside. Planned and plotted on it. Call
it a childhood dream, making good on her vow. Call it

redemption, making it up to Hope. Call it revenge, making them pay for Hope's death.

It would help if Momma's oft-heard mantra—patience... reconnaissance always comes first—didn't keep popping up like a jack-in-the-box to wave a scolding, white-gloved finger at her.

Momma. What a fun sucker.

A single light, green through her goggles, shone over the steel back door. She zoomed in on it as her breath fanned against the midnight air. Her camera *click, click, click*ed. No exterior handle. They'd have to pop it. And no security cameras. Figures. See no evil. Hear no evil. Or at least, record no evil.

She snapped photos of barred and blackened windows and a rusty fire escape that led up to a metal-gated door secured with thick, elephant-proof chains.

These guys weren't taking any chances. Which meant more surveillance and late nights for her. Unlike her other siblings, she always got saddled with recon for the family's underground railroad.

Not for long though. After two years of planning, the mission as dear to her as her own heartbeat—breaking up a human trafficking ring—was only a few weeks away. *Yeehaw!* She was going to bust heads.

Her earpiece clicked, and her brother's voice came through. "Justice, youse...uh, you in position yet?"

Tony. He worked so hard to weed out his South Philly. She liked his accent. But being adopted into her big, crazy family had taught her people could have some weird issues.

"Aw, Tone, can't spot me? Is it my expert camouflage or that stealth gene you're missing?"

Tony snorted. The sound tightroped between amused and annoyed. "Yeah, you know as much about being a Choctaw as I do about being a Chihuahua."

"It's in my blood. Only thing in your blood, paisano, is cement shoes and boosting cars."

Laughter feathered through her headphones, making her want to scratch through her face mask to dig the tickle from her ears. "Just get the pic—"

The massage parlor's back door crashed open. A dark-haired girl, maybe fifteen, sprinted out, wearing a too-loose bustier and a thong as inconsequential as her chest.

A man broke out after her, hauling back with a belt thick enough to double as a swing.

"Tony."

"No. Think larger mission here. Not one girl. All of 'em."

The heavy slap of leather on flesh ricocheted like a gunshot.

Soundless, the girl tucked her shoulder and veered to the side, toward the woods, toward Justice.

Justice's chest tightened and heated until it became as hard and fixated as the steel on her Sig. Adrenaline flooded into her body. The scene slowed and intensified.

The girl's eyes were wide and frantic. The desperate eyes of a hunted child.

She couldn't sit here—ass on haunches—and do nothing. As ineffective as government raids that took months to organize and ended with not one conviction of a principle. Not one.

This was what the League of Warrior Women was about: Stopping the shit that other people stood by and let happen. It's what her sister would have done. It's what Hope *had* done for her.

Every nerve in Justice's body begged to act. But she kept absolutely still. Movement attracted attention. Stillness went unnoticed.

The man grabbed the girl's hair and yanked her back. The girl struggled and flailed, twisted and fought. The man drove a belt-wrapped fist into her neck. She sagged, gasped.

Tony's voice came through the headset, smooth and controlled. "Stay put, Justice."

Too late. She'd already stood, raised her gun, and was in fact mid-motion of pressing the trigger when he'd spoken.

There was a sharp snap, like a broken twig, as the bullet fired from her suppressed Sig. The man's head flung back. He dropped to his ass, surrendered to the gravel.

The girl skittered away. Her eyes swung left and right before she darted for cover behind the derelict propane tank.

"Not for nothin', J, you don't listen to shit."

Justice flipped up her NVGs, pulled down her face mask, and ran across the gravel. She checked inside the doorway for movement. All quiet.

She spotted the girl crouching by the propane tank, squeezed between the building and the rusty cylinder. The kid looked like a terrified skeleton—all haunted eyes and jutting bones.

Tony ran up, checked the dead guy for weapons. "Glock. Figures," he said and slipped the weapon into the back of his belt.

Justice reached forward. "It's okay. It's okay. I'm on your side."

The girl's copper-brown eyes tracked Justice's gloved hand like it came equipped with teeth and venom. For a moment, she was sure the girl wouldn't take her hand. But she did.

Brave kid. Justice pulled her out. She'd shouldered heavier backpacks. Shrugging off her jacket, she helped the girl put it on. Keeping eye contact, she pointed at the dead man, then at the building. "How many more men inside?"

The girl held up her arm and poked two rabbit fingers from the long sleeve. Two more men inside. Justice shrugged at Tony. "No choice."

His dark eyebrows knitted tightly together, but he started for the house. He bumped Justice's shoulder as he passed. "Call it in."

She elbowed him hard in the ribs. He *oomphed* and kept walking.

Justice put a hand on the girl's shoulder. Even with the gloves, it felt like she'd grabbed a coat hanger.

Shielding Tony's view, she held out the G19. Tony could be pissed later. And not just because she'd so expertly pickpocketed him. "Can you use this?"

The girl hesitated. Then with a face as starved and empty as a runway model, she took the gun, capped her fingers across the top, and racked the slide.

Justice pointed toward the woods. The girl dashed away, and Justice pressed the button on her earpiece. Gracie answered on the first ring. "You're kidding me, right, Justice?"

Why were her siblings always giving her such shit? "Just get a van to site six, Gracie."

She hung up and went inside. A dangling, red lightbulb lit a narrow stairway and slim corridor.

On the stairs, Tony gave her a what-took-you-so-long

look? She shrugged. He motioned he'd go up. She nodded and crept the other way, down the hall.

At the end of the dim hall, gun raised, she sighted around a doorway. Ugh. That smell. BO and whiskey.

Once a living room, the space had been turned into an office. A desk, a television turned to QVC, a potbellied man in boxers passed out on a saggy couch.

She reached for a zip tie, stepped inside, and...*crash and churn*. Shit. The bottle of Jim Beam sailed across the hardwood.

Drunky leapt up, saw her, and lurched forward like Frankenstein's monster. Biggest guy she'd ever seen, but slow and lethargic.

Justice skated around him, reached up, and slammed her gun into his head. One, two, three times. He dropped.

Still conscious? If anything, the hits had woken him up.

He grabbed her ankle. She fell in slow motion. Skull cracked against floor. Hand cracked against desk. Gun dropped.

Drunky reared up and slammed into her like a wrestler, pinning her neck with one beefy limb. He held her right hand. Her left arm was trapped and pressed between them.

Justice's heart pounded electric currents through thinning veins. Pinned. It felt like the dream, the nightmare that still haunted her. Her gaze bucked around the room. She couldn't move. Couldn't breathe.

She fought off panic. Off the memory. She wasn't a little kid. She wasn't helpless.

Hand trembling, she groped past his boxers, located one sweaty ball. Squeezed.

Drunky cursed and pressed harder.

Justice's eyes watered, black spots clouded her vision. She couldn't black out. She'd die if she did.

No. Not like this. Not like Hope.

She kicked blindly again and again. Her foot connected with his ankle. He jerked, lost balance.

Justice thrust up her right hip, swung her foot flat, got leverage, and pushed. Drunky toppled.

Snakebite fast, she rolled and belly-crawled away. Where was her... Gun. Justice grabbed it.

Drunky came for her. She rolled, aimed. "Stop."

Bam. The guy crashed back and down.

She looked up. Standing in the doorway, the girl lowered the Glock.

Holy shit. The kid had killed the guy.

Wheezing through a throat still aching, Justice lurched to her feet. She sucked in hot, rank air as her legs Jell-Oed under her.

Ignoring the twist of nausea and the feeling of wrong, she picked up her night vision goggles and staggered away from the corpse. She went over to the girl. "You didn't have to."

Tiger-fierce red-brown eyes scanned away from her over to the body. The girl spit on the floor. "I wanted to."

Justice knew that anger, wasn't sure she disagreed with it, but still... "You wait here. Right here."

She went back down the corridor and up the narrow stairs. She swung her gun around as she checked the upstairs hall. Tony had taken out the other guard. He was passed out and hog-tied in the hallway.

Tony stepped from one of the corridor doorways. "Did I hear a problem?"

"Not anymore."

"Seriously, J? Stop killing people."

She glared at him. Definitely not the time to explain. "Guy had a hundred fifty pounds on me."

Literally.

Tony pointed to the man knocked out, hands bound behind his back and tied to his feet. "That guy's no featherweight. It's called training."

Dick. What did he know? Sometimes the only thing that made her equal to those she went up against was a gun. She gestured at the doors in the hall. "Where are the girls?"

He reached past her and pushed a door open. He nodded toward the occupants. "Salvadoran."

She walked into the room. The young women and girls who'd been stolen, tricked, or coerced from their lives and countries huddled together in a dark corner. The windows had been painted black. There was one dresser and a full-size bed. Probably the same setup as every room up here.

She automatically gave the instructions in Spanish. "Stay calm. No one will harm you. We are rescuing you. You will be cared for. You will not be harmed. Stay calm. Follow us."

The group began to panic. Cry out. Someone threw a shoe at her. *Ouch. Great.* She stepped back to Tony. "You got this?"

He nodded and lowered his gun. "Always a people pleaser, J."

At the pickup location designated as Site 6, they loaded the freed slaves into the white panel van. The girl who'd saved Justice refused to get inside.

Justice put her hand on the kid's bony shoulder. "What's your name?"

She looked away, then down. "They called me Cookie."

Cookie? That wasn't a name. That was a dessert. Well, if she'd learned anything from *Sesame Street* it was that *C* was for Cookie.

"Thank you for saving my life, Cee."

The girl's fiery-brown eyes, prematurely set to suspicious, appraised Justice. "Am I free?"

Justice pointed at the back of the fifteen-passenger vehicle. "Get in the van. Freedom is your next stop."

The girl shook her head. "I want to go where you go. I want to…" She hesitated as if looking for words in a language she didn't know that well. "I want to be what you are."

Kid had no idea what she was saying, what would be required of her, but rules were rules. If they asked and showed any kind of real promise, they got to try.

"Get in the van. A woman with red hair will be at your destination. Her name is Gracie. Tell her what you told me."

The girl nodded, turned, climbed into the van, and dragged the door shut.

Justice hit the door twice. The van pulled away, trailing a cloud of exhaust. When the taillights faded, she turned and slipped into the front seat of the black rental, next to the elephant in the room. Tony.

She cast her brother a sideways glance. Every inch of his five-foot-eleven frame looked ready to pound her to a soft, mushy pulp.

Tony ripped off his hat and gloves. He ran agitated fingers through black, wavy hair damp with sweat, causing it to stand on end.

Justice started the car and adjusted the heat to "off." She let out a breath, tightened gloved hands against the steering wheel. *Aw, hell.* "Stop pouting."

Tony hit the dash. "You gotta get over this cowgirl, *Kill Bill* bullshit. Why not send up a signal flare telling the Brothers Grim we're after them?"

The wheel spun through her fingers as she turned the corner. She flicked on the headlights and accelerated onto the highway.

Tony was so uptight. If only she'd known when she'd first seen him—a twelve-year-old runaway scrounging for scraps—what a pain in the ass he'd become. Never should've begged Momma to adopt him. The first boy in the family. "Get over it, Tony. An eye for an eye."

He flung himself back against the seat. "You know, an eye for an eye eventually leaves the whole world blind. It's stupid. Like your stunt tonight. We don't bust into a place like some eighties Schwarzenegger movie. You think this won't get back to them? Raise suspicions?"

He had her there. The League of Warrior Women wasn't just smash and grab or brute strength. It was the velvet hammer—negotiations, forums, and charities that supported women. And the chain saw of assassination, deceit, and violence.

Sometimes things just get messy. "Sorry, Tone. Really."

He made a sound of dismissal, stripped off his dark jacket and bulletproof vest. His tight muscle shirt showed off a navy-blue tattoo on his right arm. Half of the family motto: "One for all."